"The historical setting is redolent and delicious, the townspeople engaging, and the plot a proper puzzle, but it's Rose Carroll — midwife, Quaker, sleuth — who captivates in this irresistible series debut."
— Catriona McPherson, Agatha-, Anthony- and Macavity-winning author of the Dandy Gilver series

"Clever and stimulating novel . . . masterfully weaves a complex mystery."
— *Open Book Society*

"Riveting historical mystery . . . [a] fascinating look at nineteenth-century American faith, culture, and small-town life."
— William Martin, *New York Times* bestselling author of *Cape Cod* and *The Lincoln Letter*

"Intelligent, well-researched story with compelling characters and a fast-moving plot. Excellent!"
— *Suspense Magazine*

"A series heroine whose struggles with the tenets of her Quaker faith make her strong and appealing . . . . imparts authentic historical detail to depict life in a 19th-century New England factory town."
— *Library Journal*

"Intriguing look at life in 19th-century New England, a heroine whose goodness guides all her decisions, and a mystery that surprises."
— *Kirkus Reviews*

BOOKS BY EDITH MAXWELL

Quaker Midwife Mysteries

Delivering the Truth
Called to Justice
Turning the Tide
Charity's Burden
Judge Thee Not

Local Foods Mysteries

A Tine to Live, a Tine to Die
'Til Dirt Do Us Part
Farmed and Dangerous
Murder Most Fowl
Mulch Ado About Murder

Country Store Mysteries
(written as Maddie Day)

Flipped for Murder
Grilled for Murder
When the Grits Hit the Fan
Biscuits and Slashed Browns
Death Over Easy
Strangled Eggs and Ham

Cozy Capers Book Group Mysteries
(written as Maddie Day)

Murder on Cape Cod

JUDGE THEE NOT

A
QUAKER MIDWIFE
MYSTERY

EDITH MAXWELL

BEYOND THE PAGE
PUBLISHING

Judge Thee Not
Edith Maxwell
Beyond the Page Books
are published by
Beyond the Page Publishing
www.beyondthepagepub.com

ISBN: 978-1-950461-13-4

For all those who are wrongly judged

AUTHOR'S NOTE

EVERY HISTORICAL NOVEL brings new research challenges and delights. Amesbury reference librarian Margie Walker continues to be helpful with whatever I ask her about local history, and I thank her. The Amesbury Carriage Museum provides local maps and details about daily life in a small industrial city of the time, not to mention period carriages I can touch and study. I also perused the Museum of Printing in Haverhill, Massachusetts, and consulted with Vincent Valentine at the Telephone Museum, Waltham, Massachusetts.

For this book I visited the Perkins School for the Blind, which was still in South Boston in 1889 and had not yet moved to Watertown. Research librarian Jennifer Arnott generously gave me a tour and access to the archives, including materials on the history of braille and several other articles about attitudes toward the blind in the second half of the nineteenth century. Having read the Laura Ingalls Wilder series several times as a child (and again as a parent), I discovered *Mary Ingalls: The College Years* by Marie Tschopp.

I referred to *A Guide to Midwifery* from 1870 for information about twin births of the era. Barbara Pouliot shared stories about the French-Canadian immigrant Marie Tremblay, her great-grandmother, who lived on Thompson Street in Amesbury and who gets a bit part in this book. The historical interpreter and author KB Inglee read the manuscript and alerted me to Pickering's Women at Harvard College, who spent years cataloging the firmament.

I mention the Massachusetts Institute of Technology. In 1889 it was still in Boston and hadn't yet moved across the river to Cambridge.

ONE

I COULD SMELL CONTEMPT as soon as I entered the Amesbury post office.

At the front of the line, Mayme Settle raised her patrician nose and sniffed. "I'd like to be helped by your assistant, if you don't mind." She didn't meet postmistress Bertie Winslow's gaze.

I'd come into the postal facility to speak to my friend Bertie on this fine Sixth Month morning, but I paused, watching the encounter between her and the florid matron.

"Miss Stillwell is occupied with other tasks, Mrs. Settle." Diminutive Bertie clasped her hands in front of her crisp shirtwaist. "What can I help you with today?"

"I'll return at another time." The woman lowered her voice to a threatening whisper. "I do not support the likes of you, Miss Winslow, holding the position of public servant." She nearly spat the word "likes."

"As you wish, ma'am." Bertie smiled. Her face was framed by wisps of blond curls that always managed to escape her Newport knot, but her eyes were steely.

Her accuser turned with a rustle of tan silk taffeta, coming face-to-face with me. "Ah. Miss Rose Carroll." More than a few years over the age of fifty, Mayme was taller than me by several inches, putting her close to six feet tall. She must have weighed half again as much as I did, too.

"Good morning, Mayme."

Her lip curled at my use of her Christian name. I was accustomed to such a reaction from people not of my faith.

"We met at the Ladies Circle several months ago." I smiled at her.

She gave a single nod and a faint smile. "Yes, when you Quaker ladies came to assist in our spring clothing drive for the Little Orphans home." Despite her imperious manner, Mayme headed up a goodly number of charitable projects here in our busy mill and factory town. "And you're the midwife, as I recall."

1

"I am."

Mayme inclined her head toward me. "I'd watch out for that one. She's a danger to all proper ladies."

Beyond her right side I spied Bertie mocking horror, her twinkling eyes wide and a hand over the O of her mouth.

"It was a pleasure to see thee again," I said. "I wish thee a lovely day."

"To you as well." She swept past me and out the door.

No one else was in the office, so I approached the counter. "My goodness, Bertie, why does she dislike thee so?"

She rolled her eyes. "She doesn't approve that I live in the manner which suits me. And it suits me to reside with my beloved Sophie."

"As well thee might, despite it being not precisely what others expect of a nice lady in her forties." I'd known about Bertie and Sophie's living arrangement almost as long as I'd known Bertie herself. As a member of the Religious Society of Friends, I didn't find fault with their love. We were all equal in God's eyes. I knew a few elderly Quakers who did not extend our principle of equality to couples like Bertie and her sweetheart, but I did. And of course Mayme Settle's views had plenty of company here in town.

She shrugged, letting out a decidedly unladylike snort. "I think Mrs. Settle is afraid I will accost her or corrupt the children of our fine town."

I stifled a giggle. "Watch out, here comes the bogeylady?"

"Exactly." The smile slid off her face. "I hope she doesn't create a ruckus with town officials."

"Surely there has been talk before. Thee still retains thy position."

"Yes, but you know Mrs. Settle. She's a force of nature. I think she only recently learned of my inclinations. And if she sets her mind on something, it usually comes to pass."

I gazed out the door Mayme had left through. "Bertie, I recall something I heard about a daughter of hers."

My friend clapped me on the shoulder. "I know the one you mean. She attended Smith College and now teaches calisthenics and physiology there." The college was off in the western stretch of Massachusetts, far from here. Amesbury nestled in the northeast corner of the Commonwealth on the New Hampshire border only a few miles from the great Atlantic.

"And let me guess," I said. "She isn't married and isn't interested in the male of the species."

"Indeed she is not, and one can only surmise our Mayme Settle is none too pleased about it," Bertie said.

"Therefore she harbors a degree of anger against anyone else with similar tendencies."

Bertie nodded. "But you didn't pop in to talk about Mrs. Settle's prejudicial attitudes, did you?" She leaned her forearms on the counter.

"I was hoping to convince thee to sup with me at Lake Gardener after thy workday is over. It's quite warm today. The breeze would be refreshing, and of course the sun doesn't set until nearly half past seven."

"I can't think of a single thing I'd rather do otherwise, Rosetta. Sophie went to New York City and won't be back until late this evening."

"And my David has a meeting with his father about the health clinic."

"Perfect, my dear. I'll meet you there at six o'clock sharp. As long as you promise we won't encounter a murderer."

TWO

BACK IN THE HOME I shared with my brother-in-law and my younger niece and nephews, I spread the day's *Amesbury Daily News* flat on the table in the kitchen. I was due in my parlor, which served the dual purposes of midwifery office and bedroom, at one o'clock. I expected one of my pregnant ladies for an antenatal visit, but I had time to peruse the news as I ate my midday meal. A breeze blowing through the screened door ruffled the paper and brought the rich warble of an oriole.

The family was all off at school for the day, even Frederick, the man of the house, who taught at the Academy. Alas, Faith, my oldest niece, no longer lived here. She'd been married to her sweet beau Zebulon Weed in the winter and now resided with him and his family several blocks away on Orchard Street. Even Lina, our kitchen girl, had finished her duties for the day and left, so the house was blessedly quiet. Faith's yellow cat, Christabel, napped in a pool of sunlight. She was such a good mouser I'd convinced Faith to leave her with us when she'd moved. Our kitty's mother was Zeb's family's cat, so they already had a mouse solution in their own kitchen.

The *Amesbury Daily*'s masthead read Tuesday, June 4, 1889, and below it was the horrific news of the flood that had wiped out the town of Johnstown in western Pennsylvania. I paused in my simple repast of bread and cheese to close my eyes and fold my hands. I held the deceased and their poor families in the Light of God, that their grief not be unbearable and that God might welcome all those newly released souls to his loving embrace.

The next page held a much more welcoming item, a review of a new novel set in Louisiana, *The Awakening*, by Kate Chopin. The article intrigued me, stating that the author portrayed an unconventional attitude toward femininity. The review was rather negative, and it recommended censoring certain sections of the story, which piqued my interest. I made a note to read the book and discuss it with Bertie.

I glanced at the clock on the wall and jumped up. No more dallying for this midwife. By five before the hour I was in my parlor and ready when the front doorbell jangled. I hurried to let Jeannette Papka in.

"Please wait for me," Jeanette said to her driver, a deferential man in his fifties, after she'd greeted me. He had walked her up the steps to my door.

"Yes, Mrs. Papka." He tugged at his hat and trotted back down the steps.

Jeanette turned to me. "Shall we, Rose?" She was quite tall, with thick dark hair and a delightful smile. A bulge at her waist indicated the stage of her pregnancy. But her eyes were milky and didn't allow her even a glimpse of her world. She'd been stricken with an illness as an infant that had blinded her for life.

I extended my elbow so she could tuck her arm through it, a method she preferred to her guide taking her by the arm. She stretched her other hand to touch the wall as we made our way to my office. I led her to the chaise that doubled as examining couch. She felt behind her and sat.

"I detect thee is with child again," I began.

She laughed. "It appears I am. Mr. Papka is most pleased, I can tell you."

"How fares young Rebecca? She is three by now, if I'm not mistaken."

"She's a sturdy and strong-willed girl, in the rose of health and a challenge to her nursemaid and me."

"Excellent. I have checked back through my notes. Thy labor and birth with Rebecca were uncomplicated despite her weighing ten pounds."

"That's right. What can I say, Rose? I am a tall woman with an even taller husband, and I make large babies." She clapped one palm atop the other for emphasis.

"How is Stanley, by the way?"

"You know, I only see him at the week's end, because of his professorship at Harvard College. We were determined to stay here in Amesbury to raise our family, so we have my husband with us only three nights per week. But he is well, and we have sufficient finances to hire the help I need to run the household." A small smile played around her lips. "If anything, the heart grows fonder when it is not overtaxed. The arrangement quite suits me."

"I am happy to hear it." I was, although mention of a husband made my own heart pine for David Dodge, my betrothed and beloved. Obstacles still remained in the way of declaring our marriage vows. The situation was growing more trying for both of us each day that passed with us living apart and unwed. I let out a sigh unbidden.

"I hope you haven't been involved in any more murders recently," Jeanette said, lifting one eyebrow.

Would people ever stop saying that to me? "Thank the dear Lord, no." It was true, I'd somehow become associated with more than one case of homicide in Amesbury over the last year and had found a bit of previously undiscovered aptitude in the solving of same. "And I'd like to keep it that way. Now, how many monthlies has thee missed?"

"Three, I think. But it could be four. You know how busy I am with my work." Jeanette, whose maiden name was Voyant, spoke several languages fluently and was much in demand as an interpreter at the Second District Court here in Amesbury.

"With all the French and Polish immigrants, there must be a great need for thy services."

"Indeed. Even those who have acquired some facility with our language prefer to use their own in times of strife, which being accused of a crime most certainly is."

"But will the court allow thee to continue working while carrying thy baby?"

She wrinkled her nose. "We'll see. I didn't have the interpreter position when I was pregnant with Rebecca. I confess I'm not even wearing a corset today, although I do at court. The fool things are so very uncomfortable. But I'm having several new garments made for me in the Aesthetic dress style. You know it? The garments have no defined waist and feature much free-flowing fabric."

"Wearing such dresses sounds wise for thy condition. I have tried to encourage other clients of mine to adopt such comfortable, unrestrictive clothing but most are reluctant." I normally didn't wear a corset myself, being naturally slim of build. "Does thee know the lawyer Sophie Ribeiro? She adopted Aesthetic dress some time ago. She always looks so at ease."

"I know her, of course, from my work at the court. It was from her I acquired the idea. I hope the new dresses will conceal my state for a few more months, depending on how fast this fellow grows." She patted her belly. "I don't know, of course, but I have the distinct feeling this one will emerge a son and even bigger than my first-born."

"Lift thy skirts and let me check thee. We'll see how he's faring." I proceeded to take her pulse and then measure the distance from her pubic bone to the fundus, the top of the uterus. I applied the wide flare of the Pinard horn to her belly and listened through the small end.

I straightened. "It's faint because it is small yet, but thy fetus has a good regular heartbeat. From the measurement I would say thee is about halfway through. I'd put thee at about four and a half months along, possibly five."

She narrowed her eyes, thinking back. "I suppose it's possible. So I'll have a fall baby." She restored her skirts and sat up. "Rose, I heard some malicious gossip about Miss Ribeiro around the Armory yesterday. A society matron came in trying to lodge a complaint of lascivious cohabitation against her. She said Miss Ribeiro wasn't fit to serve as counsel."

I rolled my eyes, not that she could see the gesture. "Let me guess. The complainer was Mayme Settle."

Jeanette turned her head toward me. "How did you know?"

"She was in the post office this morning being rude to my friend Bertie Winslow, the postmistress. Perhaps thee knows she lives with Sophie."

"Of course I know. Who doesn't? And it's not a platonic friendship, either. But such talk is pure balderdash. Who gives a dead rat what two ladies do in the privacy of their own home? Luckily, the magistrate is of a similar mind and refused to lodge the complaint."

"I admire thee for speaking thy mind, Jeanette, and I'm glad we are in agreement on this matter." I patted her hand, even though I knew she could hear the smile in my voice.

"Land sake. It's the only sensible way to think. Mrs. Settle ought to be shut up and banned from polite society." She gave a vigorous nod. "Indeed she should."

I held up a hand in a reflexive but useless move. "In her defense, she does perform a great many acts of charitable service for the poor among us."

"I know, I know. And it's not Christian of me to speak ill of her." She pursed her lips, then slapped her thigh. "But you know what else she did?"

"Do tell."

"Mind you, this is fact, not gossip," Jeanette began. "I was standing in the hall outside the courtroom as plain as day, and I heard her talking to the banker, Mr. Irvin Barclay. I know his voice because Mr. Papka and I have our accounts with him at the Powow National Bank. The two were having a disagreement. He must have seen me because he tried to hush her, saying I would overhear. But Mrs. Settle claimed I was a deaf-mute and a moron and couldn't comprehend their conversation."

I gasped. "She didn't."

"She most certainly did. I hear it all the time."

"Doesn't she know you work for the court?"

"She might not, if she's never had occasion to witness me interpreting."

"But Irvin Barclay must know better, about your abilities, from you and Stanley banking with him."

"Pshh. He pays me no heed, even when my husband and I go in together. Says banking is for gentlemen." She laughed. "Mr. Papka knows well how I feel, but he still allows Mr. Barclay to have his way. My Stanley says it is a minor battle out of all those we might fight, and this way he saves me the grief of having to deal with an idiot."

Jeanette was one of the most intelligent people I'd ever met. We'd become friendly even before her daughter's birth, and she never failed to impress me with her breadth and depth of knowledge on any topic we'd ever discussed. Competent in all areas of life except vision, she knew people's identities by their voices even if she'd only met them once. She played lovely music on the violin—all by memory. Her family was enlightened, caring, and comfortable financially. Jeanette had had tutors and had completed a full course of schooling. She'd taken additional courses in the law to familiarize herself with the jargon and nuances about the matters for which she needed to interpret. She had challenging and remunerative employment, and was a caring wife and mother, to boot. Not having sight had not held her back in the slightest. Mayme Settle and the banker had each gone down another mile in my estimation.

"Don't worry, I'm accustomed to such ignorant attitudes about the blind," Jeanette said. "People who hold them? It's truly their loss."

THREE

IRVIN BARCLAY USHERED his wife into my parlor with an officious air at two o'clock sharp. He introduced his wife and himself.

"Mrs. Barclay insists on seeing you, a midwife." The corners of his mouth turned down as if the mere word tasted sour. "I advised her to consult a medical doctor but she put her pretty little foot down." The banker Jeanette had heard at the courthouse had to be at least twice his wife's age, old enough to be her father and then some. Such marriages were not uncommon among men of his apparent financial standing. He looked like an affluent spouse, judging from the cut and quality of his suit and the circumference of his well-fed midsection. His young wife, by contrast, was both petite and slender except for her growing womb.

I smiled. "I am pleased to meet both of you. Rest assured I will provide excellent care for thy wife, Irvin."

His nostrils flared. His bushy reddish sideburns bristled and he lifted his chin at the affront of my not addressing him as Mr. Barclay. "My driver will deliver me to the bank and he will return forthwith and wait for Mrs. Barclay to be finished with her appointment."

"I thank thee for bringing her."

"Goodbye, dear," Sissy Barclay said to her husband. "I'll see you tonight."

He clapped his top hat on his pate and bustled out without saying goodbye to either of us.

"Shall we?" I gestured for her to sit on the chaise.

"Miss Carroll, I don't know how I will ever make it to my baby's birth alive," Sissy said. She perched upright, clearly still encased in a corset despite being well along in her pregnancy. She looked exceedingly uncomfortable, her breaths coming shallow and fast.

"Sissy, I insist thee calls me Rose." Despite being at least six or seven months pregnant, in my estimation, this was her first visit to me.

She made a moue with her plump lips. "It's not proper, Miss Carroll." The pout made her appear even younger than her twenty years.

I kept my sigh inside. "Be that as it may. Has thee been under the care of a different midwife for thy pregnancy?"

"No. When I married Mr. Barclay last year, I moved here from Portland, Maine. Portland is where my mama and grandmamma are, and my sisters, too. It took me a while to realize I was in the family way. And when I wrote to Mama, she said I must find a midwife right away, even though Mr. Barclay wanted me to see a physician. You know, a man." She rolled her eyes. "As if I'd let any man but my husband look at me down there."

"I'm glad thee found me. I do, however, insist thee abandon thy corset from this day forth until after thy child is born. Lacing thy belly so tightly is not good for thy health or that of the growing child inside thee."

"But what if Mr. Barclay rejects me? He so admires my wasp waist." She gazed down at the sprigged fabric straining over her thick and bulging midsection. "The waist I once had, that is."

"Surely he loves thee and wants the best for thee and the baby."

"Of course he does." She lifted her pointed chin. "He's been wanting to be a father for a long time. His first wife couldn't bear babies and then she died."

"Then let's loosen this corset right now. I can't do a proper examination if thee cannot breathe adequately, nor if I can't fully palpate the baby's position in thy womb."

Sissy allowed me to unhook the back of her dress and let out the binding restricting her. She let out a little laugh of relief, then filled her lungs and exhaled before speaking. "Miss Rose, I have to admit you were correct in your estimation. I haven't been able to breathe well during the day for several months."

She was halfway to using only my Christian name, which I preferred, but I didn't mention it so as not to make her aware of her slip. I surveyed her shape, which looked like she harbored a very large ball attached to the front of her belly. It was a big ball, but more well-defined than the more voluminous wombs of some gravid women.

"Thee will respire easily now. And as for thy waist? Thee has put on barely more weight than that of the baby and the womb. I daresay thee will return to thy prior shape within several months of the birth." Or near to it, anyway. I did find that younger mothers more easily regained a facsimile of their pre-pregnancy figures than older ones. I lifted her wrist and measured her pulse against the sweep of my grandmother's clock on the mantel.

"A healthy pulse," I said. "Does thee remember when thee last had a monthly?"

She blinked, thinking. "It was in the cold months. Maybe November? I know I began to feel sick in December and could barely enjoy Christmas dinner, but I thought I had a touch of the flu."

Not realizing one was pregnant wasn't uncommon for a young primigravida, but I would have thought with a husband so eager for children, Sissy might have been more alert for the signs she was carrying a baby. "So that would make thee about seven months along. Now, please lie back and lift thy skirts."

She complied, but fanned herself with her hand. "It's a warm June, isn't it, Rose?"

I smiled at hearing her drop the final barrier to simply calling me by my name. "So it is." I measured the mound of her belly. The number seemed a bit much for the seventh month. I laid my hands on her warm, taut skin and gently pressed in, palpating the baby's position. Good. The head was down and the rump up. Then I stared at her belly. Next to the rump pressed out another shape, and it wasn't feet. I moved my hands there and palpated more. Unless I was seriously mistaken, what I felt was another head, with its rump behind the other twin's head. No wonder her belly was so large.

I picked up the Pinard horn and listened in a number of spots, keeping my suspicions to myself. Try as I might, I could only detect a single heartbeat. This wasn't unusual, though. Often one twin hid behind its sibling until the very birth. Should I tell her she was going to have not one baby but two? I was obliged to say so but I dreaded it. Not the telling as much as the birth itself. Multiples were always risky. The labor often started early and the babies were too small to survive. There could be other complications, too. Seven months along, Sissy's pains could commence at any time. At least the single fetal heartbeat I'd heard was a good, fast, strong one.

Still, I had to let her know. "Sissy, I have discerned thee is carrying twins." I smiled, doing my best to keep my expression reassuring.

"Twins?" Her hazel eyes flew wide open. "Two babies? Sweet mother of Jesus." She crossed herself. "My little sister's twin brother was born sickly and died before he was a year old. It about broke Papa's heart, especially since all the rest of us are girls. Is that going to happen to one of my babies, Rose? Is one going to be poorly and go to heaven before it has a chance to live?"

"No one can say." I pressed on her ankles but blessedly didn't notice any appreciable swelling. Oedema could indicate problems she didn't need. I restored her skirts and helped her up to sitting. I perched on my chair facing her. "So thee already had twins in the family. They can present a more difficult birthing situation, but most are born alive and healthy." If they didn't come early, that is.

She picked at a thread on her cuff for several moments. When she spoke it was softly. "Rose, I'm sure the only reason Mr. Barclay married me was so I could bear him children." Her voice caught. "What if neither baby survives? What if he tosses me to the side and sends me back to my mother?" She looked up with tears threatening to spill over. "What if he finds another girl to bear his babies?"

He wouldn't be the first. I mustered a reassuring smile. "Only the good Lord knows what will come to pass." I patted her hand. "It won't serve thee to worry without cause. Thy job now is to breathe deeply, nurture these babies in thy womb, and partake of all the lovely green vegetables, fresh fruit, meat, and milk we are blessed with in this plentiful season. Go home and tell Irvin the happy news. He will surely be delighted." He would likely imagine it was his prowess as a male that produced two babies at once, but he'd be wrong. I hoped he wouldn't insist that Sissy deliver in a hospital. She'd seemed quite set against doing so.

After she left I closed my eyes and held her and her growing fetuses in the Light for some time. I opened my eyes when I heard the three younger Bailey children arrive home from school, but I had found no sure solace in prayer.

The field of medicine had made great strides of late. We now knew disease was caused by germs, and we could prevent much sickness by acts of cleanliness. But two babies passing through the birth canal one right after the other and often at dangerously low weights? If only it were possible to delay natural labor. There was no medicine to successfully halt uterine contractions once they had begun in earnest. If only it were safe to surgically remove babies at term. Surgery wasn't a real option, either. The procedure called a Caesarean section often led to the mother dying of infection and didn't always guarantee the survival of the newborns, either. It was simply too risky.

I would consult with my darling David when next we spoke. He might be aware of some new medical advance I hadn't yet heard about. But I was afraid Sissy's near future would be fraught with peril. And I would be her trusted provider. I wasn't looking forward to receiving a call telling me her labor had begun.

FOUR

I ARRIVED AT LAKE GARDNER before Bertie. I'd packed our picnic supper into the basket on my bicycle after I'd donned my new split skirt, a cleverly designed garment which resembled a skirt in the front but was actually full-legged trousers. Wearing it made bicycling so much safer than when one's skirt always threatened to get bound up in the spokes of the back wheel. After I'd seen mention of it in a publication, I'd had the garment made in a lightweight brown wool, so it was comfortable for warm-weather cycling but also didn't show dirt as much as my pale gray work dress.

David had insisted on lending me a horse and buggy for the winter, which had been a great help during the cold, icy months. Now with the weather warm again, I was just as happy to return the ever-patient Peaches and the conveyance and resume riding my simple bicycle. It took me everywhere I needed to go and kept me in good health at the same time by virtue of the vigorous pedaling required in our hilly town. In addition, keeping a horse was more work than it was worth for someone like me without a real stable or someone designated to care for the animal.

I spread a cloth under an arching oak tree and plopped down. Winnie Hanson, my brother-in-law's lady friend, had been at the house before I'd left, bustling around making dinner for the family. I quite liked her, and expected Frederick would be asking her to marry him any day now. She had a gentle way with everyone, particularly the younger children, who still sometimes expressed the pain of losing their beloved mother two years earlier in their behavior. Winnie wasn't trying to replace my sister, but she was so warm and welcoming none of us could help but love her. And she was indeed a positive influence on moody Frederick.

However, she'd asked me to accompany her to another meeting of the Ladies Circle at Mayme Settle's home tonight, one I wasn't keen on attending. Chitchat with women who liked to talk mostly of fashions and recipes was not my favorite way to pass an evening. Still, what harm would there be in a gathering of civic-minded knitters? I'd told Winnie I'd meet her there at the appointed time of seven thirty.

A horse's *whuff* aroused me from my reveries to see the smiling face of Bertie as she slid off Grover's back. She patted his neck and tied him to a nearby tree. She unlooped a sack from the pommel and handed it to me before flopping onto the cloth. Pulling off her leather gloves, she fanned herself and undid the top button of her shirtwaist. She turned her back to the sun sinking across the lake.

"This was a splendid idea, Rose. If only I'd thought to bring my bathing costume."

In truth, several young ladies and men were splashing in the still-cold waters. While yearning to cool off myself, I still found the garments a touch scandalous, despite the ladies' black stockings.

"Let's eat, instead." I drew out the two meat pies I'd absconded with from Winnie's baking session and proffered a bowl of strawberries I'd purchased from the fruit vendor in Market Square. "As it happens I must be off by sunset. Winnie convinced me to go a-knitting again, as long as I'm not called to a lady in labor. This time the gathering is to be at Mayme Settle's home."

"Eat it is, then." She took a bite of pie and uncorked her flask of sherry. "But going to Mrs. Settle's? Are you sure you want to socialize with the likes of her?"

"Not really." I lifted a shoulder and dropped it. "But it's for a good cause." I sipped from the bottle of lemonade I'd brought for myself, being a non-imbibing Friend, as nearly all of us were.

"Mm," Bertie murmured around a mouthful. "Delicious pie."

"It's Winnie's doing."

"Think she and Frederick are going to tie the knot before you do?" Bertie wasn't one to soften a blunt inquiry.

Were they? It was possible, given how long it was taking David and me to fix a date for our union. "Oh, Bertie. I don't know what to think. David told me back in Second Month his mother had given her blessing. But now she's fussing about all kinds of details." I grimaced. "Makes a body want to run away and find a justice of the peace somewhere."

"Elope?" She whistled. "Now wouldn't that make a headline? 'Unitarian doctor and Quaker midwife tie knot in secret!'"

"Stop, now. It's not funny."

She tilted her head and gazed at me. "Come on. Sure it is. And anyway, what's to stop two adults from getting married if it's what they want? You've been wearing his ring almost a year now. What more are you waiting for?"

"Thee knows very well. Family and faith are important to both of us. I think, and I say 'think' for a reason, the elders of the Women's Business Meeting might be leaning toward not exacting quite the penalty they had threatened for my marrying a Unitarian. And Mother has assured me my home Meeting in Lawrence would welcome our celebration of marriage. But . . ."

"But Clarinda Dodge?"

"Yes. David's mother wants all kinds of parties and dinners, and I don't even know what else."

"Poor Rosetta." She patted my hand.

"Thee witnessed Faith and Zebulon's marriage, Bertie. They each had a new piece of clothing made, which will be serviceable for years to come. In the presence of family, friends, and members of our Meeting, the couple vowed to love and honor each other and signed the certificate. During worship, various people shared memories and gave blessings, and after Rise of Meeting, all present signed the certificate as witnesses to the union. Then our two families had a simple repast at home and the affair was over. Faith moved to Zeb's family's house that same night. I long for such a straightforward rite." I gazed at a red-haired woman in a well-cut sprigged lawn dress strolling alone along the water's edge with her hands clasped behind her. Her brow was knit and she chewed on the inside of her cheek as if worrying whatever problem plagued her, as if mirroring my own concerns.

Bertie clapped. "Enough of this! I see the prospect is dragging you down something fierce, my friend." She chucked me under the chin. "What's good in your life? How are the happy expectant mothers coming along, bless their sainted souls?"

I laughed. I well knew Bertie hadn't a maternal bone in her body, or so she'd told me. She'd never felt the urge to procreate, and as her physical longings tilted sharply toward her fellow woman, she had nothing to worry about.

"Well, I have a most interesting client at present. Does thee know Jeanette Papka?"

Bertie took a swig of her drink and thought for a moment. "I believe I do. Tall lady, blind? And gainfully employed translating at the courthouse?"

I nodded. "That's her. Smart as anything, and what she does is interpret. She set me straight on the difference. Translating from one language to the next is what one does with a written text. Translators have time, dictionaries, not much pressure."

"And interpreting is the spoken word?" Bertie asked, clearly engaged in the idea of Jeanette's talents.

"Yes. Interpreting is much harder. She listens to one language and speaks the meaning of the utterance in the other at the next moment. And then goes back in the other direction. I've no idea why her head doesn't explode." I mimicked my own head shooting into the sky. "She's much in demand interpreting for immigrants who aren't yet fluent in English, and you know we've had a recent surge of workers coming into town, especially from French Canada and Poland."

"And this Mrs. Papka is pregnant, I gather?"

I nodded, finishing my own pie. "She is, with her second. She is doing well, although I fear she might birth a quite large baby." I frowned. "I have another client I'm not so happy about. She is the wife of the banker Irvin Barclay."

Bertie's mouth took on a shape as if she'd tasted a rotten piece of meat. "Barclay is as bad as Mrs. Settle. Ruder than a peasant to me."

"Well, Sissy is his child bride, very nearly. And she's quite distressed something will go wrong with her birth. Or births, I should say."

"Births?" Bertie stared out over the sparkling lake. "She's having twins, is she?" She spoke slowly and deliberately.

I gazed at her. "Yes, it appears she is. And such births can be quite difficult even if the babies go to term, which they often don't."

Bertie didn't move except to lift her chin.

I knew her too well. "Bertie, darling." I stroked her arm. "This topic has disturbed thee. Has thee had a painful experience with twins thee was close to?"

She nodded once as the sun dipped below Whittier Hill beyond the lake. "You could say so, yes."

I waited for more. Bertie picked up the cap to her bottle and tossed it over and over in the air, her gaze on the water, on the trees, anywhere but at me.

She turned to me with a too-bright smile. "Listen to that bird!"

We passed the rest of our supper talking about the song of the wood thrush. We discussed the upcoming carriage opening, when all the town's world-famous carriage factories opened their doors to the public and the town was flooded with visitors both American and international. We talked about the recent shenanigans of President Harrison, Bertie's stylish new hat, and Mark Twain's latest detective story, "The Stolen White Elephant." Anything—except twins.

FIVE

I RODE IN THE TWILIGHT to Mayme's home a short distance away out on Whitehall Road, thinking about Bertie as I pedaled. I was no more the wiser about her experience with twins, one which clearly had affected her deeply. I hoped she'd tell me by and by.

A man stooped over a neat flower bed in front of the big house with a mansard roof as I approached. Water streamed out of a copper watering can onto freshly planted snapdragons and campanula. The bed was edged with the glossy pointed foliage of lily of the valley, although their tiny white bells of spring flowers were long past.

"Good evening," I said, putting my foot down after I'd slowed. "Given how warm it's been, I should say those young plants are grateful for a long drink of water."

He straightened and faced me, but he was still bent over, as if his back hurt him to stand up straight. Ash-gray hair hung long on his collarless shirt, and brown suspenders held up loose dark pants. Nearly skeletal in appearance, he smiled at me with dark gaps where several teeth used to be.

"Hullo, miss. 'Tis a lovely night, indeed."

"I don't believe we've met. I'm Rose Carroll." I smiled but didn't hold out my hand. Typically a man of his age and social class wouldn't accept a handshake with a young woman, anyway, and I didn't want to cause him discomfort.

"The name's Riley, miss. Adoniram Riley."

I blinked. The last time I'd heard the unusual name had been four years earlier. I'd still been apprenticed to my midwifery teacher, Orpha Perkins. A young woman named Alice Riley had sadly bled out and died after delivering her baby boy. Her distraught father was this same Adoniram if I wasn't mistaken.

"How fares thy grandson, Adoniram?"

He stared at me, his watering can forgotten. "How do you know about the lad?"

"I was assisting midwife Orpha Perkins when he was born, and when thy daughter so tragically left this world, despite our best efforts. I hope the boy is well."

He nodded slowly. "I remember you now. Young Donny is a strapping fellow, smart and funny, thank you, miss. He lives with my boy and his wife, over to Carpenter Street, so I see him most regular like."

Now I remembered. He was a widower. Alice, the poor thing, had refused to reveal the identity of the baby's father. Orpha had whispered to me she suspected it was Mayme Settle's son. Alice had been working as a maid in Mayme's household when she became pregnant. I didn't know what had become of the son, whether he had owned up to being the father or had skipped town instead.

"I'm glad he's thriving," I said.

"By rights his mama should be looking after him." He raised his eyes to the imposing square house with a cupola topping the third floor. "But having his mother with him wasn't God's plan, after all." His expression was grim.

"It is sometimes hard to fathom His ways."

He nodded without speaking.

"Does thee live here on the property?"

"Yes, miss. I'm the jack-of-all-trades to the Settles, I am. Or to Mrs. Settle, more so. She's the one wears the pants in the family, if you get my meaning. She lets me have a room in the carriage house for my quarters."

So that was why the boy wasn't living with his grandfather. A single room wouldn't be suitable, and if what my teacher had said was true, the Settles would be faced with their son's illegitimate child at every turn. If they knew about his parentage, that is. But why was Adoniram still working for the Settles?

He went on. "These be my flowers, and I grow most of the vegetables the family consumes, too."

"Really? I have been trying to plant more vegetables where I live. I'm afraid I'm no good at nurturing baby seeds. My starts always perish from one thing or another."

"You come by here when you're ready to plant, miss. I always have seedlings aplenty. Too many for the space out back."

I thanked him, promising I'd be back. Maybe he stayed because he loved his work and had free lodging, to boot.

21

After Adoniram turned back to his flowers, I spied Winnie coming around the side of the home from the carriage house and hailed her. I leaned my metal steed against a hitching post and waited while she came up the walk.

"Thee has my supplies?" I'd asked her to bring my knitting project so I didn't have to cart it along to the lake. Winnie, a widow and a nurse at the same hospital across the Merrimack in Newburyport where David had his practice, drove a drop-front phaeton. She wasn't obliged to carry everything on her person as I was.

She held up a large quilted bag. "Of course, and extra yarn. Shall we?"

SIX

OH, DEAR. Inside the house I wondered what I had gotten myself into. The last time I'd gone to a Ladies Circle it had been an afternoon gathering held in the hall at Saint James Church on Main Street. Here we were ushered into an ornate parlor with a circle of women in their best visiting gowns perched on stiff-backed chairs. Not a one was knitting. Instead they sipped tea and nibbled daintily on sweets.

I almost backed out of the doorway, but Winnie was behind me and I would have knocked her down. I smoothed down the front of my bicycling garment and clasped my hands in front of me.

Mayme spotted us and rose. "Miss Carroll and Mrs. Hanson, do come in." She glanced down at my cycling garment and blinked with a set to her mouth that indicated disapproval, but she seemed to catch herself before saying anything about it, and introduced us to the group.

I'd delivered the babies of two of the younger women but didn't know most of the rest of them except Georgia Clarke, the wife of a prominent carriage factory owner. She'd nearly hemorrhaged to death last summer after her fifth baby's birth. In her case I'd managed to arrest the flow and she'd easily regained her health.

"I'll come see you soon," Georgia whispered to me when I came to her. She pointed surreptitiously to her stomach.

I gave a single nod. I'd thought she hadn't wanted to bear more children. She'd said five was enough. She wasn't a young woman, either. Anyone over forty giving birth could encounter challenges to her health. Sometimes the baby was born Mongoloid, as well. Sadly, the prospects for such children were dim, at best.

I followed Winnie to our seats and exchanged a small glance with her, trying to signal "What are we doing here?" but it was no use. If I hadn't been raised to live according to Quaker values, one of which was integrity, I might have attempted a white lie and said I had only stopped in to pay my respects, that I was needed at a labor. Instead I sat where I was directed.

Sissy Barclay appeared in the doorway. "Am I too late?" She smiled and handed a wrapped box looking like a candy container to her hostess. "Mr. Barclay sends his greetings and wanted you to have this, Mrs. Settle." She smiled sweetly. "But he said it was for your personal enjoyment and not to be shared."

Mayme raised a single eyebrow at the gift, then thanked Sissy. "Of course you aren't too late, Mrs. Barclay." She set the box on the piano instead of adding the candy to the refreshments table.

I gave Sissy a little wave and noted that her breathing seemed more normal. But from the fit of her gown I suspected she'd merely kept her loosened corset, not abandoned it, perhaps so as not to be looked down on by the other ladies. So many women lost their independence when carrying a child. Upper-class ladies were banned from social occasions, and working women were made to leave their jobs. As a result, many expectant mothers restricted the expansion of their thickening waistlines as long as they could.

After Mayme poured tea for us newcomers and offered around the three-tier dish of cookies and other sweetmeats, she surveyed the group.

"Ladies, this new project is a very exciting one for me. We'll be knitting baby blankets for the young mothers at Alms Farm."

Everyone knew Alms Farm was the town's poor farm, where lived the destitute and desperate. I'd helped several unwed mothers give birth out there, the arrangement being for their newborns to be offered for adoption. The farm wasn't affiliated with a particular church, but rather was paid for out of town funds.

A buzz of soft comments filled the air. "Now, now." Mayme clapped her hands. "I know doing so might make it appear we support the unmarried mothers residing there. But they need our assistance." Her smile was very much one of a person who thought she occupied a superior position to many. "Their poor bastard babies didn't ask to be brought into the world, so let's make certain they do not suffer from lack of comfort."

Their poor bastard babies, indeed. Like Donny Riley, perhaps? I chafed at her condescending tone as well as the notion of "bastard" imposed by society. A baby is a baby, and if it is loved and provided for by its mother, who should care that the father isn't a part of the baby's life? Of course the ideal was a loving couple raising their child together, as David and I planned to do. But I'd seen enough alternatives to such an ideal to know there was more than one way to bring up a healthy and loved human being.

"So let's get started, shall we?" Mayme spread her hands. "You've all brought your needles and yarn, I assume." She gave the dimensions of the baby blankets and sat, then leaned over to draw her own project out of a knitting bag mounted on a folding frame.

It occurred to me how curious it was that Mayme had selected this charity as her latest. Wouldn't it call attention to her own bastard grandson? I watched her work. Perhaps, because of her distinctly uncharitable comments about Bertie, I hadn't allowed that she might have a bigger heart than I'd imagined. She did lead quite a few activities designed to benefit the less fortunate: filling and giving away a hundred or more Christmas boxes, an educational program for mill girls, a children's shoe and warm coat collection in the fall, festive food baskets at Easter, and more.

On the piano next to the candy box sat a large framed photograph of two teenage children, a boy and a girl. The angular girl, in a white dress, was around fourteen. Old enough to have put up her hair and let down her hems, but she looked awkward and stiff in the attire. The boy, a couple of years older, wore a cap at a rakish angle and had his arm slung around his sister's shoulders. His cocky grin matched his stance.

"Are those thy children, Mayme?" I asked.

She pressed her eyes closed for a moment, then twisted to regard the picture. Her face still looked wistful when she returned her gaze to me. "Yes, when they were younger." She turned to the woman next to her and checked her handiwork, clearly dismissing any discussion of family.

Wistful because of the daughter she couldn't bring herself to accept? And where was the wayward son? I felt sorry for her, despite her imperious approach to the world.

We'd been knitting and conversing in soft voices for several minutes when Mayme raised her head and regarded the gathering. "I wonder how else we might help these unfortunate mothers. If they promise to tread the straight and narrow path, would any of you have a position of service to offer one? After she gives birth, of course."

Georgia nodded with approval. "I think that's an excellent idea, Mrs. Settle. I might be able to use an additional girl in my household."

Another woman raised a finger and said she would consider it, as well.

"Excellent." Mayme beamed. "Frankly, the fewer residents at Alms Farm, the better, since funds to feed them come out of your taxes and mine."

A thin man poked his head in. "Mrs. Settle? May I have a moment of your time?" His spectacles perched crookedly on a head of sparse—and mussed—half-silver hair. His head was disheveled but his tie was neatly in place under his waistcoat. He wore a blue silk smoking jacket embroidered with a paisley design over his clothes. I detected a hint of an accent in his speech but I couldn't place where he might originally be from.

This had to be Mayme's husband. No butler would wear a smoking jacket. The contrast between the thin fellow and his matronly wife could have been an illustration for the Jack Sprat nursery rhyme. I sat nearest the door, and I could smell whiskey on his breath.

The long needles flew out of Mayme's hands. "Mr. Settle! You startled me. What are you doing here?" She did not smile at her husband. "What can you possibly want? I told you I was having Ladies Circle here tonight." She pressed her lips into a line as straight as a ruler.

Merton Settle batted at the air with both hands. "Pardon me, ladies. I've misplaced my spectacles and I need my wife's help to locate them." He smiled abashedly. "She can find anything."

He obviously didn't realize his glasses were on top of his head. I held a hand in front of my mouth to hide my amusement, as did several of the other ladies. Georgia winked at me.

Mayme was not so entertained and didn't even try to disguise her contempt. "Merton, they are atop your foolish head. Now go." She leaned down again to pick up her knitting. "He asks me a hundred times a day where things are when they're sitting out in plain sight," she muttered to her neighbor, who nodded in sympathy.

As I watched, Merton's ineffectual expression was replaced by narrowed eyes and a determined set to his jaw. And he aimed the hatred directly at his wife.

SEVEN

I was working on my accounts at a quarter before ten the next morning when the telephone rang in the sitting room. Lina, scrubbing pots in the kitchen, wouldn't answer it. She'd said she was afraid of the device, and I hadn't pressed her about it. I hurried into the next room. We'd had the candlestick telephone installed primarily for my business. I thought fast. Did I have a client due to begin her travails about now? I didn't think so. Foreboding filled me. Was this Sissy calling to announce her labor?

"Good morning. Rose Carroll speaking."

"Rose, this is Georgia Clarke."

I greeted her. "Is thee calling to arrange an antenatal appointment? I have several appointments open today."

"Well, in a way. But more urgently, have you heard the news?" Her words rushed out.

"News? No, I haven't looked at a newspaper yet today."

"May I come over now? Are you free? I have something I want to tell you, and it's not suited for the telephone."

I reviewed today's schedule in my mind. "Yes, if thee comes now. I have an antenatal appointment at eleven but I am entirely free until then."

"I'll be there in ten minutes." The call went dead.

I stared at the part of the device one spoke into and then at the trumpet-shaped listening piece. Finally I depressed the lever and replaced the piece. What news could this be? If the president had been assassinated, Georgia wouldn't have need for secrecy. She'd already signaled she was with child, so it wasn't that, and why would I have heard it from anyone but her?

I shook my head. I'd find out soon enough, although she'd whetted my curiosity sharper than a butcher's carving knife. Georgia lived only two blocks away, and the ten minutes would be for summoning her driver, donning outdoor shoes, and climbing into a Clarke carriage. I headed back to my parlor to straighten it and await the tidings, whether glad or bad.

When I opened the door, Georgia swept in with a rush of fresh air. She turned and faced me in the hall, her mouth open, ready to speak.

"Georgia, stop. Come along and sit down. We have a full hour at our disposal."

"Of course." She'd been to my parlor before.

She perched upright on the chaise and I in my chair facing her. Her white-streaked brown hair was in a neat chignon, and the lines around her mouth seemed deeper this morning.

"Can I bring thee tea or coffee? Or a glass of water?"

She batted away my suggestion. "No, thank you. You won't believe the news." She leaned toward me. "Mayme Settle is dead." She watched me with wide eyes, her hand to her mouth.

I stared at her. "Good heavens. What happened to her?"

"I don't know for sure."

"Poor Mayme. We were with her only last evening." She'd been a difficult woman, certainly, but she was far too young to be meeting her Maker.

"I know," Georgia said slowly. "It's terribly sad, and she was such a charitable lady." She dabbed her handkerchief at the corner of her eye.

"Is thee sure?"

"I am. I heard it from . . . well, it's a long chain of who told whom. But it's most surely true." She glanced right and left, even though she knew we were alone. She whispered, "And they're saying it was murder. Murder, Rose!"

I sat back as if I'd been punched. No wonder Georgia had wanted to tell me. How many homicide cases had I been involved with to date? Four, I thought, or five. "Murder. Exactly who is saying so?"

"Well." She sniffed and folded her hands in her lap. "My cook said the maid at Mayme's told her the Settles' cook saw a police detective going into the house this morning. He was that policeman, the one you know. Dinnegan or some such Irish name."

"Kevin Donovan. That doesn't mean she was murdered, though. He might simply be investigating something untoward in her demise, an accident, perhaps." I'd leave aside for the moment how Georgia's cook was acquainted with Mayme's maid. Asking would only complicate things, and people who worked in the serving trade of course knew each other. "Does thee know the method by which Mayme died?"

"The maid was the one who found poor Mrs. Settle dead in her bed. She said her mistress looked awful. Her face was mottled with red and she had some white substance under her fingernails. The maid screamed, of course, and ran out. Later she overheard the detective speaking with Mr. Settle. The husband was beside himself, as you can only imagine, even though we both saw how she berated him last night." She hurried to add, "May she rest in peace."

"But of course he was devastated." I pictured poor Mayme having a difficult passage, even if it hadn't been a violent one. And if it had, who would have reason to kill her? Even as I wondered what the white substance had been, I pressed my eyes shut and held Mayme Settle in God's Light, that her released soul might go easily. I held Merton and his children in the Light, too, for comfort in their grief.

"Penny for your thoughts, Rose," Georgia murmured. "It's not every day one gets to witness a detective's brain at work. Do tell."

I opened my eyes and folded my arms. "You know very well I'm not a detective, Georgia. We've had entirely enough talk about murder. Calling her death that might be entirely the result of gossip."

She tried unsuccessfully to hide her disappointment. "Are you sure?"

"Of course I'm sure. We know nothing about what happened or how she actually died, and it's not our business." I smiled to soften my words. "Now, what's this about another pregnancy? I thought thee was all done bearing babies."

She lifted one shoulder and dropped it, giving a little smile. "I haven't gone through the change yet, and Robert, I mean, Mr. Clarke is so very smitten with baby Rosie, he wants another daughter."

After I'd saved Georgia's life, she'd named her first daughter after me, despite my protestations.

Georgia lowered her voice. "And I do love the marital act, Rose. My pleasure in it keeps increasing as I grow older." Her cheeks were pink with her confession. "Isn't it strange?"

"It's not at all unusual. Thee clearly loves thy husband, as he does thee. And why shouldn't a woman derive as much pleasure from intimacy as a man, or more? I have heard other mature ladies confess the same to me. Thee is not alone."

"At any rate, I can't bring myself to refuse my husband—nay, I seek him out," Georgia said. "Rosie is still nursing and I thought perhaps I wouldn't conceive."

"Once a baby isn't exclusively suckling, women usually become fertile again. Thy daughter was born eleven months ago, so she must have been eating real food for half a year or so, am I right?"

"Yes. She has little teeth now and a tremendous appetite. She's as round as Humpty Dumpty. And as cheerful and sweet a child as a mother could dream of. So here I am, carrying baby number six."

"Then I congratulate thee." I looked at her waist, which was in fact somewhat more thickened than usual. "How far along does thee think the pregnancy is?"

She patted her belly. "Who knows? Three months? Four? My monthlies hadn't yet resumed a regular schedule."

"Has thee felt quickening?"

"Not that I have noticed, no."

It seemed a little late not to have already sensed the fetus moving, but as she said, it was hard to tell without regular monthlies. "How about aversion to foods? Nausea? I don't remember if thee suffered from morning sickness with thy earlier pregnancies."

"Only with the first, and none now, either."

"I'll add a new page to thy chart. Let me have a listen. It might be too early to pick up the sound of the heart, depending on thy dates."

She lay back and lifted her skirts, familiar with my examination procedure by now. I pressed the Pinard horn into various spots where the heartbeat was likely to be most audible but I didn't hear a thing. I might have guessed she was going through the change of life except for her thickened waist.

I shook my head. "I can't hear anything, but the fetus could simply still be too small. Come back for a check after thee notices the baby move and when thy belly is more enlarged, and I'll make an estimation of thy due date." I supposed I should mention the possibility of Mongoloidism, but decided not to. That could wait.

"Splendid." She stood. "Rose, you can share the facts of investigating poor Mrs. Settle's death with me if you want." Her tone was tentative. "I mean, if you can."

I didn't sigh out loud but I wanted to. Georgia was far too interested in the prospect of learning how Mayme expired. She seemed already to have lost sight of the fact that a lady had died, and apparently violently. Such an event was cause for mourning, not for excitement.

EIGHT

I RAPPED ON THE DOOR of Orpha's home at a little after one o'clock that afternoon, my bike leaning against the fence. Throughout the two additional antenatal appointments after Georgia had gone home, my mind had roiled with questions about Mayme's death. About Alice Riley's four years ago, too. And about how I would handle the births of Sissy's twins once she began her travails. Luckily, my apprentice, Annie Beaumont, had been doing the rest of the examinations today. Neither client had experienced any complications so far. I'd sat back and only spoken when Annie had had a question or had forgotten to carry out part of the visit. Annie and I had discussed both pregnancies after the second client left, then Annie had gone on her way, too.

But my thoughts hadn't left with her. To only one person — besides David — could I unload my burden of concerns, and it was my former teacher. I'd grabbed a bite to eat and set out on my bicycle.

Orpha's granddaughter Alma opened the door of the house she and her family shared with Orpha. The dressmaker's face lit up. "Rose, have you come to see Granny? You are exactly what she needs today." Alma wore a tape measure draped around her neck, and a square of flannel attached to her dress with a safety pin near her left shoulder was full of straight pins. "She seems to be carrying a burden in her mind, and you always cheer her soul."

That would make two of us, then.

She stood back. "Come along in, please. Granny, Rose is here," she called out.

I found Orpha in the parlor, rocking and reading her Bible, with her chair pulled over to the window. The room smelled, as it always did, of books and peppermints. Orpha loved to have a supply of candy about and was as inveterate a reader as I had ever met. She looked up and beamed at me, then laid the ribbon in the center of the book and closed it.

"Come to brighten an old lady's day, dear Rose?" She held out her arms but did not rise.

We embraced and I sat. "More like seeking a wise woman's counsel."

She let out a guffaw. Her strength was much diminished from her prime but not her hearty laugh. "I'm quite sure I've forgotten any wisdom I once had. When you're on the fast train to cross the Dark River, memory is the first thing to go." She shook her head and made a clicking sound with her mouth.

"Thee *is not* on thy way out, Orpha," I insisted, although in truth I doubted she had five more years to live.

Alma hovered. "Can I fetch you water or tea, Rose?"

I smiled at her. "No, thank thee. I am fine." The temperature had cooled to a more normal one for this time of year. It was sunny and a breeze had cooled me as I cycled.

"As am I." Orpha made a shooing gesture at her granddaughter. "Back to work with you before those girls come home."

"Is the younger one already attending school?" I asked. I thought she was only about four.

Alma laughed. "No, but she calls it school. My sister takes her to play with her own young ones so I can work. Off I go, then. Good to see you, Rose."

"And thee." I watched her disappear down the hall and turned my focus to the old lady in front of me. "Alma said thee is carrying a burden. Will thee share it with me?"

She gave a hearty laugh. "'Tis only the burden of living more than four score years. I find my mind dwelling on memories new and old, sometimes in something of a jumble. Births, deaths, joys, and pains, as well as the quotidian. Bread I have baked. Letters written. Even doilies tatted. It's nothing to be concerned with, Rose."

"Very well."

Orpha gazed at me. "But I can see your own troubles on your face. Which shall we hear of first?"

"Does thee remember Alice Riley's delivery? It was four years ago. The mother who hemorrhaged."

"Of course I do. Miss Riley's was a severe case of it. We tried all the tricks in our bag and nothing helped. Why do you think of it now?"

"I encountered her father yesterday evening at the home of

Mayme Settle. I inquired about the little boy and he said he was well, and living with Adoniram's son and his wife."

"This is a blessing, then, not a worry."

I nodded. "I seem to remember thee suspected Mayme Settle's son was the baby's father, but that Mayme had hushed the whole thing up because she didn't want her son marrying a lowly maid. Do I remember correctly?"

Orpha rocked a few more times before speaking. "It's a long sad story, Rose." Her rocker continued to creak with the back-and-forth movement. "Miss Riley hadn't been well in the last months of carrying her child. Her father's sister urged her to come and see me, but Mrs. Settle wouldn't give Alice time off. We were called once the labor started, but the puerperal eclampsia from which she suffered complicated the birth so. And once the baby was delivered, we couldn't save her. I do believe Mrs. Settle made a one-time payment for the boy's upkeep." She gazed into my face. Her eyes were rheumy but I'd always felt she could see directly into my needs and wishes.

"And the son didn't step up and do the right thing by marrying Alice before the baby was born?"

"He did not, more's the pity. I believe his mother exerted pressure on him not to, and off he went to join the merchant marine."

It was my turn to speak. "I learned this morning Mayme was murdered. How I do not yet know, but someone was angry enough with her to end her life."

"I learned this, as well. You wondered if the long-suffering gardener was the culprit?"

"It crossed my mind, yes." I let out a long breath. "If Mayme played a part in Alice's death by not allowing her time off to seek antenatal care, one could understand Adoniram's wish for justice. Although why he would wait four years to exact his revenge escapes me."

"Have you shared these thoughts with your detective friend?"

"No." Not yet, that is. "I haven't heard officially that her death has been deemed a homicide, and perhaps Kevin already has someone in custody."

"No doubt you'll be having a good chat with Mr. Donovan

sometime soon." Orpha tilted her head. "I suspect you have another worry pressing on you, Rose."

"I do. I saw a new client yesterday, Sissy Barclay. She's about seven months along and is carrying twins."

"Did you detect two heartbeats?"

"No, only one. One fetus is vertex, but next to its rump I palpated another head. Sissy said her younger sister had been one of two, but the twin boy had been born sickly and died quite young. Now she's worried about the delivery, and I am, too, for all the reasons thee knows."

"And at seven months she could go into labor any time from now to August," Orpha observed.

"I know."

"How is your French-Canadian apprentice working out?"

At last I had something to smile about. "She's learning fast. She's read the *Guide to Midwifery* cover to cover and has started taking over some of the easier antenatal visits for me. Annie is a real treasure."

"Good. It was what I thought about you when you began your apprenticeship with me. I'm glad Annie will assist you with the twin births and learn from the doing." Orpha reached out a knobby and spotted hand to pat my knee. "I trained you well, Rose Carroll. You will do your best. Your best is all you can do."

NINE

I STOOD WITH MY BICYCLE on the sidewalk in front of Orpha's, not sure where to go next or what to do. I had promised Frederick I would make dinner for the family tonight, since David was coming over and Frederick would be dining at Winnie's. I heard the bluefish were running and that the fish market had gotten in a supply. Picking up a few fillets wouldn't take long, and neither would making biscuits to go along with them. Add late asparagus and early strawberries and we could call it dinner. As long as it was tasty, no one would mind simple fare, and that would yield more time for me to spend with my beloved.

Of course what I truly wanted to do first was visit Kevin at the police station and learn what the situation of Mayme's death was. However, despite commending my efforts at the end of the most recent case, his new chief frowned on my presence at the station and on my participating in investigations even away from there.

I snapped my fingers. Kevin's wife, Emmaline, and I had become friendly. I'd been her midwife for their second child, a girl born only a month ago. Of course I had conducted my postpartum visit to check on both mother and daughter in the days after the delivery. It wouldn't hurt to see how little Rosalie—whom they had also named for me, much to my embarrassment—was faring a month later, and I always welcomed a chat with Emmaline.

It didn't take me long to ride to their home on Boardman Street. Their extremely bright son, Sean, whom Emmaline was schooling at home, sat cross-legged under a tree in front of the house, his nose in a thick book.

"Hello, there, Sean." I smiled when he looked up.

"No horse for me to watch today, Miss Rose?" He jumped up.

"No. Only this metal one, and she doesn't need much watching." I had left Peaches and the buggy in his care earlier in the year when I'd visited Sean's mother.

"I'll be sure no hooligans run off with her."

I smiled. "I thank thee. What is thee reading?"

He picked up the book from where he'd dropped it. "It's a medical textbook on children's ailments."

I nodded once. I had no doubt his genius brain could make out the words, despite him being barely seven, but I wasn't sure why he was reading it. Unless . . . "And why does thee read a thick tome like that on such a pretty day?"

"My friend is still at regular school until four o'clock. And my little sister is poorly, so I thought I'd see if I could figure out what's wrong with her."

"My goodness. What are her symptoms?"

He raised his chin. "She's hot and sweaty."

"Has thee come up with what it might be, Dr. Sean?" I kept my tone serious.

He regarded me for a moment to make sure I wasn't joshing. "Those are symptoms of fever. The etiology could be any number of diseases."

Etiology. But he was correct. Fevers could have many causes. "I'd better get in there and see her."

"Oh, and she hasn't been wetting her diaper."

I stared at him. This could be more serious than a low-grade fever. "Does she have spots, or a rash?"

He shook his head. "You're doing differential diagnosis, aren't you? I read about that."

I smiled. "After a fashion, yes. I'll go in and check her right away. Thank thee, young man."

By the time I knocked on the door he was seated and perusing the textbook again.

"Oh, Rose, I'm so glad you're here," Emmaline said when she opened the door. Little Rosalie was dressed only in a cotton diaper and the lightest of lawn gowns. The petite mother's face was flushed, too, and her curly dark hair hung in a messy braid down her back. "Please come in." She stood back, then stuck her head out and checked on her son before closing the door.

"Thy physician child told me Rosalie is feverish and not passing water. How long has she been so?" I took the baby from Emmaline when she handed her to me. The infant's torso and head were far too warm.

She didn't even smile at my remark about Sean. "Since yesterday, but she's much worse now." Her eyes were wide and welling with tears. "I can't find Kevin anywhere today. They said he's out on an important case. The doctor we normally see is away and didn't leave anyone in his place. And my own mother left on a long trip last week. What shall I do?"

I sat on the sofa and removed Rosalie's nightgown and diaper. She cried, but no tears trickled down her cheek, and the sound was weak. Her diaper was indeed dry. She hadn't been a big baby at birth, and if anything she seemed to have lost weight in the few weeks since. I glanced up at a hovering Emmaline wringing her hands.

"When is the last time she nursed?" I asked.

"I've been giving her the breast constantly but she's getting too weak to suckle." Emmaline's pale green day dress bore the telltale patches of leaky breasts. "Sean was never sick when he was little. I don't know what to do!"

I took a deep breath. I would give this a try, but if the solutions I could think of didn't work, I would get on the telephone and not give up until David was on his way here.

"It's a good sign she doesn't have spots." I gazed into Emmaline's face. "Listen to me. We need to do several things and they're all important. First, I need for thee to take a deep breath. If thee isn't in a condition to care for thy daughter, there's no hope. Does thee understand?"

Emmaline nodded, still frantic. The act of breathing deeply in and out helped, as did seeing I was serious. She smoothed down her dress, tucked her wayward hair behind her ears, and straightened her shoulders.

Good. I continued. "We need to cool Rosalie down and get fluids into her. Please bring a basin of cold water, some cloths, a towel, a clean soup bowl, and the smallest spoon thee has."

The water, towel, and cloths arrived first. I laid the towel on my lap and began to press the cool soaked cloths against the baby's hot body. When one warmed I dropped it on the floor and started again, leaving moisture all over her skin. I blew on her until the moisture dried, repeating and repeating. Windows stood open at each side of the room and a blessed cross breeze helped. As I worked I held her in God's Light, that such a new and welcomed life should not be snuffed out so soon.

Emmaline returned with the bowl and a silver baby spoon.

"We'll dispense with modesty for the moment," I said. "Thee needs to express milk into this bowl and we'll see if we can get some into her mouth with the spoon."

Emmaline wasted no time unbuttoning the bodice of her dress and pulling it and her shift down off her shoulders, sliding her arms out. She set the bowl on a cushion in her lap and soon the bluish-white milk dripped into the bowl. "I feel so much better. I thought I would explode."

"It's fine to express it anytime thee needs to until she improves enough to nurse on her own. Here, give me the bowl. Keep thy top down and hold her. The smell of thee will help, and the feel of thy skin against hers."

Once we were situated, with Rosalie in Emmaline's bare arms, nestled against her breasts, I laid one wet cloth on the baby's chest and another on her forehead to continue the cooling. I touched her cheek with my finger, glad to see she still had enough strength to root toward it, opening the tiny rosebud of her lips. I spooned in a few drops of milk. She swallowed and I did it again.

I glanced at Emmaline. "She's taking it. Sing to her, or tell her a story. Anything so she hears thy voice and feels it through her body, too." I kept feeding Rosalie until a little milk dribbled out the side of her mouth and her eyes closed.

I closed my own for another moment of prayer. May God keep this baby safe and bring her back to health.

"Rose, how can I thank you?" Silent tears crept down Emmaline's cheeks.

"We're not out of the woods yet. But now thee knows what to do. Keep her cool. Make sure she gets milk into her every time she's awake until she's strong enough to suckle. Wake her if she sleeps more than an hour. And next time? Call me earlier, please. If I can't help, my betrothed might be able to. David Dodge is a doctor in Newburyport." Although what more he could have done I hadn't a clue.

She wiped her cheeks and sniffed. Her expression grew puzzled. "You didn't know our baby was sick, and the timing of your visit makes me think it wasn't a purely social call." She raised a single eyebrow. "Are you working on this new case, too?"

"No . . ." I drew out the word. "But I might have a few ideas for Kevin if he's interested."

"I thought so!" The old Emmaline was back, grinning. She'd helped get messages back and forth between Kevin and me in the winter. "I'll tell him."

I stood. "Is thee all right for me to leave now?"

"Yes, as long as you don't mind if I don't get up." She gazed down at her only daughter, then slipped her arms back into her shift. "But call Dr. Sean in, if you would. He'll be as happy as an Ipswich clam to help with baby cooling and feeding."

Before I reached the door, though, the telephone rang on the small table next to the door.

"Could you please answer the telephone, Rose? If it's Kevin, the device has a long cord."

I lifted the receiver. "Good afternoon. Donovan household."

"Do I hear your voice, Miss Rose?" Kevin's voice blared through the line.

"Yes." I nodded at Emmaline and lifted the telephone to carry it over. "I've been helping thy wife with a feverish baby. I think we have her cooled at last and with a bit of milk in her, as well."

"Thank my sainted stars, Miss Rose. Our little girl was right poorly this morning. I felt like a wretch leaving them behind, I can tell you. I had no choice but to come to work on an urgent matter, not if I wanted to stay employed."

"Mayme Settle's murder?"

He fell silent for a flabbergasted moment. "I won't even ask how you know about it. But yes. And I'm afraid your friend Miss Winslow is in a spot of trouble."

It was my turn to be shocked. "Bertie? What in heavens does thee mean by a spot of trouble?"

He lowered his voice as if he didn't want to let others nearby know what he was saying. "We have several witnesses saying Mrs. Settle was continually insulting Miss Winslow about her, ah, personal life. Another citizen—one of high repute, mind you— attested to seeing Miss Winslow in the vicinity of the Settle home last evening."

"This is pickled hogwash, Kevin, and thee knows it. I was at the Settle home last night and I saw no trace of Bertie."

"That's strong language for you, Rose. But don't tell me you were with the Settles at ten o'clock last night?"

"No, earlier. Tell me, has Bertie been arrested?"

"She might be soon, she's putting up that much fuss."

"Thee knows a witness account isn't enough for an arrest. I'm coming straight over there and don't thee dare try to stop me."

"Yes, Miss Rose." His tone was infuriatingly placating. "Now, might I speak with the long-suffering Mrs. Donovan?"

TEN

I RUSHED UP THE STAIRS to the police station and hauled open the heavy door. If they didn't let me see Bertie, I wasn't sure what I would do. Like Emmaline with her feverish baby, I had temporarily lost my own calm and reason, and I knew it. Somebody had to be an advocate for Bertie. She needed a lawyer, not a midwife, but a friend would have to do for the moment.

I halted as soon as I entered. And smiled. Sophie Ribeiro stood at her full height, as tall as Jeanette, at the front desk. I pushed my spectacles back up the bridge of my nose and listened.

"I am Roberta Winslow's legal counsel and you may not prevent me from speaking with my client," she told the befuddled desk officer. "It is her right under the law. I have requested a meeting with her. You and your superiors have not been forthcoming. If you don't allow me access to Miss Winslow within five minutes' time I shall consult with your chief's superior and as far up as I need to go. You are a disgrace to your profession, young man."

The fellow turned and nearly ran into the back of the building.

"Nice work, Sophie," I said. I blotted perspiration from my brow with a folded handkerchief. I'd ridden like a madwoman to get here.

She whirled. "Ah, Rose." She smiled at me. Her garments today were cut in the loose, flowing style she always sported but were sewn out of fabrics much more muted and professional-looking than I'd seen her in when she relaxed at home. Today she wore a deep blue outer garment with a pale blue beneath, and a snowy white jabot at her neck. Her dark hair, which bore a silver stripe at her left temple, was twisted into a knot on top of her head, as always. "These fellows have no idea who they are up against."

"I only now heard the news. What a travesty, to haul Bertie in here. Is there anything thee can tell — "

At a sound from within, she laid a finger across her lips. A moment later Kevin pushed through the door, the nearly cowering desk officer close behind.

Kevin smiled. "Ah, Miss Ribeiro. We were awaiting your arrival." He glanced past her at me. "Good afternoon, Miss Rose."

I held up a hand in recognition, not trusting myself to speak to him.

"Detective Donovan, I assume you are here to bring me to my client without another wasted moment?" Sophie said.

"Indeed I am. Please follow me, Counsel."

Sophie glanced back at me. "Go on home. I'll telephone as soon as I can." She and Kevin disappeared through the door.

At least Kevin cooperated with Sophie and was respectful to her, not that I'd ever seen him disrespect women. What a relief Bertie was in her able hands.

The officer looked at me with a nervous smile. "Is there anything else you need, miss?"

In fact, I needed quite a lot. Since I believed Bertie wasn't at the Settle home last night, I needed to know who lied and said she was. I needed to know who actually killed Mayme. Most urgently — and most important, really — I also needed to buy fish and make my way home to prepare supper.

"No, but I thank thee." I turned toward the door. Sophie might be able to extract Bertie for now, but clearing her name might be quite the task.

The outer door swung open. Chief Norman Talbot strode in. His eyes narrowed ever so slightly when he saw me. "Miss Carroll, what brings you to the station today? I hope it isn't to report a crime in our fair town." He smiled with his mouth alone.

I mentally rolled my eyes but smiled back outwardly. "Good afternoon, Norman. The only crime would be if the postmistress of that fair town were to be falsely accused of a wrong she did not commit."

His lip curled. "I assume you refer to Miss Winslow? An immoral and disgusting disgrace to ladies everywhere, that's what she is."

I leaned away from him, as if that would distance me from his distasteful views. "Luckily she has legal counsel with her. Good day." I slid by him and out the door, which he still had hold of. I truly didn't care what he thought of me, even if it would have behooved me to. What he thought of Bertie? I hoped he wouldn't try to block justice because he disapproved of her.

Now for the fish market.

ELEVEN

MY ELEVEN-YEAR-OLD NEPHEW Mark and I were in the middle of making biscuits for dinner at half past five. With Sophie tending to Bertie's legal problems, I'd resolved to put them out of my mind. For now, anyway. The twin boys and nine-year-old Betsy were my only companions until David arrived. Betsy played in the sitting room while Matthew read next to her.

When the telephone rang, Betsy answered the call. "Hello. Betsy Bailey speaking."

After we'd had the device installed last winter, I'd taught the children the polite way to greet a caller.

"Yes. One moment, please. I'll fetch her." My younger niece appeared in the kitchen doorway cradling her doll in one arm. "Auntie Rose, it's for you."

"Fold into thirds and roll gently, four more times," I reminded Mark, whose apron and one cheek were white with flour. He'd asked me to help him learn to cook. How could I say no? His twin, Matthew, didn't have the slightest interest in helping in the kitchen, but Mark was acquiring cooking skills right and left. It was an unusual interest for a boy. Still, I welcomed it. I wiped my hands and hurried into the other room.

"This is Rose."

"I extricated Bertie," Sophie said, "but she's quite shook up. We have to go back for more talks with the detective tomorrow."

"What a relief she's free. I thank thee for remembering to let me know. Did thee learn who falsely accused her?"

She cleared her throat. "The thing is, Bertie did pass by the Settle home last night. She'd been at a meeting of the Woman Suffrage Association at a home out on Whitehall Road."

"Passing by is very different than going in and —" I glanced at Betsy, who hung on my every word. *Uh-oh.* "Doing something bad."

"Of course it is. Rest easy, Rose. I won't let them lock her up. But to answer your question, no, the detective refused to say who leveled the accusation."

"Will she be at the post office tomorrow?" I asked.

"She insists she must. And you know our Bertie. There's no changing her mind once it's settled on a course of action."

I heard the smile in Sophie's voice. "I know her well. I appreciate the call. Please give her my love."

We said our goodbyes and hung up.

"Rose, what's 'accused' mean?" Betsy asked.

Matthew, who was absorbed in *The Adventures of Tom Sawyer* nearby, chimed in without looking up. "It means when someone says you did something bad, whether you did it or not."

"Thee is correct, Matthew," I said.

"Who accused Bertie of something bad?" Betsy pressed.

"We don't know, sweetie."

"Aunt Rose, should I start cutting out the biscuits?" Mark called from the kitchen.

I hurried to join him. I checked the oven temperature. It was hot enough, but so was the entire kitchen. The home of the poet and abolitionist John Whittier, an Amesbury Friend and a mentor to me, had a kitchen separated from the house in which to cook in the summer, but our modest abode included no such luxury. I wished it did have a summer kitchen, as did many larger homes. My dress was damp with perspiration around the neck, and I swiped an arm across my brow to dry it.

I pulled the dish of bluefish out of the oven. The dark flesh was cooked through but still juicy, so I withdrew the pan and placed it on the cooler area of the stovetop, setting a sheet pan on top to keep the heat in.

"Yes, cut away." I handed him the round biscuit cutter. "Thee can place them close together on the pan." Between the two of us we formed all the dough into biscuits and slid the pan into the oven. I asked Mark to clean up the biscuit-making mess and called Matthew and Betsy to set the table.

"Wash your hands first." I threw a chunk of butter into the cast iron skillet and added the asparagus spears when it was melted. But where was my darling David? I hadn't seen him in two days and had much to discuss with him after we dined.

He arrived at the side door at the exact moment the biscuits were ready and the asparagus was lightly cooked. The children were all back in the sitting room by now.

"Knock, knock," he said through the screen door.

"Door's open," I called, not looking around. I drew out the biscuits and slid them into a cloth-lined basket. The asparagus went onto a plate. The fish I left in its baking dish.

David slid one arm around my waist from behind, kissing the back of my neck. Shivers went up and down at the deliciousness of feeling him so close. His other hand appeared in front of my eyes, and it held a big bouquet of fragrant heliotrope and sweet peas.

"My, isn't thee sweet!" I twisted to face him. "Where in the world did thee find those?" How I longed to be cooking dinner in my own kitchen and have David—as husband, not beau—come home with flowers.

His blue eyes sparkled. "I have my sources."

"I thank thee." I kissed him on the lips but kept it chaste. This was family dinner time, not canoodle time. When I pulled away, my stomach growled something fierce.

He tossed his head back and laughed. "Never stand in the way of Rose Carroll and her supper."

"Words to remember, my dear. Children, dinner's on," I called. "David, help with putting the serving dishes on the table, please?" He was a man atypical for his time who didn't object in the least to being asked to help with domestic matters. I stuck the bouquet in a blue-and-white earthenware pitcher with water and set the flowers on the table before joining the others.

After the manner of Friends, we joined hands, closed our eyes, and held a moment of silent grace and thanksgiving. David joined us in the practice, of course. He'd told me after his first time sharing our repast how much he appreciated the quiet respite. The next half hour passed in a flurry of eating, Betsy trying to recite a new poem she'd learned vying with the twins sharing jokes they'd heard in the schoolyard. Queen mouser Christabel lurked beneath the table anticipating fish scraps.

"Where's teen Luke tonight?" David asked.

"He's studying with a friend and eating supper there, and I think I mentioned Frederick is out with Winnie."

"The fish is delicious, Aunt Rose," Mark said, gesturing at his empty plate. "It was a good idea to add the dill weed to the bread crumbs, wasn't it?"

"A very good idea," David said.

We'd had a jar of dill I had dried last summer, but it had been Mark's excellent idea to add some to the bread crumb topping. Maybe the lad would end up a famous chef somewhere when he was older.

"Auntie Rose," Betsy piped up. "What's a moron?"

Mark put his hand to his mouth and stifled a laugh. Matthew rolled his eyes.

"It's a word people use to talk about someone whose brain doesn't work very well," I said, thinking of Irvin's comment about Jeanette. "But it's not a nice name to call someone with a simple mind. We shouldn't judge them faulty simply because they're different."

"A moron would still be a child of God, wouldn't she?" Betsy asked.

"Yes, indeed, Betsy," David said. "Where did you hear this word?"

"Father said that girl who lives next to our school is one. And anyway, she isn't! Her mind is keener than most children's."

My heart turned to lead. Quaker Frederick? How could he be so ignorant? Saying such a thing reflected the views of many in our world, but it surprised me he would use that word.

"I play with Ginny sometimes before I come home," Betsy went on. "She can't see so she can't go to school. Sometimes I read my primers to her because she really wants to learn."

"And well thee might, my darling. I shall have a word with thy father about his ignorance." And maybe with Jeanette about helping this girl.

"I have a new joke," Matthew spoke up. "Did thee hear this one? If all the seas were dried up, what would Neptune say?"

Mark screwed up his face, thinking.

David opened his mouth to answer but I smiled and nudged him to let Matthew have the pleasure of giving us the answer, which doubtless included some kind of pun.

"I really haven't got a notion," Matthew announced triumphantly.

Mark gave a hoot, but Betsy looked confused.

"A notion," Matthew told her. "An ocean, Betsy. Neptune doesn't have an ocean. Get it?"

She smiled and clapped her hands. "Yes!"

When would David and I have our own table full of lively little ones? My betrothed caught me gazing at him, and I knew he had understood my thoughts.

"Soon," he mouthed.

TWELVE

WE LEFT THE CHILDREN to clean up and retired to the sitting room. Already I could hear giggles and protests, but they knew how to do dishes and put away food—not that we had much left over—and were plenty old enough for regular chores.

David and I sank onto the cushioned settee. He laid his arm over my shoulders and stroked the hair off my brow, letting his fingers trace the shape of my cheek and outlining my mouth. A frisson of thrill rippled through me. I had no choice but to pull his face to mine and engage in a long and luscious kiss.

At a giggle from the doorway we pulled apart.

"Back to your cleanup, Miss Betsy," David mock scolded my niece, who disappeared into the kitchen.

I stroked David's hand, basking in my warm cheeks and tingling insides.

"What adventures have you been up to, Rosie?" he asked.

"Hmm. What haven't I been up to?"

He peered at me. "Meaning what?"

"For one thing, I helped Kevin Donovan's wife with a dangerously fevered month-old infant today."

"Little Rosalie, your namesake?"

"Yes. Poor Emmaline was overwhelmed, and the baby was dehydrated. I resolved to do what I knew how, and if it wasn't enough I was prepared to call you. Their usual doctor was away and left no one to back him up, more's the pity. But cold cloths and spoon feeding the baby milk that Emmaline expressed did the trick."

"Alas, I have no other fever-reduction tricks in my bag besides willow bark extract. You know, salicylate," David said.

"I suspected as much. But surely thee wouldn't give salicylic tea to an eight-pound infant."

"Not without diluting it. It's far too harsh. I have read of a chemist attempting to synthesize salicylic acid, the active ingredient of willow bark, into a pill form, and adding something to buffer the acid's irritating effects. But I don't believe it's on the market yet."

"Such a pill would be a boon for ill people. At any rate, I think I helped Emmaline regain her calm," I said. "She'll call me if the baby doesn't improve. The fact she hasn't yet is a good sign."

"Very. What else has been happening?"

"I have a twin birth coming up. Sissy Barclay came to me yesterday for the first time at about seven months along." I repeated what I'd told Orpha. "She is young and a first-time mother. I confess to being full of trepidation for when I receive the call about her labor."

"Understandably. But I think you have successfully delivered twins who lived to be healthy children, haven't you?"

"Only once by myself, although I did assist Orpha with several. In one case, the mother's cervix kept starting to close, and Orpha had to reach in and nearly drag the first baby out." I smiled. "But he was fine, and his sister wasn't a difficult second birth, despite being bigger than her brother."

"What about your twin nephews?" David asked. "Were you there for their births?"

"No. It was before I moved to Amesbury, but Matthew and Mark's births turned out to be pretty easy for Harriet. She'd already borne two children by then and neither twin presented complication. They went to term but were not overly large."

"I was reading in the medical journal only last week of a new technique for Caesarean sections which might make them safer for the mother."

"Perhaps one day. For now, I hope Sissy goes another month, so the babies are big enough to survive, but no more, so they aren't too big to be born without giving her problems."

"Sissy Barclay." He frowned. "I know the name Barclay. Is her husband Irvin?"

I nodded. "A banker. Considerably older than his wife."

"What did I hear about him?" David rapped his fingers on his thigh. "I can't recall at this moment. It wasn't good, whatever it was."

"Sissy said his first wife couldn't bear children, and then she passed away."

He stared at me. "Right." He leaned closer on the settee and lowered his voice to a murmur. "At the time some gossiped that the wife's death was possibly not a natural one."

"You mean Irvin might have killed his wife to make way for a more fertile version?" I whispered. "Sissy did mention he had always wanted to be a father. She suspects he only married her to be able to have children. She said she's worried that if her babies die, she might be discarded, too."

"Or worse," David muttered.

"Or worse." We sat quietly with our own thoughts for a moment.

He snapped his fingers. "Now I remember. She expired from apparent heart failure, but she was fairly young and otherwise healthy. Certain poisons can cause the heart to stop, too."

"None were detected?"

"No, but toxicology is an inexact science. A Frenchman named Orfila made great strides earlier in this century, but one still has to know what poison to test for, and the results are not always conclusive."

"Speaking of killing," I kept my voice low, "Mayme Settle was murdered last night."

"I heard about the murder." He twisted to gaze at me. "Did you know her?"

"Only through the Ladies Circle, and I didn't particularly enjoy her company, may God keep her soul. I was with Winnie at the Settles' home last evening, though. This morning I heard Mayme was dead. And not from natural causes." I blew out a breath.

"Don't tell me you're involved."

"Well . . ." I let my voice trail off.

"Again, Rose?"

His question might have sounded like a challenge to an outsider. On the contrary, the sympathetic look on his face confirmed for me his concern without including a trace of opposition to my actions. Of course he wanted his beloved to be careful, but he'd never once cautioned me not to investigate wrongdoing when I felt called to do so. He knew my urge for justice was a strong one.

"Not involved, exactly," I said. "Except they brought Bertie in for questioning this afternoon, and I went to the station to protest."

He sat back. "Why in the world would Bertie kill Mrs. Settle?" The rising pitch of his question brimmed with incredulity.

"She wouldn't, of course. But Mayme had a serious and public objection to the way Bertie lives openly with Sophie Ribeiro. I mean, she was so opposed to their living arrangement that in the post office yesterday morning, Mayme wouldn't even let Bertie wait on her. She said she would come back when Bertie's assistant, Eva, was at the desk."

"Bertie didn't care, did she?"

"No," I scoffed.

"I'd be surprised if she did. Why was Mrs. Settle so incensed about Bertie and Sophie?" he asked.

"I understand her own daughter was estranged from Mayme, and Bertie thinks it's because the daughter also practices lesbianism."

"Interesting. She doesn't live with the family, I gather."

"No," I said. "She teaches at Smith College. In addition, the Settles' son also went outside what society tells us is appropriate, by impregnating a maid and then abandoning her and her child."

David made a tsking sound.

I thought about what Jeanette had said. "Mayme also insulted my client Jeanette Papka. She's a highly intelligent, multilingual court interpreter who happens to be blind. Mayme Settle called her a deaf-mute and a moron. Can thee believe it, David?"

"Alas, I can, although such an attitude seems to contradict what I have heard of her good works. Mother has mentioned the many charities Mrs. Settle was well known for supporting."

"That's very true. She had a large heart in that regard. I wonder if that's why Mayme was so conscientious about doing charitable works, something society looks on with favor."

"To make up for what she regards as her children's failings, you mean?" David asked. "That sounds plausible to me. Although, considering a woman loving her own kind a failing is rather different than Mrs. Settle's son not acknowledging nor supporting one's own offspring."

"Very true," I agreed.

"I didn't know the woman, may she rest in peace, but in the case of her views on Bertie's and her daughter's choices as well as your interpreter friend's abilities, Mrs. Settle was clearly the ignorant one."

"What's 'ignorant' mean, Uncle David?" Betsy asked, suddenly back in the room and at David's elbow.

I wondered how much she had heard of our conversation.

"It means someone who isn't educated on a particular topic, either because they haven't learned better or because they don't want to learn." He held out his arms and Betsy scooted onto his lap.

"Tell me a story," she murmured, leaning into his chest.

Her father, Frederick, loved her, but he battled his own demons. He often wasn't able to offer easy love like David did. It filled my heart she already called my husband-to-be Uncle and slid into his lap with such ease.

"Once upon a time a Quaker princess lived in a castle," he began. "But she was lonely because she didn't have a pet to keep her company."

A Quaker princess. He was most surely spinning a tale of fantasy.

"What was her name?" Betsy asked.

"Elizabeth."

My niece smiled to herself. I did, too. Of course David would name the princess for her.

But as he spun a well-crafted yet improvised tale of conflict, change, and happy resolution, my thoughts turned to the not-so-fanciful, and the real-life conflict swirling around us. Who had killed Mayme Settle? And why?

THIRTEEN

ANNIE BEAUMONT YAWNED as she and I trudged toward home the next morning at six, already two hours past sunrise. We were only three weeks from the summer solstice and the days were longer than long.

David and I had never had a chance to talk about our marriage arrangements last evening, because I'd been called to a woman in labor while he was still making up the story of Elizabeth, Quaker princess. He'd offered to stay with the children until Frederick returned.

The laboring client's home was only a few blocks distant on Orchard Street, so I had tidied my hair, grabbed my birthing satchel, and walked over. Annie had already been there sitting vigil with the woman, a first-time mother, during the early stages and had only called me when the contractions seemed to be coming fast and furious.

The labor had slowed again after I arrived, and it had taken the baby another ten hours to finally emerge. The woman pushed for a full two of those hours, with Annie doing the bulk of the coaching. Despite the long labor, a little son was born in good health, if with a temporarily pointy head from his passage through the birth canal. The new mother also suffered no injuries or other complications. We'd stayed until both she and her newborn boy were stable. After he had nursed and both mother and child were drowsing, we departed, leaving them under the joyous watch of the new father.

"How did thee find the birth, Annie?" I asked my red-headed apprentice. I suppressed my own yawn. The cooler temperatures of yesterday seemed to have gone into hiding again. The sun was already warm and had barely made its way above the treetops to the east. "I think this was one of the longest labors at which thee has assisted."

"It was. Why did her contractions slow down after you arrived, do you think?"

"It's hard to say. She might have needed to rest, but she could have been worried to do so without her primary midwife in attendance."

At this, Annie's brow knit. "Do you think she didn't trust me? Because I'm French Canadian, maybe?"

"I'm sure it's not thy background. She's an Irish immigrant herself, isn't she?"

"You're right."

"I know thee does an excellent job, Annie." I patted her arm. "I trust thee completely. But this client had visited me, not thee, for all her antenatal visits. Thee has seen how we women become somehow more primitive during our laboring, when the animal body takes over for the rational mind. It is no impugning of thee if she felt she could relax and rest for a bit once I arrived. Her body might have dictated its own actions. Anyway, all's well that ends well, as Orpha taught me."

"It was indeed a good outcome, Rose."

We walked on a few more paces. "We'll be having a difficult birth coming up this summer, though." I told her about Sissy Barclay. "I'll need thee to read everything thee can about birthing twins. About best practices as well as possible complications. Start soon, please."

"I will."

"She could go into labor any day, or not for another two months."

"I'll not disappoint you, Rose."

"We have another client due in early fall." I smiled. "She's a delight. Has thee ever met Jeanette Papka? Her maiden name is French, Voyant."

"*Mais, oui!*" Annie clapped her hands. "She's some kind of relative of mine. I haven't seen her in ages, though. She can't see, and she has a little girl, yes?"

"Yes, and yes, this will be her second child. Her daughter was a large baby, something like ten pounds, and Jeanette suspects this one will be even larger."

"I will be so happy to work with her." Annie's expression turned darker. "I knew a girl who was half French and half Irish, a few years older than me. Things did not go so well for her when she was carrying her baby."

"Oh?"

"She died from complications after she gave birth." Annie slowed to a stop. "Her name was Alice Riley." She pronounced the girl's name like *ah-Leese rai-Lee*. "Her mama, she was a Rousseau, from our village of Gentilly in Quebec. The girl worked as a maid here in Amesbury after her mama died. But the son of the family where she worked, he made her pregnant, and then said he hadn't. And the lady of the house wouldn't let her see a doctor when the pregnancy made her sick."

I stopped, too. "I know this story," I said. "So thee was acquainted with Alice?"

"Of course. We French Canadians all know each other. Her mother moved here a long time before my family did. She married Mr. Riley and upset her parents because he was Irish, and upset the priest at home, too, but she didn't care. She said he was a good Catholic boy and his faith was all that should matter. Alice was born, then her little brother. The children and their mama came home every summer to visit."

"I attended Alice's birth when I was apprenticed to Orpha," I said. "We tried everything after she began to hemorrhage, but we weren't able to save her. I talked with Adoniram Riley, her father, yesterday. He works for the Settle family."

"Settle? I never knew Settle was the name of the family." Annie took a step back. "But that's the name of the lady who was killed yesterday."

"The same."

She crossed herself, then pressed her hands to her cheeks and stared at me. "Are you helping Mr. Donovan with the case?"

"No, although I will tell thee they are questioning my dear friend Bertie, which is a travesty."

"Miss Winslow? Oh, she never would." Annie's mouth pulled down at the edges and she shook her head.

"Of course not. But . . ."

"But now you want to find out who did kill Mrs. Settle." She cocked her head. "Where did the bad son go?"

"Orpha told me he joined the merchant marine."

"And never supported the girl he made pregnant." Her mouth formed an O. "What if Mr. Riley killed Mrs. Settle to make revenge for his daughter's death? He would have committed a mortal sin."

FOURTEEN

THE REST OF THE MORNING was spent in work, worry, and anything but rest, despite my not having grabbed even a wink during the night. The coffee I brewed upon my arrival home had stood me through making breakfast and helping the family off to school and work. The second cup kept my eyes from shutting during my only antenatal visit of the morning at nine o'clock.

Throughout the hours I worried about Bertie. Had she had to return to the station for more grilling? Had Kevin found someone else to be interested in? He and his team should be looking for evidence, checking people's alibis, querying Mayme's enemies, who must be legion. I longed to telephone Bertie, but I didn't want to get in the way, either, nor disturb her at work.

I also spent some time thinking about my conversation with David last night. Yes, Mayme's children and Bertie all stepped outside the normal paths of behavior. But didn't I, as well? I was an independent businesswoman. I rode all over town alone at any hour of the day or night. I didn't curtsy to ladies or use titles for men in power, and I barely followed the strictures of fashion. I knew I was a moral, principled person but knew some didn't see me that way. I was likely as judged for my rather tame unconventional behavior as others were for theirs, no matter the reason. I shook my head and returned to my notes on the visit that had just ended.

Now, at ten thirty, I couldn't decide whether to venture into town seeking information or collapse on my bed in search of sleep. I compromised by laying my head on my arms where they rested on my desk.

I apparently fell fast asleep, because I sat up all a-startle at an insistent bell ringing at ten past eleven. Spittle marred the ink of my notes about the day's first client as well as my cheek. I swiped the drool off my face and headed for the front door. Only then did I realize the clang had been the telephone ringing, not the doorbell. Changing course, I lifted the receiver in the sitting room—only to hear nothing.

I depressed the hook switch twice. "Gertrude, this is Rose Carroll. I missed a call."

"Yes, Miss Carroll," came the tinny reply. "I'll put you through to Miss Ribeiro."

Sophie's voice came on the line. "Rose? I'm so glad you're there."

"Is Bertie all right?" My urgent words tumbled out. "What's happened?"

"Nothing's happened. Not to worry. She's fine, and went along to the post office at her usual time."

My relief made my knees nearly buckle. I slid my back along the wall and sank to sit on the floor.

"But I have to take the next train into Boston for a critical trial and she could use some steadying," Sophie said. "Can you possibly stop by her workplace during the afternoon and then spend the evening with her?"

"Of course I can, unless I'm summoned to a woman in labor." I'd have to check my schedule, but I was pretty sure I could support my friend in such a way. "But Sophie, nothing further from the police?"

"No, not since Detective Donovan had said he wanted her back. One does wonder, but I daren't call and jog their memory."

I laughed. "I agree. Go off to thy trial. I'll watch out for our Bertie."

"I'll be home on the last train." She thanked me and disconnected the call.

I *whooshed* out a breath not unlike those Peaches exhaled, the horse I'd had on loan during the winter. I shook my head all about like her, too, trying to clear it. So far Bertie had escaped arrest, despite her accuser's false claim. Her freedom alone made things right in my world.

Today was our kitchen girl's midweek day off, so the house was quiet. I pushed myself up and headed into the kitchen for a hearty snack. An involuntary nap, a bite to eat, and some interim good news—or lack of bad, more accurately—did wonders for my mood and motivation. After I tidied up both kitchen and person, I headed into town.

FIFTEEN

FIRST I NEEDED TO STOP by Emmaline's and make sure Rosalie was on the path back to health. One month postpartum could be a risky milestone for both mother and child. Mothers with plentiful milk sometimes suffered from infections in their breasts. For first-time mothers, the lack of sleep and sheer amount of work it took to care for a newborn could trigger serious postpartum melancholia, as I'd witnessed in a mother over a year ago. Babies were sensitive to the amount of milk, whether too much or not enough. And all of it was apart from infants catching any of the many illnesses besetting our world.

I leaned my bike against a tree, surprised not to see Sean out playing, and rapped on the Donovans' front door. To my surprise, Kevin himself pulled it open.

"Miss Rose, top of the morning to you. Would you be looking for me, then?" His native brogue was much more in evidence at his home than at the office.

"Not exactly, since I didn't expect thee to be at home. I wanted to be sure thy wife and daughter were back on the path to good health."

Kevin beamed and stepped back. "Please come in and see for yourself." He turned his head. "Emmie, Miss Rose is here. Make yerself decent, now."

I stepped inside. Emmaline was stationed on the love seat almost exactly as I'd left her yesterday. She sat bare-chested, but this time with a diapered Rosalie latched on and nursing like a champ, judging from the slurping sounds filling the room.

"Decent? Listen, husband, Rose Carroll has seen me with nary a stitch on my body and howling like a banshee. She doesn't care about your decent when it comes to birthing women, or afterward, either, I daresay." Emmaline laughed. "Oh, Rose, did you ever save our lives yesterday. Look at our dearie now." She gazed down at her daughter.

Kevin cleared his throat behind me. "I'll be in the kitchen."

"We mortified him good and simple," Emmaline said with a grin. "Come feel how cool she is."

I laid my hand on the baby's bare back. She wasn't cool, but her temperature was normal. I touched her bottom, happy to detect a damp diaper, which indicated she was getting sufficient fluid. I perched next to the pair.

"Thee can't know how happy I am to see this," I said. "So the cool moist cloths and spoon feeding helped?" I prayed the fever would not return.

"It was like a miracle." Emmaline frowned. "But Rose, why was I so addled? I'm usually a sensible person. I have never been afflicted with panic about Sean's health, even when he got the influenza last year. Yesterday? I was like an imbecile, or a helpless child." She searched my face with puzzled eyes.

I stroked the baby's head. "Thee is a new mother again, Emmaline. Thy woman's body is in a state of enormous change. It can affect thy mind a bit, and add to that a very real worry about Rosalie's fever? Thee had every reason to become a little crazed."

"I should say so." She shook her head.

"The thing to remember is it's always fine to ask for help. Thy doctor, thy husband, me, thy neighbor. Even Sean. He could have summoned someone. Thee isn't alone. Does thee understand?" In one sense it seemed odd to act as her counselor. Emmaline was a good ten years older than I. Still, I was the expert in the room, and she clearly didn't mind my words of advice.

She nodded and wiped away a tear. "All's well that ends well. Isn't that what you're fond of saying?"

"Indeed it is." I stood. "I'm going to have a word with Kevin, if I may."

"You may." She waved me away. "And Rose?" she called after me.

"Yes?"

"Thank you."

I gave a single nod. I pushed open the door to the kitchen and stopped short. Kevin Donovan, stalwart police detective, sat with his arms folded on his knees, his shoulders shaking with sobs.

"Oh, Kevin," I murmured. "All seems to be well now." I ventured to pat his shoulder.

He scrubbed at his face with his fists and sat up straight. "I apologize, Miss Rose. It hit me like an andiron dropped from the sky how close I came to losing little Rosalie, and maybe my Emmie, too." He gazed at me from an extra-ruddy face, this time with reddened eyes I'd never seen on him.

"No need to apologize." I determined that getting down to business might be the best approach to avoid further embarrassing him. I sat at the table across from him. Over his shoulder I spied a sink full of dirty dishes and two crusted pans on the stove, the plight of every mother with a newborn and a busy husband. If I had a chance to clean the kitchen before I left, I would. "Where is thy son, by the way?"

"Our Sean's got himself 'apprenticed' to Mr. Jonathan Sherwood down to the Lowell Boat Shop." He emphasized the word "apprenticed" to indicate he knew it wasn't a real apprenticeship. "My son told the man he wants to learn the practical application of the mathematics he's been studying. The boy's only seven years old, but Sherwood, bless his heart, took him on."

I smiled at the image of a child younger than Betsy wielding saws, planes, and hammers to construct sturdy wooden dories. "Anyone can see how bright Sean is. Yesterday he seemed to be leap-frogging directly into medical school." I rose and moved to the sink, pumped water into a basin, and rolled up my sleeves.

"The good Lord only knows how he'll apply that brain of his. He must have gotten it from his sainted mother. His intelligence is certainly not an inheritance from my side." He rolled his eyes. "Now, Miss Rose. I'm quite sure your own brain's been working overtime on this business of Mrs. Settle's death. Homicide, more's the pity."

"I confess the murder has been uppermost in my thoughts. Thee must know Bertie Winslow cannot in any way, shape, or means have had anything to do with Mayme's murder." I fixed my sternest gaze on his visage.

"I tend to agree with you. But a certain influential businessman in town is exerting pressure on Chief Talbot to arrive at a resolution."

"Might the man be Irvin Barclay?"

Kevin bobbed his head once without actually saying it was.

"I assume thee knows a controversy surrounds the death of his first wife," I went on. "His second — and pregnant — wife is under my care, but I heard — from sources other than wife number two — he might have engineered wife number one's death."

"Hmm. I had heard rumblings of same. A poison-induced heart failure."

"A number of people seem to know, yet he has retained his position as a banker. Curious."

"If nothing was proved, of course he would," Kevin pointed out.

"In addition, the childbed death of Alice Riley, the Settles' gardener's daughter, seems to have direct ties to both Mayme and Merton Settle and their wayward son."

"Said gardener's name?"

I hesitated as I scrubbed a particularly stubborn pot. Adoniram had been nothing but nice to me, and he'd been in the Settles' employ for years. Why would he kill Mayme now?

Kevin drummed his fingers on the table. "Miss Rose?"

"You won't forget this one. Adoniram Riley."

"I should think not. Duly noted," Kevin said, despite having pencil and paper nowhere in sight. "Anything else?"

I thought back to the Ladies Circle gathering. "Thee might want to look into Merton Settle. He seemed quite the browbeaten husband. His wife humiliated him in front of a gathering of her friends the evening before she died. I was there. He smelled strongly of alcohol, and I glimpsed a flash of a look from him, as if he were shooting daggers of hatred at his supposed beloved."

"Or of poison, one supposes."

"Was Mayme poisoned, then?"

"They are thinking so. You know it's near impossible to ascertain something like poison in the autopsy. My men confiscated a cup we found by her bedside. Apparently she made a practice of taking a hot drink before bed. Our chemist is examining the dregs in the vessel."

"Surely a murderer would have rinsed out the cup."

"If he had a chance. You know very well that killers are often not the smartest among us."

"Will thee let me know what he finds?"

"Surely. Curiously, the deceased also had remnants of something white under her fingernails." Kevin glanced at the clock on the wall.

"Crikey!" He leapt to his feet. "I'm late for a meeting with the boss. Let yerself out, Miss Rose." He smashed his hat onto his head and dashed in to kiss his wife and baby before rushing out.

SIXTEEN

I PEDALED TOWARD MARKET SQUARE after I'd cleaned up the Donovans' sink. I barely avoided being run down by a dray piled high with bales from the first haying, likely bound for stables and carriage houses at homes like Georgia Clarke's or even Jeanette Papka's. I'd love to chat with Jeanette about Mayme's murder but assumed she would be working at the courthouse.

What Kevin had mentioned about a white substance under Mayme's fingernails intrigued me. Someone else had mentioned it, too. Oh, yes, it was Georgia Clarke, courtesy of the Settles' maid. I mused on it as I rode. What could the substance be? Face powder wouldn't be white. Besides, I didn't remember seeing her with powder on her face. Perhaps talc? Or a lotion? But any cream or lotion would have been absorbed by the skin. I wished I could find out more. Maybe Georgia could manage an introduction to the maid for me.

My lack of sleep was catching up with me again as I made my way to the post office. I'd promised Sophie to check in on Bertie. Maybe I could pretend it was my idea to have some fun tonight. Right now I wasn't sure I could stay awake until the evening. My nerves were afire with the edgy sensation of being beyond tired, and every push of a pedal seemed twice as hard as usual.

I parked my bicycle outside the post office and took my place at the end of a line of citizens wanting to buy stamps, pick up parcels, and who knew what else. The queue threatened to spill over onto the sidewalk, but I couldn't spy Bertie at the counter. Young Eva, Bertie's assistant, was barely keeping up with customers asking this and demanding that. Where had our esteemed postmistress disappeared to? I slid out of the line since I had no postal business to conduct and headed to the right side of the facility, where the post boxes were lined up on the wall in rows and columns worthy of a military battalion. Bertie's office lay beyond the boxes, but the door labeled *Postmistress Winslow* was shut tight. I knocked anyway and got no answer, and when I tried the knob the door was locked. Where was my friend?

Confound it, as my mother often said to avoid any more inflammatory language. I knew Kevin uttering "Crikey" when he'd realized he was late was only a disguised version of saying "Christ," as were so many other presumably mild expletives. For me, I knew God had a window into my soul. If I were upset, He would know it no matter what I said. Still, there was something satisfying about letting loose with a vehement utterance in times of strife, even if uttered silently or under one's breath.

I made my way to the end of the queue again and waited as it inched forward. This was a new building, as the previous post office had burned down in the Great Fire of 1888 over a year ago. The ornate metalwork of the little post boxes shone, and the public telephone box near the door contained a stern-looking man conversing with someone at the other end of the line. When at last I approached Eva Stillwell, a fellow Quaker, I didn't even need to ask where my friend was.

"She said she had to go somewhere," Bertie's young assistant offered, glancing at the wall clock with a look of desperation in her light eyes. "She left at eleven thirty and it's now half past one, Rose." She beckoned me closer and whispered, "And I've a need to use the necessary. I don't suppose thee could—"

Her face fell and she stopped speaking when I shook my head.

"I'm sorry, but I don't know the first thing about the duties of post office clerk," I said, and it was true. "But thee must have a notice at hand saying the clerk will return shortly?"

She nodded, light dawning.

"I suggest thee place it here on the counter and go do thy business. Be expeditious, but no one will fault thee for doing what we all must."

"I don't know why I was waiting for Bertie's permission." She grinned, reached under the counter for the engraved sign, and placed it facing out on the counter. "I owe thee a favor, Rose." Eva, no older than Faith, tucked an auburn curl behind her ear before disappearing through the back door.

I smiled back, despite feeling distinctly uncheerful. Where was Bertie? I turned to leave. I apparently had been last in line, because not a soul fumed impatiently behind me.

Once outside, I stood gazing up and down the busy

thoroughfare. I didn't usually feel at a loss for where to go, but right now I surely was. I supposed I could investigate Bertie and Sophie's cottage on Whittier Street and see if she was there. Kevin didn't have her in custody, that seemed clear. Or, speaking of Whittier, I could seek counsel with the great man himself. Yes, calling on John was what I'd do.

And if I couldn't locate Bertie after my visit, well, it was Sixth Month. I would pass by the shop that sold tomato starts at this time of year. I'd been trying to expand our vegetable and herb garden at the house a little every year. There was no time like right before the solstice to plant our tomatoes. Frost had surely passed us by until the fall.

Or . . . I exclaimed, startling a well-dressed couple passing arm in arm. Adoniram had offered me tomato seedlings. I had a plan. I'd go see the Settles' gardener before I went to Friend John's. Maybe I could learn something in the doing.

SEVENTEEN

I DID PASS BY BERTIE'S home on my way to visit Adoniram, but she was not in evidence.

"Damnation," I muttered to myself, as Bertie herself often exclaimed. "Where are you, woman?"

Not being present, she didn't answer. If she had, I would have jumped right out of my skin.

On I cycled, five minutes later pulling in behind the Settle house proper, where I heard the *scritch* of hoe on soil. I leaned my bike against the wall of the carriage house, which had white trim and gray paint matching that of the main house. The fragrant blooms of stock in a bed against the carriage house were lovely shades of pinks and purples.

I followed my ears to Adoniram. The gardener was busy cutting weeds off at the roots between two long beds of infant flower plants. He pulled the long handle of a stirrup hoe, scuffling up the dark, rich-looking dirt and covering the decimated weeds so they wouldn't resprout.

I knew he'd seen me, but I sensed he needed to finish the row before speaking. Sure enough, at the end he leaned on the hoe's handle and wiped his bony brow with a green kerchief.

"Miss Carroll. Come for tomato starts?"

"Good afternoon, Adoniram. Yes, I'd be happy to, if thee still has some to spare."

He regarded me with a faint smile from under bushy gray eyebrows. "Follow me." He gestured off to the side with his chin.

I paused when the hair stood up on my neck and arms. Wasn't this gardener a possible suspect? Didn't he have cause to kill Mayme, no matter how delayed a revenge it was? I might be putting myself in danger by following him.

On the other hand, we walked in the full light of afternoon. Neighboring homes and gardens flanked us on both sides. I heard children squealing with joy nearby and the sounds of carpentry under way somewhere not too distant. I should be fine, but thought I'd throw in a bit of insurance.

"I thank thee. I told a friend about thy seedlings and she said she'd be along in a minute, as well, to see if any are in surplus." I figured God wouldn't mind a minor Friendly prevarication in the service of personal safety. Even if He did, it was done now.

"Why do you talk funny like that, anyway? I heard about them Shakers, up to Canterbury way. You one of them?"

"No, I'm what people call a Quaker. I am a member of the Religious Society of Friends. More than two hundred years ago Friends began using 'thee' and 'thy' for everyone, because we believe we are all equal in God's eyes."

He grunted. "Some wouldn't have you think so." His gaze cut to the big house at the other end of the property. It seemed he didn't like his employers one bit. Why had he continued to work here, then? Perhaps they paid him well, or for some reason he thought he couldn't garner other work that also came with lodgings.

"I know. But now, curiously enough, our speech sets us apart again." I laughed softly. "I daresay the oddities will be abandoned at some point in the future."

"Interesting." The gaunt gardener led me along the side of a glass greenhouse some thirty feet in length. At the end he halted so abruptly I nearly ran into him.

"There." He pointed at a makeshift table with rows of small earthenware pots, each nurturing a plant five or six inches tall. The ones with textured and serrated leaves were tomatoes, while others with glossier spade-shaped foliage had to be peppers. The leaves on all were a healthy green. This man knew his horticulture. "Take as many as you'd like."

"I can fit only a half dozen in my bicycle basket, but a small number is all I have room for in the garden, anyway." I surveyed the extensive yard. It wasn't quite an estate, but had to be at least an acre of well-tended flower gardens, plus the vegetable garden at the back beyond the greenhouse. Tall hedges shielded the property from its neighbors and buffered the noise from the street, creating an oasis in the hubbub of daily life. "We don't have a large piece of land like this."

"That's fine, then."

"I'll return the pots after I've emptied them."

"No need. Mr. Settle can afford the cost of new ones."

"Very well. So do the Settles have a big family? All these seedlings will yield quite a crop." I smiled at him.

"No. A grown daughter, lives out Amherst way. The son joined the merchant marine four years back, few months before my Alice died. He was lost at sea, they say. And good riddance." He folded his arms and watched my face, as if daring me to challenge his speaking ill of the dead.

"What a pity." His death, in combination with Mayme and the daughter being estranged, had left her essentially childless. No wonder she'd wanted to help children in need. I waited to see if he'd say something similarly negative about Mayme. When he didn't, I ventured, "And now his mother is dead, too. Did thee see anyone lurking about on the evening of Mayme's death?"

"No. And I told the copper as much." He narrowed his eyes. "What are you, some kind of Pinkerton girl?"

"No, not hardly. Put simply, Mayme's death is the talk of the town."

"I suppose."

"I hope they find the culprit soon. The police have the wrong notion that a friend of mine was involved, but I know she wasn't."

"Who's the friend?" he asked.

"Bertie Winslow, the postmistress."

"Her? She's a queer one. Seems she leans the other way, if you know what I mean. Like the Settles' daughter."

So what Bertie and I had conjectured was true.

"Don't matter none to me, though," Adoniram continued. "Miss Winslow's always been right nice to me when I been in the post office. She's a good egg, she is."

"Bertie has a good soul," I agreed. "Does the Settle daughter come to visit often?"

"Her?" He shook his head slowly. "She'd like to, but her mother won't accept her ways. Mrs. Settle nearly spits at the thought of her name. Mr. Settle, now, he travels out to that college to see the girl now and then."

Despite her mother's disapproval, the daughter still loved her and wanted to see her. They must have been closer when the daughter was young. *Interesting.* "Well, I'd best be going."

He gestured at the seedlings. "Take a pepper or two, as well, if you like. What the family don't eat I supply to my son and his kin, but we have plenty. And now the family here be down to only Mr. Settle." He handed me a flat pan. "Load 'em in here to carry to your bicycle."

"I thank thee kindly."

"Come back for more if you're needing them."

I nodded, loaded up, and headed back to my metal steed. The gardener didn't accompany me. I transferred the starts to my basket. Before I rode off, I glanced back at Adoniram. Hands in his pockets, he was staring at me. He wasn't an effusive man, but he'd seemed friendly enough when I'd encountered him this week. His look now? It was stern and unsmiling. Maybe this good Catholic boy, as Annie had put it, had turned irrevocably bitter after the loss of his only daughter.

EIGHTEEN

Mrs. Cate, John Whittier's housekeeper, led me through into the garden, where the elderly poet sat in the shade of one of his prized pear trees.

"Ah, Rose. Do join me on this fine afternoon." He smiled at me from under snowy brows, his thin face showing the passage of time in its furrows and loosened skin. His dark eighty-one-year-old eyes were clear, though, and had the same intense focus I'd seen in them ever since I'd met him.

"Mrs. Cate, please bring Rose a cool drink, if thee would be so kind."

After the lean woman had gone back inside, I said, "I thank thee, John. Tell me why thee doesn't address her by her Christian name, after the manner of Friends?"

He smiled. "I respect her and her husband's wishes. I am a weathered and seasoned Friend, Rose. One must not be rigid in these matters."

I winced inwardly. I had often displeased people by refusing to call them by their title and surname.

"Also, Mrs. Cate simply wouldn't stand for my addressing her as Caroline or her husband as George. Neither she nor her esteemed husband are Friends, as thee must know. I rely so on both of them, I don't know what I would do without the pair living upstairs here and caring for the house in my frequent absences to hither and yon. So Judge and Mrs. Cate it is."

"I understand." I smiled as I sank down to sit on the grass in front of him. "This shade is most welcome."

"One never knows which day will be one's last. When God gives us a perfect day, aren't we obliged to venture forth and enjoy it? Even though right here in my garden is as 'forth' as I'll be venturing this day." He gazed down at me. "I daresay thee didn't pay me a call simply to enjoy a pearish shade with me. What is on thy mind, Rose?"

Mrs. Cate came back out with a glass of lemonade for me. I

thanked her and waited until she disappeared into the house before speaking.

"Amesbury once again has a case of a violent death being visited upon one of its citizens," I began.

John nodded, looking somber. "I've already heard talk of Mayme Settle's unfortunate death."

"Yes, Mayme is who it was. At the moment, Bertie Winslow is under suspicion, but only because someone lied about her actions."

"Our unconventional and most delightful postmistress. Thee has introduced me to her as thy friend."

"Yes, and a very dear one." I smiled, thinking of her.

"By unconventional I mean her loving cohabitation with the lady lawyer, of course."

"Yes, although Bertie feels free to reject many of society's other strictures against the fairer sex, too." Riding astride, holding a position of power in town, and speaking her mind were high on the list.

"As well she might," John said. He softened his voice. "Our Mrs. Cate calls Boston marriages an abomination, did thee know?"

I made a sound in my throat. "Is this true?"

"Yes, I'm afraid so. As thee knows, I find her employ so valuable I am willing to overlook a number of what some might call minor transgressions."

"It wouldn't be minor to Bertie. Abomination or not, she is the least likely person to kill someone I know, next to thyself, of course."

A smile lurked behind John's eyes. "Tell me, who might have had cause to kill the woman? As yet I've heard no names bandied about."

I ticked them off on my fingers. "Adoniram Riley is the Settles' gardener. He has a grievance from several years back against the Settles and their son. The son has apparently perished in the merchant marine." I related the story of Alice's death. "Neither parent pushed their son to own up to fathering a child."

"The Settle father should have persuaded his son to act honorably." John tented his fingers, as he was wont to do.

"True," I acknowledged. "I confess I have been primarily blaming Mayme for the death and the child's abandonment. The responsibility in fact rested with the son."

"It appears the gardener still harbors deep pain."

"I agree. The question is whether he also harbors deep anger, and if so, why did he take four years to act on it."

"Who else has thee in thy bag of suspects, Rose?"

"A friend said she overheard the banker Irvin Barclay having an argument with Mayme. I am caring for Irvin's wife's pregnancy at present."

"If everyone who argued killed the person with whom they disagreed, we'd have a much smaller population on this blessed sphere of ours."

"I know. I think Irvin might bear further investigation, though, in part because his first wife might have died under curious circumstances." I gazed up at an oriole, its orange vest brilliant against a black head and coat, its notes rich and throaty. "And then there's Mayme's husband, Merton."

"Merton, eh? Why, I serve on the library board with him. He's wealthy by way of inheritance, not from any efforts of his own. And he happens to love books."

"He might love books, but I'm not so sure he and Mayme loved each other. The evening I was at their home—" I stopped speaking when John raised his hand.

"What evening would it have been?"

"The very night Mayme was killed, or the evening before, anyway."

"Go on."

"She was rude to her husband and humiliated him—in front of twenty women." I still could barely believe how she'd treated him. "After she turned away from Merton, the look I saw him give her in return was pure vitriol."

"This case has quite the twists and turns, doesn't it? But seriously, it seems to me I heard something intriguing about Merton Settle. I can't place who told me, but it regarded his heritage."

"The name Settle sounds British through and through, doesn't it?" I sipped my lemonade, the perfect mix of sweet, tangy sour, and cold.

"One would think so. In fact I believe it was originally some kind of appellation originating in Poland, which was Anglicized to make Merton's ancestor—or perhaps he himself—better fit in here in America."

My eyebrows went up. Was Merton keeping secrets along with a name change? Perhaps it wasn't a relative at all who had altered the surname, but Merton himself who'd revised his natal name when he immigrated to America. I had overheard a slight accent in his speech, I remembered. Had he changed his surname for naturalization purposes or a more nefarious reason? "And thee cannot recall who told thee he was Polish?"

"I'm afraid not, Rose, dear. My brain seems to wish for me to continue creating poems, and it is reserving its energy primarily for poetry of late. 'Tis the plight of those who have seen fourscore years of sunrises."

NINETEEN

RIDING MY BICYCLE the short distance home from John's home had never seemed so onerous, and not from the weight of the seedlings, either. A forty-minute rest this morning was no substitute for a full night's sleep. Such was one of the hazards of my chosen profession, however. I should be able to retire to my bed several hours early tonight and refill the sleep reservoir at least in part.

But not understanding the who and why of Mayme's murder, nor the how, sapped my spirit. It and my sleep deficit were both laden atop wondering about when in the world I might be able finally to marry David, with the question of Bertie's whereabouts permeating all of it. If I couldn't locate my friend, how would I let Sophie know?

I could address the last by popping over to her house again. It was four o'clock by now, and by rights she should still be at the post office, but nothing much was going by rights today. After I knocked and called her name and knocked again, I gave up. A whoof and a stomping of equine feet behind me in the road made me turn to look, but all I saw was a black rockaway carriage driving away with perhaps a flash of green fabric on the driver.

Sighing, I knew I lacked sufficient energy to go to Bertie's place of employment again, as it involved riding downhill and then back up, even though I'd promised Sophie I would. So I headed down Friend Street toward home.

But as I neared the Armory, I spied a tall figure standing at the edge of the street. Jeanette repeatedly waved her arm and hand at passing conveyances. I couldn't figure out what she was doing, so I pulled over and braked to a stop.

"Jeanette, what is thee about?" I didn't identify myself. She would recognize my voice. I'd seen too many people ignorant about the hearing of the blind, people who needlessly identified themselves time after time. I'd asked my friend once if her hearing was more acute than mine. She'd said no, but that she relied on her hearing for far more than I did and didn't have the distraction of sight to muddle her perceptions.

"Oh, curses, Rose. All I want is a conveyance for hire to take me home. But not a one has stopped for me. This happens more often than you can imagine."

"But how should they know thee wishes to hire them?"

She pulled her mouth into a wry expression. "Well, exactly. There's one fellow who takes me home nearly every day about this time, but when he is detained elsewhere, or if I leave work early or late, I'm left at the mercies of any driver who cares to stop. Or none, as you can see."

"Thee doesn't live too far."

"No, I don't. But can you picture me trying to walk there on my own? I'd be dead before supper." She laughed and clapped one palm atop the other.

"For today at least, I'll walk thee home," I offered. Chatting with her for only a moment had already raised my spirits. "Would strolling together suit? It's a lovely afternoon, and I would welcome a chance to visit with thee." Maybe after our conversation I'd be reinvigorated enough to make the effort to find Bertie in the last place I could think of.

"Then we've got a deal." She extended a hand toward me.

"Let's see. I'm with my bicycle, and it walks best if I have both hands on the handlebars. How about if thee holds this one here." I guided her hand to the left handgrip. "I'll place my hand next to thine and we'll walk together."

"I like the way you think, Rose. But warn me if I'm about to encounter obstacles like bricks out of place or tree roots growing up out of the paving stones." She rubbed her nose with her free hand. "I came by this crooked nose courtesy of a sawhorse set up where it oughtn't have been. I got all tangled up in it and crashed right onto my face."

"Ouch. Is thee ready?"

She laughed again. "I'm about to trust you with my baby's birth. I'd better be able to trust you with walking me home safely."

We made the turn onto School Street and past the police station. I avoided even casting my eyes up the stairs toward the doors. Bertie was not back in there. She simply couldn't be. Instead I kept a careful eye out for obstacles that could present a danger to Jeanette.

"Watch out here," I warned. "This shop has all kinds of wares displayed on the sidewalk." I steered her around an array of buckets, brooms, and shovels. So many things to trip on if one wasn't aware they were there.

"Who cares for Rebecca when thee is working, Jeanette?" I asked as we passed the Josiah Bartlett statue on the corner of School and Main Streets.

"Our long-suffering nursemaid. She's a splendid woman from Quebec, so Becky speaks French with ease now, more to Mr. Papka's dismay. But my daughter is a handful and a half, and her *nounou* certainly earns her keep. I'd trust her with my own life, too. Reliable through and through."

"Thee is fortunate in having her. I hope to start a family before long and will need to find similarly competent and trustworthy help for when I am absent."

"I'm pleased to hear you're looking forward to having your own babies, Rose." She squeezed my arm.

"I very much am."

I slowed to a stop so we could wait for the horse-drawn trolley to finish ascending the hill and round the corner on Main Street before attempting to cross. "Careful here. There's a gap between the cobblestones in the next few steps."

"Thank you, Rose. You're a good set of eyes." She sniffed. "And there's a pile of manure to avoid, too, if I'm not mistaken."

"Indeed, but it's to your left," I said. "I hear the trolley might be electrified next year. William Ellis has already begun manufacturing them on Oak Street."

"Do tell! Won't an electric car be exciting?"

"I suppose." I glanced up at her as we crossed. Her expression was more alert, listening to her surroundings, than when she'd sat in my office. "Although if a line went down, everything would come to a standstill. I should think horses would be much more reliable."

"That's very backward thinking of you, Rose," Jeanette said. "I'm surprised."

"I'm not a complete dinosaur." I gave a little laugh so she'd know I wasn't upset. "I do have a telephone, thee knows."

"Of course I know. And you're right about the lines. Still, if we don't try new inventions, no one will ever be motivated to improve them."

Two lads my twin nephews' age approached us. One carried a covered lunch bucket, the other a strap tightened around two books. They nudged each other when they saw Jeanette. One stuck his tongue out and crossed his eyes, while the one with the books put his hands by his ears and waggled his fingers.

The latter snickered. "Look at the deaf-mute idiot."

"Moron," the other called.

"Boys, for shame," I scolded, looking sternly at them. "Moron" seemed to be the word of the week.

"Careful, she'll call her policeman friend on you both," Jeanette said in a mild voice.

The boys' eyes widened and they dashed around us.

"That was despicable," I said. "What are their parents teaching them?"

"Who knows? They might have learned it from their father and mother." She lifted a shoulder and dropped it. "I'm used to such treatment. Their ignorance is their problem, not mine."

"It still doesn't make it right." I spied some edges of sidewalk brick sticking up. "Tread carefully here, my friend. There's a set of bricks wanting to escape up ahead." I slowed and watched as she paid close attention to where she placed her feet. "How were thy court assignments today?" I asked after we'd cleared the problem area.

"Funny you should ask. Remember when I mentioned Mayme Settle on Tuesday?"

"Of course. And thee knows she was murdered that very night."

"Indeed I do. Well, today's court business included a Polish man by the name of Szczepanski who recently came over from the old country."

"What's the name again?" She'd said something like "shuh-Pan-ski."

"Szczepanski. It's not so hard to pronounce, but the spelling of the start of the name is impossible. S-Z-C-Z-E, then P-A-N-S-K-I."

"My goodness."

"Quite a string of consonants, isn't it? The man speaks about six words of English, which include 'I no speak English.' The magistrate claimed the Pole didn't have papers allowing him to stay. The man claims Merton Settle is his brother, and says Merton absconded with the family riches thirty years ago. I was kept busy interpreting in both directions, Polish to English and English to Polish. It's taken the poor fellow this long to track down Mr. Settle and then to raise the money for his passage across the ocean."

"What an interesting tale. If this Polish moniker was Merton's name, no wonder he changed it to Settle when he immigrated."

She laughed. "I should say."

"John Whittier had mentioned that Merton's wealth came by way of inheritance. I hadn't known prior to speaking with him earlier. And why should I?"

"Truly, Rose. The likes of you and me who work for a living have no need to concern ourselves with this inheritance or that. Heirs are the stuff of the Brits, them and their snooty classes."

I laughed. "True words. Unless the brother's tale is true and Merton didn't rightfully inherit his funds." We were almost down to Patten's Pond and Jeanette's house, but her speaking about working had given me an idea. "Jeanette, nearly a year ago I delivered a baby boy who has ended up without the use of his eyes. I wondered if thee might be willing to speak with his parents about raising him so little Charlie can grow up with the most opportunities possible. I'm not sure they have any idea which way to turn."

"Of course I will meet with them. What a splendid idea. How did he come to be blind?"

"I'm afraid his mother had the clap and it infected his eyes during the birth."

She tsked. "It's a bad disease, and so very common. Such a shame there's no medicine able to cure it."

"I agree completely."

"You introduce us and I'll spend as much time as they like talking about schooling and ways to keep him active and out in the world. He should be as independent as possible when he reaches adulthood."

"I thank thee. Where was thee educated?"

"My parents had the foresight and the funds to send me to the Perkins School in South Boston. It's quite a forward-thinking establishment. Why, they introduced us to braille, and they even taught us world geography with relief maps."

"So you could feel the boundaries of the countries?"

"Yes, and the mountain ranges and the seas, as well. I can still remember how high the Himalayas rose up." She laughed. "They were quite strict about the girls not consorting with the boys once we entered our teen years, but you can bet we found ways. They finally instituted a series of social events, and even dances with sighted young people our age, so we would learn to comport ourselves properly."

"Why not simply gather with your classmates of the opposite sex?"

"And give us the notion that two blind people could eventually marry each other? I don't see a problem with such unions, but the school was dead set against it. If you ask me, they were willing to educate us but still regarded us as somehow defective rather than simply different."

I steered a bit to the right but an overhanging tree ahead was still in Jeanette's way. "There's a branch about to whack thee in the face. How about if thee lays thy right hand on my shoulder from behind and puts up thy left arm to shield thy face from the branch?"

She did so. "It's my neighbor's tree. I keep asking him to trim it back and he never does. It gets me every time I go out walking alone. I'm going to come out some night and trim it myself, I swear."

"And thee won't need a light to do it by either."

"So true, Rose." Jeanette gave a hearty laugh. "I never need a light to do anything. It's quite convenient, really."

TWENTY

BERTIE HAD, IN FACT, been at the post office the rest of the afternoon. When I stopped by after leaving Jeanette at her destination, Bertie welcomed me to come home with her when she closed the office at five o'clock.

"Come along and we'll have a bite to eat," she urged.

I agreed, and we walked our steeds together, one large and breathing, one compact and steel.

She whooshed out a breath once we'd cleared downtown. "People just can't mind their own business, Rose."

"What does thee mean?"

"I received a note from the head of the Whittier School. Remember I'd offered to come in and speak to the children about how the postal system works?"

"Yes. Betsy in particular was quite excited about the prospect." She had told me of the planned visit and, since she already knew Bertie, was beside herself.

"I am apparently not welcome around their children. My so-called immoral ways might corrupt their tender souls. I would surely turn them all on the path to the dreaded lesbianism."

"No!" I halted and stared at her.

"Yes, indeed. As if I would ever bring harm to anyone, especially a child, or try to persuade someone to . . ." Her voice trailed off in frustration. "I just want to live my life. Is that too much to ask?"

"It shouldn't be. They have no right to judge thee."

Twenty minutes later, our transports stowed—and watered and fed, in Grover's case—I was in Bertie's sitting room speaking on the telephone with my brother-in-law.

"No, Frederick, I will not be home to cook thy supper, nor the children's." I paced up and down Bertie's kitchen at five thirty, ranging in my frustration as far as the telephone cord would take me. I'd joined the Bailey household back when we all were sorely grieving Harriet's—my sister's—sudden death. I'd done my best to state my position: Frederick had his job and I had mine. I was happy

81

to help with the meals and the children, as I was able, in return for a rent-free room, but I'd told him it wouldn't always be possible. He'd agreed to my conditions at the time, grateful to have even a portion of a woman's presence in the home. And of course I loved being with Harriet's children, and they with me.

"What are we supposed to do for our meal, then?" Frederick now growled over the line. "Everyone had a long day and is hungry. Doesn't thee care about thy family?"

I held out the receiver from my ear and stared at it as if it was my curmudgeonly brother-in-law in the flesh. His moodiness had generally been improving since he'd been spending time with Winnie, which had been since mid-winter. Tonight? He'd reverted to form. I'd had an even longer day than any of them and did not find it in my powers to deliver a calm, understanding response.

"Frederick, as I made clear when I first moved into thy home, I am neither thy cook nor thy housekeeper."

He made a *harrumphing* sound but didn't interrupt me.

"Thee has many choices," I continued. "Thee and the children can eat bread and cheese. Mark can make omelets and biscuits. He's quite good at both, in case thee hadn't noticed. Thee can walk with the family into town and purchase dinner at the new hotel. The only choice not available is for me to return home at thy beck and call and provide dinner out of thin air. I am needed elsewhere." He didn't need to know I wasn't at a long labor but instead was spending time with my good friend, a friend who needed me.

"Very well," he said, despite sounding as if nothing I'd said had gone down very well at all. "I will take this opportunity to tell thee I plan to ask for Winnie's hand in marriage soon. She might not want thee occupying her parlor once we are wed and she moves her belongings here."

Good try, brother. Threaten me with expulsion and assume Winnie will accept thy proposal in the same breath. "Good night. Please give the children my love."

He grunted. I hung up with rather more force than necessary. David and I still did not have a date certain for our union. If Frederick ejected me from the house before I was able to marry and live with my dear husband, I would have to return to the boardinghouse where I'd lodged before Harriet's death. It would be unseemly, even for an independent Quaker female like myself, to live alone, and I doubted I could afford to rent a small house by myself. I would no longer have an office in which to conduct my business unless I was able to rent a suite that included a sitting room.

I turned to see Bertie staring at me. She had her stocking-clad feet up on the chair opposite her and a half-empty glass of sherry in her hand.

"Well, well. Rose asserts herself to the man of the house. Cheers and well-met, my friend." She raised her glass toward me and sipped. "I was more than ready for a glass after what I went through this afternoon."

"What did you go through?" I sank into the third chair at the round table and removed my shoes. Bertie didn't stand on ceremony. I rested my own feet on the fourth chair.

"Are you quite sure you don't want a drink?" she asked with a sly grin.

I was so tired and upset I made a snap decision. "Pour it." I could barely believe the words had left my lips. I'd played with a few sips of alcohol in a fit of teenaged rebellion against the strictures of my faith, but my last drink had been nearly a decade ago. At this moment I wasn't really able to summon up the sensation it had left me with at the time except it had been momentarily pleasurable. Why not rediscover the pleasure?

A moment later a lovely pink stemmed glass with floral etchings was in my hand, which Bertie had filled nearly to the rim. She topped up her own, too.

"It's my very finest aged sherry. Cheers, Rosetta." Bertie extended her glass across the table, so I did the same. When our glasses gently touched, they made a delightful tinkling sound.

She sipped. I did the same. The amber liquid was lightly sweet but not syrupy. It left a round feeling in my mouth, and warmed me in the gentlest of ways as it went down.

"What do you think?" she asked.

"It's so . . . soft." I sampled another taste and smiled at my friend. "I very much like this." I resolved to not dwell on what my fellow Friends would think if they could see me now, or worse, if they got word after the fact of my imbibing.

"So Freddy wanted you to run home and be the obedient little sister-in-law, making his dinner?" She raised a single eyebrow. "The man needs to learn to cook. And acquire some manners while he's at it."

"Thee knows how he gets. Charming and polite one moment, full of temper the next, and somehow it's always the other person's fault. Frankly? I have no idea what Winnie sees in him. She's such a dear. And Frederick? The furthest from a dear I can fathom."

Bertie gentled her tone. "I'm sure she sees in him the same thing your sister loved about her husband. You know, Rose, none of us can truly know what goes on in the hearts of two people who care for each other."

I nodded, tears filling my eyes unbidden. I thought about my dead sister. I thought about my beloved David, about Faith and Zeb, Bertie and Sophie, about all the couples who loved each other. I sniffed and swiped at my eyes. And sipped again. Then laughed without restraint as my stomach complained loudly of emptiness.

"Bertie, I will need to put something nourishing in my stomach soon or I will fall drunk and asleep on thy kitchen floor before the hour is out."

She laughed, too, and sprang up in a flash. "Then you're in luck. I made a delicious ham and cheese pie last night and a full half remains." She padded over to the pie keep in the corner and drew out the dish. "What do you think? I don't have the stove going. Is eating it at room temperature acceptable?"

"Of course it is."

"Let's take it outside and eat in the arbor, shall we? It was a long, cold winter. I, for one, am ecstatic about the coming of summer."

"I shall follow thy lead."

She divvied the pie in half, placing one piece on each of two plates. She darted outside with a folded cloth, then came back in and handed me both plates. "Please."

I accepted the plates and set them on a tablecloth-covered low table in the cool, fragrant arbor behind the house. Bertie and Sophie had a rather wild garden back here, with flowering trees, all shades of greenery, and annual flowers in every hue tucked in here and there. It was a most welcoming respite from the noisy world beyond the fence. The time was past six by now, and the heat of the sun had diminished along with its position on the western horizon.

I'd turned to fetch more of whatever she handed me when Bertie appeared with forks and knives, our glasses, and the bottle of sherry.

"I can't keep drinking like some lushey," I protested. "What will the Meeting elders think of me?"

"They're not going to find out unless you tell them, Miss Goody Two-Shoes." She grinned.

I snorted, not something I thought I usually did. Clearly evidence of my already being under the influence. Still, I sat and raised my glass. I decided to ignore whichever path of corruption down which I was apparently tiptoeing. I was determined to enjoy the evening with my dear friend, and that was that.

She once again clinked glasses with me. We both sipped and began to eat. I couldn't quite believe I hadn't even asked for God's blessing on the meal, but this was apparently Rome, and I would do as the Romans did. Or Bertie, in this case.

"We've done quite the job at creating a private room out here, haven't we?" She gestured around the garden.

"True." The growth shielded where we sat from the eyes of inquisitive neighbors. "Was that by design?"

"Yes, indeed. We have one particularly nosy fellow over the fence to the back. The man, Mrs. Settle's match in his attitude, goes to great lengths to snoop into matters that are none of his business. He even tried to peep into our bedroom window a few years back."

"He didn't!"

"He did, the rat. That was when we realized we needed to draw heavy curtains every day at dusk. He took himself downtown and wanted to lodge a complaint of indecent behavior against us. But my Sophie countered with a charge of trespassing, pointing out that he had to come onto private property to get anywhere near that window. The scoundrel withdrew the complaint."

"What's the aphorism? Let he who casts the first stone . . . something or other." I felt a laugh bubble up at my inability to finish it.

"I think it's more like, 'Let him who is without sin cast the first stone at her.' Which in that case was an adulterous woman. But the point Jesus was making is also in Matthew. 'Judge not, lest ye be judged,' by which he meant we should live righteous lives without hypocrisy."

I pointed my fork at her. "I had no idea thee was a biblical scholar."

She smiled to herself. "I am far from that, but I did have a solid Christian education."

"Now, this is quite a delicious pie, my dear." I stared at the green bits in it. "And asparagus, too? Thee could open a restaurant." I had to work a little to get the last word out clearly. *Uh-oh.* Rose Carroll, Drunkard Midwife might have to be my epitaph. I giggled, thinking of it, and then sobered. If Sissy Barclay went into labor tonight, I would be in hot water. I'd have to hope Annie could handle the birth, which was entirely irresponsible of me. Still, I was feeling gloriously relaxed. Guilt could wait.

"Slow down a little, Miss Rose." Bertie made a pressing-down motion with both hands. "You don't have to drink the whole bottle at one sitting. You'll feel mighty bad tomorrow if you do."

"Very well. I will slow down. But thee has to tell me where thee disappeared to at midday today." I gestured with my fork, sending an errant speck of pie sailing past Bertie's shoulder. "Poor Eva was at her wit's end, and Sophie was worried about thee, too. That's one reason I'm here." Except the way I pronounced "that's" came out sounding like "thash." I'd lost control of my tongue.

Bertie stood and whisked away both my glass and the bottle. While she was gone I drained the rest of her glass and giggled again. She returned with a big glass of cold water for me, but stood with arms akimbo staring at her empty glass.

"And now Miss Carroll has taken to thieving, too?" She winked and sat. "Drink your water, girl, and I'll tell you what's what."

TWENTY-ONE

AT THE CROWING OF A ROOSTER, I awoke fully clothed on the chaise in Bertie and Sophie's sitting room the next morning. My head pounded, my mouth seemed to be full of a foul-tasting cotton, and I was fiercely thirsty. Someone had left a glass of water on a small table next to me as well as a small brown bottle. I donned my spectacles and peered at it with bleary eyes. The label indicated it was some kind of tonic claiming to cure "the effects of dissipation."

What did I have to lose? I downed the bitter tonic, chasing it down with the entire glass of water. Dissipated I certainly was. Whether cured or not, only time would tell. Why, oh why, had this good Friend fallen for the lure of an easy escape from her troubles? I could scarcely believe it. Sudden distress seized me. I rushed outside to the necessary, barely seeing the fanciful painting on the outhouse door.

Being cleansed from both ends was not my idea of a happy Sixth Day. Being saved from my young relatives witnessing my intoxication and subsequent distress tempered the pain to a degree. I scrubbed my hands and rinsed my mouth at the pump then fell back onto my makeshift bed inside, moaning only twice before I lost awareness of the dawn.

When I again awoke, Bertie was in the kitchen bustling about. From what I could see, she was washed, dressed, combed, and laying rashers of bacon on the stove. Very gingerly I swung my feet onto the floor and came up to sitting. By some miracle my head had returned halfway back to normal. I stood and stumbled toward the kitchen.

"Well, look who's arisen from the dead, or the den of intoxication, more accurately." Bertie grinned and held her arms out for an embrace.

I ignored the gesture, instead collapsing into a chair. I set one elbow on the table and my poor chin in my hand, staring at her from under heavy lids.

"Why did thee corrupt me so, Bertie? Here we have a case to solve, and instead thee entices me to drink myself senseless."

She chortled. "Come now, Rosetta. What's a one-night intoxication spree? I wouldn't have lured you if I'd thought you were susceptible to needing alcohol day and night. Wasn't it fun at the time?" She leaned her head down and peered at my face. "Am I right?"

I groaned. "Yes, thee is right. It was great fun. But now I will need an entire day to recover. And it's a day I do not have at my disposal."

She set a steaming mug of coffee before me. "I've already dosed it with fresh cream and sugar. I don't suppose you'd like to try the hair of the dog, too?"

"Whatever that is, it sounds completely distasteful and I'd rather not." I took a sip of the full-flavored, aromatic, dark-roasted beverage and moaned with pleasure. "Bertie, this coffee is the best drink I have ever tasted." I sipped again. "In my entire life. In the entire universe. In the history of the world."

"Thank you," Bertie said but ended up laughing until she was bent over. "Oh my, Rose. You were the easiest drunk ever."

"What does thee mean?" I couldn't help but smile at her amusement, despite it being at my expense. "Thee tempted me, certainly, but imbibing was my own decision."

She perched on the chair opposite me, spatula in hand. "Of course it was, dear." She opened her mouth to speak, but shut it. Then opened it again. "I apologize for finding amusement. I do hope you can write off last night as one of life's rich experiences and not berate yourself for it."

"I shall try."

My friend tossed her head. "I'll tell you, girl. If I chastised myself for every 'life experience' I've ever been through, chastisement would occupy my every waking hour." The skin around her eyes crinkled in amusement.

I drained my coffee and struggled to dredge up memories from last night. "As I recall, I had asked thee where thee had been during the midday hours yesterday. Thee absented thyself from the post office, leaving poor Eva to tend to all the customers and her bladder, too."

Bertie winced at this reminder, the amusement sliding off her face.

"Alas, I appear to have lost my memory of thy response," I continued. "Please remind me, if thee will?"

Sophie appeared in the doorway. "Remind you of what, Rose?" she asked in a sleep-husky voice.

"Good morning, Sophie," I ventured. She hadn't had her coffee yet, either, but Bertie soon remedied that state of affairs.

"Good morning to you both. This kitchen smells heavenly." After she kissed the top of Bertie's head, Sophie pulled an Asian-looking wrapper closer to her body. She snugged up the tie and plopped into the chair next to mine. Her dark hair hung loose about her shoulders, the first time I'd seen it out of its customary bun. She tucked a silver-streaked lock behind her ear.

"I must apologize," I began. "I did track down our Bertie yesterday and accompanied her home after the post office closed. Thee asked for someone to be at hand looking after her. But"—I cleared my throat—"apparently I myself was the one needing looking after. I quite blissfully slept there in thy sitting room from I don't know when last night until ever so recently." I yawned. "I had not slept at all the previous night because of a birth, so I had some catching up to do."

"Assisted by our friend on the sideboard there." Bertie gestured with her chin to the half-empty bottle.

"Yes." The thought of the drink sent a shudder through me. I pointed at Bertie. "No more avoiding. Where did thee get thyself off to yesterday?"

She turned the bacon, one rasher at a time. She finally looked up. "I had to get away. I've been accused of immoral behavior before but never suspected of murder. Your detective was in the post office in the morning asking me to come back to the station for more questioning. I told him I couldn't talk to him at work, but I was afraid he'd be back."

"You were running from the law, my darling?" Sophie asked.

"In a way. I rode Grover up to the top of Po Hill and sat there pondering my situation for more than an hour. And when I came down, I went straight to the station and answered his questions. He added a few new ones to the original set, which were mostly about my whereabouts that evening."

"New questions?" Sophie frowned, immediately looking more awake.

"Yes. Did I garden? What did I have in my shed? What cleaning supplies do I keep in the house? Do we have a problem with rodents? Had I ever made study of mushrooms? That kind of thing."

"So he's trying to find poisons on this property and learn what you know about them," I said.

Bertie nodded. "I believe so. And then he pressed me about my cohabitation." She laid her hand on Sophie's. "I told the man in no uncertain terms that I had never been arrested for a crime, and that what I did in the privacy of my own home was none of his business."

"Well done, love," Sophie said. "All true."

"It's not that nobody has ever cast aspersions on the way I choose to live, but it's not criminal and that's that." Bertie gazed at us. "I also apologized thoroughly to the ever-patient Eva upon my return."

"Detective Donovan has no evidence against you, Bert," Sophie pointed out. "And I was able to convince him to tell me your accuser was Irvin Barclay."

"Barclay?" Bertie set her fists on her hips. "That windbag? He's got the nerve."

The nerve, indeed. But why would he want to cast suspicion on Bertie? Unless it was to divert it from himself — or someone he was protecting.

TWENTY-TWO

I STAYED EATING BREAKFAST at Bertie's until she left at a quarter before eight. I knew the Baileys would have left the house for the day by the time I arrived home. Frederick was going to have to learn to step up and care for his children in all kinds of domestic ways. Faith and I had carried the burden for over a year, but she had now started her own life with Zeb, and I was hoping to do the same soon with David.

Once outside, I stared at my poor seedlings languishing in my bicycle's basket. I'd ridden all over town with them yesterday and forgotten them completely last evening. I drew a cup of water at the outside pump and gave them each a drink, then pedaled home, thinking as I went.

A thick fog lay over the town this morning, coating everything with heavy moisture, so the plantlets weren't as dry as they might have been. The fog made even commonplace sights look mysterious. I rode past the Friends Meetinghouse, whose tall windows loomed dark and grim, giving no hint of the inspiring sight they presented from the inside. I pedaled up Whitehall Road, but turned off onto Thompson before I reached the Settle home. I coasted down to the bridge over the Powow River and slowed to a stop. A mother duck trailed eight yellow puffballs behind her. On the opposite bank I spied the fluffy tail of a fox, and I suspected fewer ducklings would be waddling single file tomorrow.

I rode on. Bertie and I hadn't done a thing to solve the case. Kevin was clearly still interested in her, despite my protestations. Mayme's killer was still somewhere walking as freely as the fox, as far as I knew. I'd laid out the facts for John Whittier yesterday. Truly, talking with the wise poet hadn't helped, either. I now knew Merton's childhood surname. But was his name even relevant?

Irvin Barclay. I thought again about his arguing with Mayme at the courthouse. Had Jeanette heard what it had been about? I didn't think she'd told me. It must have been a serious matter if they were both in court. How could I delve into the topic of their argument? I had a home visit scheduled with Sissy for this afternoon. Perhaps she could tell me of the issue between her husband and Mayme. I also pondered Sophie's information about Irvin's claim he'd seen Bertie at the Settle home. It didn't make sense.

Turning onto Powow Street, I pushed on the pedals to get me up the sloping road until I reached Center Street. Powow became a sharply steeper hill a hundred yards farther along, but the highest point in town wasn't my destination today. I'd settle for ascending the summit of the investigation, instead.

Once home, at the middle house of the triplets that had been built for the Hamilton Mill workers a decade earlier, I removed the seedlings and stashed them safely on the ground in a spot where the house would shade them when the fog burned off. I pumped water and made sure they were all well wetted before I trudged up the side steps and unlocked the door.

Lina wasn't here yet, and goodness, did she have her work cut out for her in the kitchen today. Dirty dishes and pans seemed to be everywhere. Porridge stuck to the sides of a pot. A porcelain cup was stained with leftover coffee. Half a loaf of bread had been left out unwrapped to stale on the cutting board. Drops of egg yolk congealed on the table. A saucer of milk sat on the floor for the cat, except half the milk was on the floor itself. And more, much more. Four males and a little girl could do a lot of damage without someone to rein them in. My brother-in-law had never been much of one for enforcing the children's chores, either. They knew better. Frederick himself had probably never washed a dish in his life. The state of the kitchen smacked of him punishing me for not coming home to cook yesterday.

I spied my name on a missive propped up on the sideboard. The note was written in Betsy's girlish hand on paper torn from an exercise book.

Uncle David called for thee, Aunte Rose. He wood like thee to return his call at thy erlyest cunveenyense. Love, Betsy

I smiled at her phonetic spellings, and my heart lightened at the prospect of hearing David's voice. The kitchen clock read eight fifteen. He would certainly be up by now and possibly not yet at the hospital. But if he'd already departed, I might be forced to speak with his mother, Clarinda. She had never approved of his courting me and had become even less happy when he'd asked me to marry him last summer.

I fingered the simple gold love-knot ring on my left hand, which he'd given me as a token of his affection. We'd been betrothed for nearly a year and still had no ceremony planned. Clarinda had finally given us her blessing a few months ago — or if not a blessing, she'd agreed to not stand in the way of our marriage. But she'd insisted on needing time to plan all the festivities, and so far David hadn't protested about the delay. Wasn't arranging a wedding supposed to be the purview of the bride and her family? I had to admit my own Meeting had stood in the way of our union, too, and still did, to some extent.

I was overdue for a visit to my parents on the farm where I'd had a happy childhood. The farm was on the outskirts of the now-thriving mill city of Lawrence some thirty miles to the southwest from here. Once this case was settled, I would catch the next train and put my head together with Mother. She was a sensible person and gentle in her forthrightness. We would come up with a plan and present it to Clarinda, plain and simple. I truly longed for a plain and simple wedding, like Faith's had been. And I longed even more to be finally united in matrimony with my beloved David.

Whom I still had not called. I went into the sitting room and stared at the phone. No, I would call him in an hour and speak to him in the safety of his office.

TWENTY-THREE

THE TELEPHONE RANG at nine as I was going through my accounts. I hurried to answer it, hoping it was David reaching out for me again. I should have returned his call by now. Instead a tearful Georgia Clarke was on the line.

"Rose, please come quickly."

"Is thee . . . is it . . . tell me what is happening, Georgia. Speak to me."

"I'm bleeding," she whispered. Her voice dissolved in a sob.

Oh. "I'll be right there." I hung up and hurried to tidy my hair and wash my hands. I grabbed my birthing satchel. She lived only a block away, but I hopped on my bicycle anyway, in case I needed it afterward. Alas, it sounded very much as if she was experiencing the end of her newest pregnancy. That she hadn't yet sensed the baby move and that I'd been unable to detect a heartbeat two days ago comported with the possibility of a miscarriage. But I would see what I would see.

A frightened-looking white-capped maid let me into the stately home and pointed upstairs. "Shall I show you the way, miss?"

"No, I know where to go." I thanked her and trotted up.

"Georgia?" I pushed open the door to her room but didn't see her.

"In here," she called in a weak voice from the bathroom.

Robert Clarke had spared no expense when he'd had this fine home constructed. He and some of the other "Captains of Industry," as the small group of factory and mill owners liked to call themselves, had formed a private water company and run pipes to pump water to their own homes. Georgia's bathroom was a roomy tiled space with a deep tub, a sink with gold fixtures, and a flush commode, on which she currently perched bent over nearly in half. Her head hung down over her forearms, which rested on her knees.

I went to her and gently laid my hands on her nightgowned shoulders. "How long has thee been bleeding, Georgia?"

"Since dawn."

Five hours. "Is it heavy? Does thee have pains?"

"Yes. It's not like labor, Rose, but it hurts more than a monthly." She sniffed and sat up straight. "I'm losing the baby." She did not make it a question.

"I think it's probable. Has thee passed a clot or any thicker matter?"

She nodded, with the saddest look I'd ever seen on her face. "Right before I called you." Tears crept down her cheeks as she reached for a red wad of flannel on the shelf next to her.

The cloth looked like a rag torn from a woman's red petticoat, the undergarment we all donned during our monthlies to minimize accidental staining of lighter-colored fabrics. When the petticoats wore out, we tore them into rags to use during the same period, that cyclic aching reminder of our fertility.

Georgia folded back the fabric to reveal a mass of deep-red bloody tissue, within which I glimpsed the shape of a tiny seahorse under an inch long. A human embryo.

I steadied myself on the sink behind me and pressed my eyes shut. I had experienced an almost identical tiny life being wrenched from my body far too early. In my case I had only recently grown out of childhood. My pregnancy had been the result of being violently assaulted. It had not been a blessed event for me, and having my body end it of its own accord had been a great gift.

But I was here to help Georgia, who had wanted this baby. My job was not to dwell on the pain of my own past. I opened my eyes to see her staring at me.

"Are you all right, Rose?" Her brow knit.

I smiled sadly. It might help her if she knew I had experienced what she was enduring. "I had a pregnancy end similarly long ago. I apologize. The memory took over for a moment there."

She nodded. "Then you truly understand how this feels. I have known you long enough not to care that surely you were unmarried when it happened."

"I thank thee. I believe I do understand."

"I never lost a baby before. Why did it happen now?" Her voice was plaintive. "I've been eating well and haven't lifted anything heavy."

"Only God knows, Georgia. In truth, we women are born with a finite number of eggs in our bodies. They grow old along with us, and their number diminishes, of course, with every monthly and every pregnancy. By the time women reach thy age, the eggs available to be fertilized by the male are much fewer. I've read medical papers hypothesizing that any toxins we might come in contact with throughout our lives can accumulate in the ovaries, damaging the remaining stock, as it were."

"Oh?"

I gave a little laugh. "I'm sorry for subjecting thee to a scientific treatise. I only meant to say that the older a woman is, the more chance she has for producing offspring with serious problems."

Georgia nodded. "I see. Better I lose the baby this way than carry to term a defective child? One whose body or mind might not form correctly in the womb?"

"Your body making a corrective move is one way to look at it, and it can be comforting."

"In fact it is, in a twisted way. Ohh," Georgia groaned and bent over again. I squatted in front of her and stroked her forehead.

"Use thy birthing skills." I spoke softly. "Thee knows how. Breathe down to the pain. Let go of constriction. Blow out a deep breath and do it again." I took in a long inhale and gently blew it out through pursed lips to model it for her. "In this situation, thee can bear down whenever thee needs to."

I was a bit worried. After her daughter had been born last summer, Georgia had hemorrhaged, but I'd been able to control the bleeding. I prayed something related wouldn't occur here. I had little experience helping women through miscarriages, except for a disastrous one in the winter which ended up not being a miscarriage at all. My clients rarely came to see me until they were halfway along in their pregnancies, and most losses like this one occurred early on. I longed to talk with Orpha for guidance. Her granddaughter Alma did have a telephone in the house, one which had been critically useful in a dangerous episode with a killer nearly a year ago, but I doubted Orpha would be comfortable using the device. Instead I held Georgia in the Light of God, that the bleeding would not threaten her health in any way.

She and I, we'd get through this. She wouldn't be the mother of six, after all, but not being pregnant again was likely for the best. She and Robert could enjoy the five healthy children they already had.

Georgia sat up again. "Being a woman isn't for the weak, is it, Rose?" She swiped her brow.

"Indeed it isn't. But we knew that, didn't we?"

"Why, if Mr. Clarke gets the least bit sick he acts as if he's on his deathbed."

"Orpha told me something funny once," I said, glad my client felt well enough to speak of everyday things. "She said labor is so painful, women can almost understand how a man feels when he runs a low fever."

She gave a quick laugh. "That's a good one." She stopped smiling and seemed to turn inward, blowing out a breath. She put one hand on the shelf and grabbed my hand with her other. She breathed in through her nose and out through her mouth.

"Good," I murmured. "Thee is doing so well."

After the current pain subsided, she cocked her head. "You know, I've been thinking on poor Mayme being killed."

My eyes flew open. "Thee has?"

"Yes. My cook said the Settles' maid—well, she's Cookie's cousin's daughter—told her the gardener fellow they have over there has always been an odd duck. One time he brought some mushrooms in for the cook, but something seemed off about them so she threw them in the rubbish. Maybe the gardener is Mayme's murderer."

Maybe, indeed.

"Your policeman might want to look into it, no?"

"I'll pass along thy tale to him." And I might see if I could have a word with the Settles' cook later today. I might just.

TWENTY-FOUR

By TEN THIRTY Georgia was feeling well enough for me to leave. I'd cautioned her she might continue bleeding lightly for several more weeks, but to summon me immediately if the flow became heavy again. She'd insisted on pressing three dollars into my hand before I left, despite my trying to refuse. She'd said Mr. Clarke would have it no other way.

Now I stood in my parlor waiting for Gertrude to put my call through to David at Anna Jaques Hospital. What was taking so long? I supposed she must have to go through the hospital's operator. Lina rattled pans and dishes in the kitchen, and the coo of a dove floated in through the open window. I normally found both kinds of noises soothing—Lina's because it meant I didn't have to clean the kitchen, and the dove's because it was such a soft sound. Neither helped at this moment. The world was still cloaked in fog. My mind was, too.

I perked up when a voice came over the line, but sagged when it was not David's deep, rich tones but the hurried high notes of operator Gertrude.

"Mr. Dodge is not available, Miss Carroll. Please telephone at a later time."

With a click, the line went dead. I paced back and forth, frustrated at not being able to talk to him. I rued not making the call earlier this morning and realized I was going to have to get over my unwillingness to deal with his mother. She was a lady in excellent health and my future mother-in-law. She no doubt would be part of our lives for two or three more decades at a minimum.

I also thought about the effect having a telephone in the house had on my patience. Before we'd had it installed, David and I would write notes to each other, sometimes every day, as a way of communicating. Now? If I couldn't reach him exactly when I wished to, it drove me a little wild.

Of course, being able to receive calls at home had made an enormous difference in my profession. Clients of means no longer had to send a driver merely to call me to a labor. And when I did get a call, I was able to summon Annie by using the telephone to leave a message with the landlord of her building, who had agreed to let her know where to meet me.

I flounced into the chair at my desk. This murder case was rattling my brain with too many unanswered questions. I wasn't due at Sissy Barclay's until one this afternoon, so I drew out paper and pencil. Sometimes writing down the known facts and questions about the unknown helped clarify things in my mind.

I made two underlined headings and pushed my glasses back up my nose. Under *Known* on the left I jotted down a list:

> Adoniram upset about daughter's death
> A. brought suspicious mushrooms to cook
> Irvin and Mayme argued
> Irvin tried to cast suspicion on Bertie
> Irvin's first wife's death?
> Merton humiliated by wife
> Mayme took hot drink before bed
> Mayme white stuff under fingernails
> Polish stranger in town claims Merton is brother

I wasn't even going to try to spell the man's name. Were those eight bits all I knew? I tapped the pencil on the paper. Maybe, maybe not, but I could add to it any time. I shifted over to the *Unknown* column.

> Poison
> White substance
> Mayme and Irvin argument
> If Polish man is Merton's relative
> If Merton made off with brother's money
> Reason for Irvin's false accusation

I sat back and stared at the sheet. Did I have means to discover the facts about any of these unknowns? The first two on the second list were the purview of the police, the man performing the autopsy, and the chemist. By now I was confident Kevin would share the information with me when he had it. Sissy might be able to shed light on her husband's beef with Mayme. Maybe Jeanette could offer or gain more information about the mysterious Pole.

"Aha." I was missing some of the very basics of detecting: opportunity and alibi. I returned to the *Unknown* list.

Tuesday night whereabouts of A, Merton, Irvin, relative

Merton and Adoniram most definitely had opportunity, living at the same property as the victim. Irvin and the Polish stranger? Somebody must know where they each had been after our knitting circle had broken up. Poor Bertie had been out and had admitted to Sophie she'd passed by the Settles' home late that evening. But of course she didn't go inside and dose Mayme's drink with poison. Why would she? Similar to what John had said yesterday afternoon, if Bertie killed every person who didn't approve of her living with Sophie, she'd have been hung for murder long ago.

TWENTY-FIVE

I TRIED THREE MORE TIMES to reach David, never with success. I hoped his call had not been about anything urgent, and that he'd merely wanted to see me and perhaps go for a drive or dine out together. I'd eaten a bowl of leftover potage after I finished my list. It was now after twelve thirty and the kitchen shone. It smelled clean, too, and I hadn't had to do any of the work to make it so. I thanked Lina for doing an excellent job, which only made her blush. I doled out her weekly wage before sending her along home.

I needed to leave soon myself to meet Annie at the Barclay home several blocks up the hill on Prospect Street. My apprentice hadn't accompanied me on an antenatal home visit before, so this was a good chance for her to see the kinds of things I looked for. I'd never found anything wrong with the bedchamber of a comfortably situated mother-to-be like Sissy, but still it was good to know the layout of the house, who the servants were, and to explain to the client the process of the birth if it was her first. With less well-off pregnant clients, it was important I made sure they had a clean enough and sufficiently private setting in which to assure the most successful outcome possible.

I'd washed my face, put up my hair, and picked up my satchel when the telephone rang. Maybe this was David, finally.

"This is Rose Carroll."

"Good afternoon, Rosie," David said.

Smiling, I set down the satchel. "Hello, my dear. I'm sorry I wasn't at home last evening, and this morning I could never get through to return thy call. Is all well in thy world?"

"In a way, with the exception of a poor patient of mine who suffered a grievous fall."

"I'm sorry to hear it."

"So was she. Say, do you have any news in this week's case?"

"I do, a little, but I'd much prefer saying it in person. Will thee have any time to see me later?"

He laughed. "This Friend speaks my mind," he said, mimicking one of the many peculiar turns of phrase Quakers use. "How about dinner with Dr. Dodge this evening? I've learned the Grand Hotel has a new chef preparing meals. They say he's quite excellent, having trained in Paris and New York. May I fetch you at six tonight?"

"I would be delighted. Must I 'dress for dinner,' as thy mother puts it?" Not that I owned any garments suitable for dinner in society's elevated circles. I didn't wish to have them in my possession, either. More than a year ago, before David had asked for my hand, I'd borrowed a lovely rose-colored gown to attend a dinner dance, an appearance Clarinda had nearly commanded.

While I'd obtained special dispensation from John Whittier for the evening's attire, I had not been comfortable at the soiree. I didn't mind being judged unworthy by Clarinda and her friends. The only eyes I wanted to be judged worthy in were David's. But perching politely on a slippery chair and smiling at the young ladies who were my apparent competitors for David's hand had given me a serious case of indigestion.

"You know I don't care about such customs, darling Rose," David now said. "Your beautiful face and companionable conversation is all that is required for our outing. Conversation and a healthy appetite."

It was my turn to laugh. "Thee never needs worry about my appetite. I shall be ready at six o'clock."

TWENTY-SIX

I WAITED IN FRONT of the Barclay home until ten after one, but Annie never appeared. When I'd arrived, a roan pulling a black carriage had pulled out of the driveway and was plodding up the hill. Irvin, perhaps.

The fog had finally burned off. With clear weather one could see the nearby coast from up here, but today the air was hazy with late-spring humidity. It was warm, to boot. I removed the shawl I'd donned before leaving the house and rolled it into the bike's basket. The brim of my bonnet blessedly shielded my face from the sun's strong rays.

The grounds of the property, situated on a southern-facing slope, were full of perennial herbs and flowers I couldn't even begin to identify, although they appeared a bit ragged, neglected. It looked like a master gardener had planted and tended them and then left with no one to replace him. The house itself was a more modest abode than I'd expected for a banker, a simple two-story home with neither a mansard roof nor the new complicated gables and rooflines that were coming into style for the moneyed classes.

I finally leaned my bicycle against the carriage house, which was also of a modest size. I prayed my apprentice had not come to harm, but I couldn't wait any longer. If I had a chance later, I'd ride by Annie's family's flat and see what was up.

Rapping on the back door of the home brought a full-figured woman in a white apron to the door. The reason for her flushed cheeks was apparent after she let me in. The kitchen was warm and redolent with smells of heaven: cinnamon and cloves, lightly browned flaky crusts, and the tangy sweetness of baked apples. I also spied a bottle of uncorked sweet wine and suspected alcohol might play a role in the rosy hue of her face.

I introduced myself. "I am Sissy's midwife, and I believe she is expecting me."

"She told me yeh'd be along, Miss Carroll. I'm Aoife O'Malley, the cook here."

Eef? "Please call me Rose, ma'am. I'm pleased to meet thee. Might I inquire, how does thee spell thy name?"

She threw back her head and chortled. "Nary a soul knows who isn't Irish. It's A-O-I-F-E, dearie, but don't you make a notice of it. Pretend it's E-E-F and be done with it. Now, I'm after baking up the last of the fall apples, I am. Care for a slice of pie before yeh go up?"

"I thank thee, but no. I would love a taste when the visit is over, though. The smell alone is enough to make a person melt."

"And well might it be. I learned to bake from my gran in the old country, I did. Nothing much a few spices and a generous helping of butter won't cure, wouldn't you say, Miss Carroll?"

"Indeed I would." I laughed. "The Barclays seem to have a talented grower on the staff. The gardens outside are lovely."

"The manual labor is done by a local lad, miss, but Mr. Barclay is the mastermind, Miss Carroll." She caught sight of my open mouth. "And no, I won't be calling yeh by yer Christian name. 'Tisn't proper, miss."

"Very well. Irvin is a gardener?" I asked. "A banker dirtying his hands surprises me."

"As it does the rest of us. But when the dear Lord gives us a gift, we're ungrateful if we refuse it, isn't it so?"

I smiled. "Thee is correct."

"Like yer midwifing, then." Aoife glanced at the ceiling. "We're that happy about a baby in the house, we are. And now we learn we're to have two at once."

"Yes, I detected twins when I examined Sissy earlier this week."

"The master, he's been after wanting to become a da ever since he married poor Mrs. Barclay. The previous one, I mean."

I gave a single nod. "I understand she was not able to provide him with a child."

The cook shot her gaze right then left, and beckoned me closer. "He was mean to her, he was. Wretched and insulting. Why, I wouldn't be surprised if she withheld her womanly favors on purpose. Kept those legs locked up tight. Who'd want to get poked by a man of his ilk?" She winked and made an O with her left index finger and thumb, followed by a poking gesture with her right pointer. "Yeh know my meaning."

How could I not know? I only smiled and nodded. "I understand she tragically passed away."

"'Twas tragic, for certain. But she didn't simply up and die one day. No, the mister was responsible as sure as I'm an O'Malley." She gave a definitive nod.

This woman was clearly an O'Malley. "What does thee mean by responsible?" I whispered, having no idea if other servants or even Irvin might be in the house.

"The mister used to bring her a special tea every night before she slept. It was the one time he was ever so solicitous. He'd make certain she was all tucked up in her bed—a separate one from his, mind yeh." At this she rolled her eyes as if the notion of sleeping apart from one's spouse was ludicrous, which it probably was in her world, and in mine, as well. "But I'm of a mind he dosed up the tea after it left my hands and before it arrived in hers. He was slowly poisoning her, Miss Carroll. Make no mistake about it."

I stared at her. Irvin poisoning his first wife, and now a woman with whom he had some kind of grievance had also perished from poison? If the cook's story were true, the two deaths were far too similar to be coincidence. I couldn't wait to share this information with Kevin.

"I think I heard she died of heart failure." I gazed at Aoife.

"Sure and that's what it looked like." She nodded knowingly.

"Mrs. O'Malley, have you seen Rose Carroll?" Sissy called from somewhere beyond the kitchen door. She pushed through and stopped. "Oh, hello, Rose. I didn't know you'd arrived." She smiled and clasped her hands in front of her tea dress, under which she'd clearly not donned a corset today. "Having a nice chat with our talented cook? Aoife alone is responsible for all this fat I've acquired." Sissy patted her belly.

"Go along there, Mrs. Barclay," the cook said. "A tiny lady the likes of you could stand to put on a bit of weight, and besides, it's the wee babes who're doing the growing in there." She beamed.

"I'd agree with thy cook, Sissy," I said. "Let's go visit thy bedchamber together, shall we?"

Sissy nodded and pushed open the door that swung in either direction.

"Oh, Aoife," I said. "My apprentice should be appearing any

minute now. Her name is Annie Beaumont." Where was Annie, anyway? I'd forgotten to worry in the respite of pleasure that meeting cook Aoife O'Malley had provided. "Please send her upstairs when she comes."

"I will." She raised a floury hand. "This piece of pie here has yer name on it, and there's pie aplenty for Miss Beaumont, too. So don't forget to stop back by before yeh both leave. "

She also elevated one eyebrow as she said the words. The signal could have indicated not the pie but the secret she'd divulged. I'd be coming back for secrets, as well.

TWENTY-SEVEN

IF THE MAIN STAIRWELL was any indication, the Barclay home had been spared no expense in its construction, despite its plain exterior. It looked to have been built not so long ago, whether sometime prior to the War for the Union or immediately after, I couldn't say. The wood of the banister was a smooth rich cherry and didn't wobble in the slightest with the pressure of a hand on it. A leaded glass window adorned the landing halfway up, casting spots of colors on the floor now the sun had finally made an appearance.

Sissy did not lack in vitality this afternoon. She lifted her skirts and trotted up as if she were a child competing in a running race instead of a matron seven months along. She turned back at the top.

"Pardon me, Miss Carroll." She giggled and brought both hands to her mouth in a schoolgirl gesture. "I simply feel so free now you've given me permission to throw that fool corset aside."

I was a mere six years older than Sissy. My experiences, my work, my circumstances all conspired to make me feel far more mature than this young mother-to-be. I could only hope the birth of her twins would go easily on her. I prayed Irvin would stand up to be a loving provider — even if he hadn't in the past.

Sissy, now with warm cheeks and lungs heaving from her exertions, led me into her bedchamber. I had entered many a rich woman's private quarters in the last five years, but none as richly adorned and feminine as this. If a shade of pink existed in the known universe, it was included in this room. Margaret Fell Fox, one of the founders of my faith, was no doubt turning in her Quaker grave at the ostentatious decorations confronting me.

Flounces, ruffles, curlicues, and general frippery decorated every corner and nook. This window featured pale pink lace curtains. That chair was embroidered in a deep pink floral brocade. A rose-colored silk bouquet arched out of a translucent magenta glass vase. And so on. And on and on.

Sissy twirled with her arms out. "Isn't it the most delightful room you've ever seen, Rose? Mr. Barclay gave me permission to decorate it however I pleased and free range with his accounts to pay for it."

I found the room confining and overwhelming, but I would never say so to a client, especially to one who quite clearly loved her surroundings. "It's very nice, Sissy." I swallowed, determined to conduct my business and be done with this space until her labor began. At least she had the shades up and the windows open on this now-fine late spring afternoon. "Thy husband does quite well in his chosen profession, I gather." Could I somehow bring up his argument with Mayme Settle?

"Indeed he does. And he has made some wise investments, he told me."

I mentally crossed my fingers. "I saw him near the court in the Armory recently," I said, even though it had been Jeanette who saw him, not me. "I hope there's no kind of trouble with the judicial system."

She gave a shake to her head. "I don't want to speak ill of the dead, but Mayme Settle was arguing with the mister about a pot of money."

"Oh?"

"Yes, they were cousins and he said there was some inheritance the two of them were to split equally. Mrs. Settle had refused to do so."

And now this entire pot of money would go to Merton, unless there was some other arrangement. Curious. I wondered if Irvin's investments had been as wise as he'd told Sissy. If he were desperate for money, he might have resorted to murder to get it—except where did he think it would come from?

A door stood open revealing a tiled floor within. "Is that a bathroom?" I asked, pointing. It reminded me of Georgia's miscarriage of a few hours ago. I really should stop by and make sure she was well after I left here. I was not at home to take her call should her bleeding have increased.

"It is." Sissy nearly skipped to the doorway. "It has all the most up-to-date conveniences. Even hot running water, Rose! Imagine."

"Hot water will be useful during thy labor, Sissy." I needed to calm her oddly effusive mood and prepare her for her impending children's births. At which event I hoped Annie would be able to assist me, and because of which I wished she were here right now.

"We usually need to depend on recently boiled water, and we might still, so it will be sterile. Tell me, Sissy, does thee expect any family members to be assisting in thy birth? Thy mother or an aunt, perhaps? A sister?"

Sissy plopped onto the bed, the air let out of her happy balloon. "No." To her credit, she neither pouted nor wept. "No one will be helping me, besides you, that is. I am on my own here, you see."

I wondered why her mother wouldn't help her through her travails. I smiled, despite my inward lack of cheer. "My apprentice Annie and I shall be thy womenfolk during the birth, then."

Annie's voice sounded downstairs.

"And there she is," I added.

A moment later Annie appeared in the doorway, a green ribbon festooning her red hair. Annie was not a Quaker.

"Désolée," she whispered to me. *Sorry.* She smiled at Sissy. "Good afternoon, Mrs. Barclay. I am Annie Beaumont, and I assure you I have never been late before."

"Please call me Sissy. 'Mrs. Barclay' makes me think someone is talking to my husband's mother. And she's not a very nice lady." Sissy's animation returned, and she beamed in return. "I love your green ribbon! Aren't hair ornaments fun?"

Annie touched her ribbon, smiling at our client, but she also cut her gaze to me for an instant, as if to say, "I'm humoring her."

"My *memere* is from Quebec City." Sissy regarded Annie like a long-lost sister.

I folded my hands, feeling like the old lady in a girl's boudoir. Had Sissy taken a mood-elevating tonic, or was she simply feeling relaxed in the company of women? She'd apparently been lacking such companionship since her marriage to Irvin Barclay and her move to Amesbury, away from every woman she'd ever held dear. Her giddiness was understandable. I didn't know what I'd do without Bertie's friendship, Faith's love and confidences, and my mother being on the other end of an efficient postal system.

Right now? We had a pre-birth interview to conduct. I cleared my throat.

"Sissy, I'd like to review what thee can expect when thy labor begins. Thee will deliver thy babies here in this room." I nodded at Annie to continue.

"You're a first-time mother." Annie took up the narrative without hesitation. "The more you're familiar with the process, the less fear you'll have. Fear can lead to an involuntary tightening of the body, and tightening can cause pain."

"But won't you have medicines to give me?" Sissy searched my face and then Annie's. "My friend in Portland said she heard the lying-in hospital gives ladies gas now, and it makes them go to sleep and forget the whole thing. You know, like the ether men take when they need to have a diseased leg removed."

I shook my head. "We don't use gas at home because it isn't safe, and there really aren't effective medicines to remove the pain without harm to thee or thy baby."

Annie again spoke up. "You'll be better off by moving about, using your breath, and letting us help you relax."

I saw Sissy about to object and held up a hand. "And thy babies will fare far better, too, not having drugs put into their bodies via thine."

She wasn't quite ready to believe me. But she didn't have any choice in the matter.

TWENTY-EIGHT

THE THREE OF US CONVERSED for the next twenty minutes about what Sissy could expect, when she should summon me, and what kind of assistance the household could provide.

I was surprised when Sissy said Aoife performed the roles of housekeeper and maid as well as cook. I would have thought Irvin had the means to employ a larger staff than he did. Nevertheless, I knew I could work amicably with the cook during the labor and delivery. Aoife was a far more congenial helpmeet than I sometimes had at hand.

"Annie, if Sissy is agreeable, why doesn't thee perform an antenatal physical examination while thee is here." I gestured toward my satchel.

Sissy nodded and sat back on the bed, pulling up her skirts.

"You look very well, Sissy," Annie said. "You must be taking good care with your health."

"I do try. Miss Rose there is a good influence."

Annie took Sissy's pulse and measured her belly. With her fingers held flat and together as I had taught her, Annie palpated the womb in several places, pressing in with a hand on opposite sides of the belly. My apprentice nodded when she felt the second baby. "Yes, you are most certainly bearing twins, Sissy."

"Goodness, I haven't even given a thought about what to name them. And . . . oh! We have only the one cradle." She pointed to the small box on rockers already outfitted with a fluffy white coverlet. "Whatever shall we do?"

I smiled. "Thee shall do what every other new mother has done — make do. If the babies are little, they'll be happy to share the cradle at first. They'll be accustomed to each other's heartbeats and bodies from all these months together in the womb."

"I suppose." Sissy frowned a little, looking doubtful.

"Or thee can line a bureau drawer with a soft blanket and one baby shall have a nice safe bed for the first few months. Truly, thy days will be too busy with feeding one then the other to worry about trivialities like cradles."

Annie laughed. "I agree with Rose. Babies who cuddled in the womb for nine months don't want to be separated, anyway. They'd cry their poor hearts out if you had two cradles."

I nodded. She'd clearly had experience with newborn multiples.

Annie glanced up at me after using the Pinard horn to auscultate the heartbeats in various places on Sissy's bare belly. It bulged up beautifully from her body, with the skin already taut and shiny with the burden of containing two fetuses, their amniotic sac — or sacs, depending if they were identical or fraternal twins — and the increased fluids and blood flow accompanying any healthy pregnancy.

"*Je n'entends qu'un,*" Annie murmured, knowing I was well up on my birth-related vocabulary in French. *I hear but one.*

I nodded that I had, too, and indicated we'd talk about it later.

"Thank you, Sissy," Annie said, clasping Sissy's hand in both of hers. "We're both so excited to meet your babies."

Sissy, in a fit of informality, clasped Annie's shoulders and kissed her on both cheeks.

I pulled out my appointment book. "I'd like thee to come in for another check in two weeks' time."

We arranged the day and time and I jotted it down. "We'll see ourselves out," I said. Once we were downstairs and out of earshot, I laid a hand on Annie's arm.

"It's not unusual not to hear both hearts," I murmured. "The babies are getting big and one sometimes hides behind the other."

"Or one could be deceased," she suggested, also speaking softly.

"Sadly, it's possible. We'll have to wait and see." I pushed through the door to the kitchen.

"There yeh two are," Aoife said. "I insist yeh sit down and sample my pie."

I exchanged a glance with Annie, who smiled.

"Thank thee kindly, Aoife," I said. "We would love to."

She served us each a wedge of pie at the wooden table to the back of the kitchen, and sat across from us. "I'm not used to cooking for so few people, I'll tell yeh. I can't wait for those wee babes to be born."

"I'm surprised more staff doesn't work here," I said.

"Mr. Barclay, he sent them off. The maid, the gardener, his driver.

The two of 'em last week, and the driver only yesterday. I'm the only one left."

"Does thee know why?"

"He wouldn't be telling the likes of me, now, would he?" Aoife leaned toward us. "But I heard him on the talking device. Sounded like he has money problems. Debts owed and such." She sat back. "Why, I don't know what he was after, letting the missus spend so much money on her fancy room up there. Gave her a bathroom fit for the Queen of Sheba, he did. Living beyond his means, and with babies on the way. Who ever heard of such a thing?"

TWENTY-NINE

I PEDALED OUT HIGH STREET after Annie and I left the Barclay home. I had much to think about. Aoife's claim that Irvin poisoned his first wife. Learning of his debts, and that he'd been related by blood to Mayme Settle. Could he somehow have poisoned Mayme's nightly drink, too?

I headed toward the Settles' home, hoping I could grab a word with the cook there. But under what auspices? I turned onto Whitehall Road. I was almost there and needed to think fast. When I was fifty yards distant from the house, I slowed to a stop. Lake Gardner was to my right, and even though the fog was gone on Powow Hill, here it still lay atop the water. It looked eerie, almost like steam rising. Brambles grew at the lake's shore on this side, and their fresh green color contrasted with the murky look of the lake. The color of the water was not unlike the yarn I'd been knitting with the night I'd been at the Settles.

An excuse for a talk with the cook popped into my brain. I would claim I'd left a knitting needle at the house. Such a reason for a visit would get me in the door. And as soon as Kevin arrested the killer, I'd quit with the white lies. Every single one seemed like a stain on my integrity. I rode on to the Settle home. The windows on the front were draped in black, making the house look like a dowager in deep mourning.

I knocked on the servants' door at the back of the house. When no one opened it, I tried again. Finally I twisted the knob and found the door unlocked. I stuck my head into the kitchen.

"Hello?" I called.

Unlike the fragrant kitchen, lit and warm, I'd left a little while ago, this one was clean, darkened, and still. No meat roasted in the oven, no soup simmered on the stove, no pies cooled on the table. Men's voices sounded somewhere in the house and grew louder with the clatter of feet on stairs. They seemed to pause on the other side of the kitchen door. Both spoke with vehemence, clearly arguing. Except I couldn't make out a word of what they were saying. It had to be Merton and his long-lost brother shouting at each other in Polish.

I wasn't going to learn a thing from them. Since the cook was absent, I thought I'd better leave before I was discovered snooping in someone else's house. The voices stilled and I heard a thud from the hall. Had the speakers come to blows?

The door from the hall pushed open and a thin man hurried into the kitchen. He resembled Merton but was younger. The cut of his clothes and the style of his hat marked him as foreign. He had to be the Polish brother. He stared at me like I was an apparition, then rushed past and out the back door.

I had my hand on the swinging door to the hall to make sure Merton was all right when Adoniram walked in, his arms full of parcels wrapped in paper and tied with string, as if he'd returned from doing the marketing. But why would a gardener be shopping for food? And where was the cook?

"Miss Carroll, what are you doing here?" He set his packages on the table.

What *was* I doing here? My world had gone topsy-turvy. "I, uh, think I left my knitting needle behind when I was here with the ladies earlier in the week. I came by to ask the cook if someone had found it."

"But she's not here. Had a death in her own family down to Cambridge, and the maid was so frightened by finding her mistress dead, she gave her notice and fled home to her mother in Merrimac. It's only me doing for the mister until Cooky returns." He rolled his eyes. "And now for the man who doesn't speak English, too. Did you see him come through here?"

"Yes. So he is staying here at the house?"

"Indeed he is."

"He and Merton appeared to be embroiled in a great dispute. I heard a thud in the hall, and then the man hurried through the kitchen. I thought I should check and see what happened. But perhaps thee would prefer to do so, and I'll remove myself."

"You come and look, too. You're some kind of a nurse, aren't you?"

"I'm a midwife, but I am familiar with basic first aid procedures, of course." I followed him through into the hall. The staircase rose up in front of us. To our right the hall ran down along to the dining room. But to our left . . .

Adoniram took two quick steps and knelt at Merton's side. He lay crumpled on the black-and-white tiled floor of the entryway. Blood stained the white tile under his head.

THIRTY

"Is HE BREATHING?" My hand flew to my mouth. Not another death. Not another one.

Adoniram bent over Merton's face. "Yes."

I let out a breath. "What a relief. They must have a telephone here. I'll summon an ambulance wagon."

"No. Don't call anyone." He dabbed at the back of Merton's head with a white handkerchief.

"Why not? He needs medical attention, and soon." I stared at the gardener.

"Mr. Settle hates doctors. He doesn't want them anywhere near him."

"Adoniram, I insist." I set my fists on my waist. "Not liking doctors is all very well when one is thriving. Merton Settle is not thriving at this moment. Does thee want his death on thy hands?"

"It would be on his brother's hands if it came to that," he muttered.

"Where is the telephone?" I used my strictest auntie voice.

He didn't look up as he pointed to a closed set of doors. "Library."

I hurried in. The telephone sat on a wide desk covered with a mess of papers. I tapped the hook switch until an operator answered. "Please, we need an ambulance wagon at the Settle household on Whitehall Road, and hurry."

"Yes, miss. Who is calling, please?"

"This is Rose Carroll. I am a visitor to the home. The house is easy to find—it's across from the lower reaches of the lake near the dam, and its windows are draped in black." I lowered my voice. "Please also send police detective Donovan. The injury is the result of an assault." She said she would also summon the police, and I hung up. There, my civic duty was done. Kevin would come, and I could fill him in on all the provocative bits of information I had learned today. With any luck, someone would track down the violent Pole, as well.

117

My gaze fell on the papers. One included the name Szczepanski, the one Jeanette had told me about. But the rest of the writing was undecipherable to me. It appeared to be some kind of legal document, though.

"Miss Carroll?" Adoniram called.

My heart sank. Had Merton taken a turn for the worse? I rushed back to the hall. "Yes?" Instead, my eyes flew wide open at what I saw.

Merton struggled to sit up. "Where's my damned brother?"

"Mr. Settle, don't get up," Adoniram urged him, touching the injured man's shoulder. "You've taken a bad fall."

"Get your hands off me, man." He twisted away from his gaunt employee. He touched the back of his head and stared at his bloody hand. "My head," he groaned.

At least he was conscious and his speech was clear, both excellent signs.

"Thee hit thy head on the staircase," I said. "We are both most encouraged thee is awake. Head wounds bleed a great deal. A doctor will be here shortly to bind it for thee."

"I don't want any cursed ambulance." Merton stared at me. "But who are you, and why do you talk so strangely?"

I clasped my hands in front of me. "My name is Rose Carroll, and my speech is a custom of my faith." The ambulance bells grew close.

"I found her in the kitchen," Adoniram said. "Said she was lookin' for the cook, that she'd lost her knittin' needle the night of that ladies affair of Mrs. Settle's, may God rest her soul."

"Be as that may," Merton snarled. "Did either of you see my brother?"

A great pounding set up on the front door. "Ambulance!"

In lieu of answering Merton, I opened the door. "He's just there." I pointed to Merton. "I believe he might have hit his head on the newel post."

The first man nodded and hurried by me carrying the front handles of a canvas stretcher. The man behind followed. Kevin Donovan was the third in line, but he remained on the landing outside and beckoned to me to join him. I stepped out.

"I heard you asked for me." Kevin removed his hat and worried the back of his head, then replaced the topper. "What were you doing here?"

"I came to find something I'd left the night of the Ladies Circle."

He squinted as if he didn't quite believe me. "Very well. Tell me what happened."

"I believe Merton Settle's brother pushed him in the heat of an argument."

He frowned. "You believe?"

"I was in the kitchen and I heard two men arguing on the other side of the door. There was a thud, then a man resembling Merton ran through the kitchen and out of the house. It appears Merton hit his head on the newel post, perhaps after the other man pushed him, and lost consciousness. He's awake now, albeit with a head wound, and appears to be lucid."

"Interesting. What was the argument about?"

"I couldn't understand the language. They weren't speaking English, but after Merton came to he asked where his brother was."

His expansive brow wrinkled. "You don't say."

"I do. Kevin, I have learned a number of intriguing things since we spoke yesterday, including some facts about the brother. Would thee like me to relate them at this time?"

He glanced past me into the house. "I think I'd better deal with this one right now. Do you know the other brother's first name?"

"I don't, and his last name is a long Polish one, not Settle."

"The devil you say!" He stared at me.

I cast him a look over the tops of my spectacles.

"Pardon my language, Miss Rose. Right when I think this case can't get any more confusing, it does. A Polish brother, indeed."

"They do rather resemble each other. Thee can see the name on a paper on top of Merton's desk in the study, though."

"Miss Rose! What in the devil's name were you doing snooping in Mr. Settle's papers?" Kevin set fists on hips. "You know what my chief would have to say about that."

"I was using the telephone to try to save Merton's life, that's what! Can I help it that my eyes fell on papers that sat out in the open? I was not snooping, Kevin."

"Fine." He gave a little eye roll. "I'd better get in there. Will you be at home this afternoon?"

"I shall be there until six o'clock."

"Very well, I'll pass by your lodgings when I'm done here, if I may."

I nodded and watched him make his way to where the medical men were bandaging Merton's head and asking him questions, apparently checking to see if his brain was concussed. I had no desire to insert myself further, so I reclaimed my bicycle and set out for home.

As the afternoon sun glinted off the lake across the road, I mused on how one would go about finding a Polish man on foot. Perhaps Kevin would set his men to visiting the several men's boardinghouses in town, and the new hotel, too. He'd have to summon Jeanette to translate if he found the brother, that was certain.

THIRTY-ONE

KEVIN AND I PERCHED on stools in the shade of the tree next to my house at a few minutes before five. It was cooler out here than in the house on this warm day. The scent of the blooming peonies in front of the fence was a delight, and the tang of the lemonade I sipped refreshed me.

Kevin set down his glass on the upended wooden box between us. "I'll tell you, Miss Rose, this case is as complex a one as I can ever recall being confronted with."

I nodded and waited for him to go on.

"At least Mr. Settle was up and about before I left." He patted a glistening forehead with a neatly folded handkerchief.

"Would he tell thee what happened? What they had been arguing about?"

"Only said it was old family business. And he didn't look a bit happy about it."

"My client and friend Jeanette Papka is an interpreter for the District Court. She told me something interesting yesterday. She said a man for whom she was interpreting—Polish to English and the reverse—claims Merton Settle is his brother. He said Merton absconded with the family riches thirty years ago. It took the brother this long to track down Merton and then to raise the money for his passage."

"I saw that name. If you're thinking Mr. Settle changed his name when he entered this country, I would agree with you. Who in blazes could ever pronounce the original?"

I laughed. "People who speak the language, of course. And if thee finds the brother, thee will need to have Jeanette interpret for thee."

"How does she come to speak it?"

"I believe her husband's family speaks Polish. As she has a remarkable facility with languages, she acquired it, with a bit of study."

"Think she could pick this Pole out of a lineup?"

"That's not going to be possible. She's blind."

He gaped. "What's that? She can't see a thing?"

"Correct. She never has seen, either."

He rubbed the back of his head and scrunched up his nose. "She's not a deaf-mute, too, then, or she wouldn't be able to do so much translating. But is she smart enough for the work?"

"Her eyes don't work, but her mind is keener than most I have met."

"Doesn't that just cap the climax!"

"Not really. It's a prejudice of our times to think the blind are also mentally deficient. She's fluent in French, as well, with a family hailing from the province of Quebec."

"Sounds like a handy person to have around the court, if she's intelligent, as you say. We're always hauling in those Frenchies for one crime or another. Immigrants cause trouble, Miss Rose. They might consider going back where they came from."

I frowned at him. "Kevin Donovan, thee disappoints me. Thy own parents were immigrants from Ireland, were they not?"

"True enough, lassie."

"They must have faced negative preconceived notions about them when they were newly finding their way. Thee mustn't judge those who arrived after thy family. Everyone wants to come to America, and life is hard when they first arrive. You'll see, in another generation French Canadians and Poles both will be simply regarded as hardworking Americans. A wave of new immigrants from somewhere else — Italy, perhaps, or Russia — will surely be struggling to learn our language and to pass as Americans."

"Fine, fine, fine." He batted away the suggestion. "Now, you said you'd learned more than one interesting tidbit since we spoke yesterday?"

"Yes. I paid Sissy Barclay a visit. She's expecting twins sometime in the next two months. I had a chance to chat with her cook a little. She's Irish, too, Aoife O'Malley."

"I know her. She's me ma's niece's sister-in-law."

I nodded, not surprised. "She told me Irvin had dismissed all the other household help, and that he does the gardening himself."

"That pompous fellow? I find that hard to believe. Man's a banker, too. Why's he hurting for money?"

"I don't know. She also said he was in the habit of bringing his first wife a hot drink before bed, one he insisted on delivering himself. Aoife insisted that Irvin had been poisoning his wife little by little, that the tea was the only time he was nice to her."

Kevin whistled. "Poison in a hot drink before bed. Mrs. Settle's death could be a repeat performance."

"But Irvin wouldn't have been able to put some toxin into Mayme's tea, would he?"

"Unlikely. You've got a point, Miss Rose." He stroked his chin. "I wonder if Barclay and Settle are acquainted."

"What about alibis, Kevin? Has thee determined where various people were during the night on Third Day?" I ticked the names off on my fingers: "Adoniram Riley, Merton Settle, Irvin Barclay, for starters."

He threw open his hands. "Nothing certain for any of them. Riley and Settle say they were asleep in their beds with no one to vouch for them. Riley has a key to the main house, of course. Barclay claimed he was in his bed, too, and his wife said he was."

"Except Sissy told me they have separate bedrooms," I pointed out, not sure if he knew.

"Well, isn't this a fine kettle of fish? Neither of them bothered to tell me."

"But it's true." I nodded. "Their cook confirmed it."

"In addition, I've had my men out asking neighbors and whatnot, but nothing yet. Despite what you say, we still have Barclay claiming he saw Miss Winslow at the house late that evening."

"Bertie told you all she did was ride by on her way home. If he saw her, he must have been there, too." I gave him a stern look.

He held his palms up. "I am aware of that. Barclay says he was merely passing by in his carriage coming back from some gathering in South Hampton. Miss Winslow's only alibi for later is that lady lawyer she lives with, who swears her friend was at home. At any rate, I had a team search their house and premises this afternoon."

My jaw dropped. I closed it and folded my arms. "They didn't find a thing to implicate her, either."

"I haven't gotten a full report yet." He lifted his chin.

"When is thee going to stop investigating Bertie? She told me about all the new questions you asked her yesterday. Doing so has to be taking you away from finding the real killer."

"Miss Rose, you know I have to follow up every clue, every possibility. Please just let me do that."

"All right. Here's one. A client of mine has a connection with the Settles' cook. Apparently Adoniram once brought mushrooms in for her to prepare but she thought something seemed off about them, so she threw them out. Maybe he knows a lot more about poisons than you think."

"I'll look into that. Anything else?"

I thought back to the Ladies Circle. "I told you how cruel Mayme was to her husband at the Ladies Circle on the evening of her death."

Kevin nodded.

"I remembered something else. Sissy Barclay brought a box that looked like it held sweets, chocolates perhaps. She gave it to Mayme, and said Irvin wanted it to be for her consumption only. Mayme obliged and set it unopened on the piano." I rocked a little on my stool, thinking. "The cook at the Barclay house told me she overheard Irvin talking on the telephone about money problems, about debts. Sissy mentioned earlier today that Mayme and Irvin were distant relatives and were supposed to split some inheritance, but Mayme was refusing."

"I can have a man look into that."

"Maybe Irvin poisoned Mayme with the candy so he would come into all the money."

His eyes widened. "You might be onto something there. I do believe we came away with a box of candy when we investigated the deceased's bedroom."

"I hope it went into the evidence room and not next to the coffee pot for the men."

"Wouldn't that be a shock? No, I told my fellow to secure it. We haven't had a chance to get the chemist to test it yet, but we will." He frowned. "Although, Miss Rose, I think your reasoning on this matter has a hole in it."

"Oh?"

"Upon Mrs. Settle's death, you see, any inheritance of hers would go to Mr. Settle."

I made a face. "That's right. Unless maybe it was restricted to go to blood relatives only?"

"Could be. I'll send someone along to the court in the morning to find out the facts."

THIRTY-TWO

THE SKY GLOWED the color of my name as David and I finished our repast, blessedly not discussing the murder investigation even once. He'd reserved a table for two at a west-facing window in the Grand Hotel dining room. The resort perched atop Whittier Hill, and on a clear day like today one could see as far as Mount Wachusett seventy miles to the west and the much closer hills of West Newbury to the south. Our view of the sun setting over the Little Farm below was my favorite.

I opened my mouth to share my good news when David spoke at the same moment.

"Mother's been at it again," David said. "She wants to hold a big garden party in our honor."

"She does have a lovely garden," I said. "And it's generous of Clarinda to offer a celebratory gathering."

"With a hundred people in the garden you'll barely be able to see the plantings."

The thought of such a sizable crowd of Clarinda's social acquaintances nearly gave me an attack of the nerves. "A hundred? Oh, my. When does she wish to present this spectacle?"

"As soon as we have a date for the actual ceremony. I'm sorry, Rose. You know how she is."

"Yes, I do." I reached for his hand, my nerves turning to excitement. "David, dear, Mother wrote today that we are clear to marry at Lawrence Meeting in early Ninth Month."

David squeezed my hand. "Rosie, what joy! I wish it were sooner, but it can't be helped." He beamed.

I smiled back. "I also would that it were today, thee knows that. I confess not to liking that our union cannot be accomplished earlier, but there we have it." The news was indeed a mix of good and if not bad, then disappointing.

"And the Amesbury Friends, your elder women, they still do not accept your marrying an open-minded and peace-loving Unitarian?"

I smiled back, but ruefully. "I'm afraid not. Their adherence to practices from the past disappoints me." The custom of Friends was to disallow marriage to people of other faiths. In earlier times, when Quakers were severely persecuted for their unconventional beliefs, the intent was to keep the religious society strong and not diluted by outsiders. In this more liberal modern era, many Meetings were easing those strictures. Not Amesbury, though. Not yet, despite John Whittier advocating for change. "I can only pray they will come around in time after we are wed."

"They will, I'm sure of it. I'll tell Mother she can proceed with planning her festivity, if I may. The garden will still be lovely in late August."

Our food arrived, so we took a moment to taste the dishes. As always when we dined here, the meals were expertly prepared and rich in the kinds of sauces and garnishes I didn't sample in my daily life. I'd chosen the sole tonight, and its sauce had been buttery and lemony in exactly the right proportions, with a few capers mixed in for a piquant touch. Rather like the man across the table from me. Serious and playful in equal measure, with a rebellious streak to spice him up.

"The chef has outdone himself tonight," I said. "Back to the garden party, if we might? I'm sure it will be lovely. Am I to invite my own family and friends, as well?"

"Oh, yes, she said to mention that. And you know how happy she would be if Mr. Whittier were in attendance."

"He's not one for crowds, and he is growing more frail with age," I said. "But it never hurts to extend an invitation. He sometimes sends a freshly penned poem in lieu of attending in person." Over David's shoulder I spied a couple being seated. My eyes widened when I saw the man was Irvin Barclay. And the woman he was with was most definitely not Sissy. His companion wore an emerald green dress in the latest fashion, with a gored skirt flaring away from the tightly fitted waist and sleeves that puffed out above the elbow. A hat in the same hue as the dress perched on her red tresses at a gravity-defying tilt. I had seen her only yesterday looking worried as she walked at the lake.

"What have you seen, Rose?"

"Don't turn around now, but Irvin Barclay has sat down to dinner with a rather stylish woman who is not his legally wedded wife."

David gave a little whistle. "You don't say?"

"I do. And if I were the betting type, I would wager this is not his sister nor his mother, nor a business partner, either, strictly speaking." I thought of Sissy alone with Aoife and my heart broke. I leaned closer to David. "I learned this afternoon Irvin has some kind of financial problems and has dismissed all the household servants except the cook. And this shortly before his wife is about to give birth to twins." I shook my head.

"You are thinking this dinner date of his might be where his money has gone?"

"Those were my thoughts, yes." I gave another glance at the woman, hoping to make it look casual. "But how to ascertain the identity of this companion is the question."

"Have you finished your meal, my dear?" David asked.

He had the twinkle in his eye I adored—and which I knew by now also signaled he was up to something.

"Yes, thank thee, darling."

He twisted in his seat, surveying the room as if searching for the man who had been serving us. David in fact caught the man's attention, but his gaze also traveled across Irvin's companion's face.

My betrothed faced me again. "I know who she is," he murmured a few seconds before our waiter reached us.

"We'd like a sweet to finish off our meal, wouldn't we, Rose?" David asked.

Repressing the urge to snicker at his solicitous tone, I simply nodded.

"We have a Charlotte Russe, angel cake, and a bread pudding with hard sauce to offer you tonight," the man said, clasping his gloved hands.

"I'd like the angel cake, please," I said.

"The Charlotte Russe for me," David said.

"Excellent choices for you both." The man gave a little bow and left.

"And?" I asked, when David didn't elaborate on the woman's identity. "Who is she?"

"I don't know her name. She came to the hospital seeking treatment for something the nurses regarded as scandalous."

"Does thee mean the clap or perhaps syphilis?" I kept my voice as low as I could. If her husband was intimate with a woman who had such a disease, Sissy would soon also be infected, as well as Irvin himself. I'd already delivered a baby whose mother was infected with the clap and didn't know it. Baby Charlie, the one I'd mentioned to Jeanette, was blind as a result.

"Something along those lines," David said. "Not that there is much of a treatment, and certainly no cure."

"If this woman is intimate with Irvin, both of Sissy's babies are at risk."

"Let us hope she is not." He nodded gravely. "But one nurse also said the woman is some kind of scientist. Possibly an astronomer."

"Like Maria Mitchell, the Nantucket Friend who studied the stars." Faith and I had both been excited to learn of fellow Quaker Maria and her informed quest to discover and name stars never before identified. She had died only recently.

"Yes."

I thought for a long moment. "A woman diagnosed with a sexual disease. A scientist-astronomer. Someone out to dinner with a banker who doesn't seem inclined toward the sciences in the slightest, and who is married to a lovely young lady and apparently thrilled about becoming a father twice over on the same day. I confess to being confused, David."

He smiled, rolled his eyes a little, and nodded. "I reside in confusion with you, my love."

My gaze traveled back to Irvin, who was on his feet, gesturing and apparently in dispute with the man serving the diners. As I watched, both Irvin and his companion rose and moved in our direction, apparently for a change of seating. True, their first table had been situated near the noise and bustle of the kitchen. I did not fault them for requesting a different location for their meal. A moment later Irvin neared us and slowed as I smiled at him.

"Ah, Miss Carroll." He came to a halt. "Ah, well, good evening." His gaze darted to David and back at me as his forehead broke out in nervous droplets.

"Hello, Irvin," I said with a smile. "May I present my betrothed, David Dodge of Newburyport? David, this is Irvin Barclay."

David stood and extended his hand. "Pleased to meet you, Mr. Barclay." He inclined his head toward the woman. "Miss."

"Ah, yes." Irvin cleared his throat. "I, I . . ." He swallowed. "I am pleased to meet you, sir. This is Miss Nalia Bowerman. My, ah, cousin." He ran a finger between his suddenly red neck and his collar. "Miss Bowerman, Miss Rose Carroll."

I smiled at Nalia. "Irvin's cousin? What a pleasure to meet thee, Nalia. I am Sissy's midwife. Has thee come to assist her in her confinement and delivery of twin babies?" I couldn't help myself from asking, despite being quite certain that was not the purpose of Nalia's presence. I inquired mostly so I could see how they both would react.

Nalia's relaxed demeanor and bell-like laugh were in distinct contrast to Irvin's case of nerves, which appeared to border on panic. "No, Miss Carroll. I actually reside here in Amesbury." Her voice was oddly nasal in timbre, and she smelled like she'd applied rosewater liberally. "Mr. Barclay and I were merely conducting a spot of business, weren't we, cousin?"

Her emphasis on the word "cousin" lingered in the air as he escorted her to a table where they, too, could observe the beauty of the sunset. And where all present could observe them. What was Irvin thinking, coming out in public with a lady not his wife? Unless Nalia was, in fact, his cousin. But then why was Irvin so nervous at us seeing him with her?

I resolved to put them out of my mind. I was out with my husband-to-be, and I wasn't letting anything rob me of the joy of being with him.

THIRTY-THREE

THE NEXT MORNING I saw Frederick and the children out the door to their half day of school, it being Seventh Day. I poured myself a second cup of coffee and sank into a chair at the table, reaching down to pet Christabel, who purred her contentment. I hadn't slept well and was not feeling so content. I wasn't sure if my restlessness had been from the rich food of my dinner with David or the mélange of facts and questions surrounding Mayme's death.

The sound of a mockingbird on a maple tree outside floated in through the screened door as it ran through its repertoire of other birds' songs. By the end of summer the bird would have acquired even more. I'd once met a man who could similarly imitate people's voices. It was uncanny how he could change the timbre of his voice to sound like other men and even some women. Too bad one couldn't get into other people's thoughts and emotions the same way, at least in a murder case. What was Mayme's killer doing right now? What was he feeling? Smug that he'd gotten away with an evil deed, or nervous he was about to be caught? Myself, I wanted to stomp my foot in frustration. I was getting nowhere in unraveling the tangled ball of string this week had become.

I drained my coffee with a sigh and took the cup to the wide black soapstone sink. At least this morning I'd been able to remind the children to clean up after themselves. The sink was full but the rest of the kitchen was relatively tidy, so Lina would be able to focus on the floors and other cleaning tasks. Right now I was going to attend to my garden for a little while and then clean my own room. I didn't have any prenatal visits this morning and I'd sometimes found doing manual labor freed up the mind to think in a more orderly fashion. Or to ignore thinking and let the mind sort things out in its own way.

As I was already wearing my oldest dress, I pushed up the sleeves and made for the outdoors, clapping an old straw boater on my head to keep the sun off my face. This near the summer solstice, the sun's rays were strong even in the morning. I had dug up and applied some of Fredericks's horse Star's manure to a new garden patch in back of the house last fall. I donned the gardening gloves we kept in the outbuilding, grabbed a shovel, and got to work. I loosened the dirt, mixing in the now-aged manure, and readied the bed. From the clouds blowing in and the humid air, it appeared we'd get a good dose of rain later in the day. This was a perfect time for young plants to go into the garden.

Sitting back on my heels some time later, I admired my several tomato plants and the pepper seedling. By Eighth Month the family would be dining on our own crop of plump sun-ripened vegetables. I rose and moved over to the herb garden, where I nurtured some of the herbs I used in my practice. I knelt again and pulled weeds from around the lavender, yarrow, and motherwort until all those little competitors for the herbs' soil nutrients and water were banished to the compost heap.

I didn't seem to be doing much thinking as I worked but trusted my brain was operating in the background. I was cleaning up around the base of the low-spreading pennyroyal when a shadow fell over the plant. A person-shaped shadow. I twisted my head to see Nalia Bowerman, Irvin's companion from the night before. A chill passed through me. How had she found my house? Could she possibly be Irvin's partner in murder, too? I was home alone. At least I was outside, and the upholstery factory on the other side of the back fence was bustling with workers making cloth and leather seats for carriages, sleighs, and other conveyances. If Nalia were so daring as to threaten me, I could easily summon assistance.

I swallowed. "Nalia, what a surprise." I hoisted myself up from my knees and dusted off my skirt. "I won't offer my hand. I have obviously been working in the dirt. What might I help thee with?"

She nodded and did not return my smile. "Miss Carroll, my cousin believes you labor under the delusion you are a private detective."

Her cousin. Irvin had introduced her as such last night, and I supposed it could be true. Or perhaps not. "Did he send thee here?"

"No." The redhead was not dressed in dinner finery as she had been last evening, instead wearing a tan linen traveling costume. She sported a boater trimmed with a matching ribbon and a daring red feather, and again wore it at an angle befitting my stylish friend Bertie. "Cecelia informed me where your residence was located."

I scrunched up my nose. "Who is Cecelia?"

"You are her midwife and you don't know her name?" Her nostrils flared.

"Oh! Thee means Sissy, I gather. She has never presented herself to me with any other name."

"Be that as it may. Mr. Barclay told me he is not certain he wants to proceed with you providing his young wife's medical care. In the matter of her impending delivery of his infants, that is."

I blinked. *His infants.* Last time I checked it took both a man and a woman to make babies. "Why has Irvin himself not told me Sissy will be under another's care for her births?"

"It's because he is disturbed at your meddling in the work of the police."

Aha. Now the truth emerges. "This is what thy cousin says, I assume?"

"Of course," she scoffed. "Do you think I have any stake in this?" Her tone indicated the sheer impossibility she would care.

I had the feeling Irvin hadn't actually asked her to make this trip. "And what is Sissy's opinion in the matter?" This conversation smelled like spoiled fish.

"She has no say. The husband's opinion is the law of the land." She folded her arms, with remarkably long fingernails splaying over her elbow on one side and her forearm on the other.

I gave my head a little shake. Nothing she said made sense to me. "I understand thee is a scientist."

"Yes, that is true. I am a computer at the Harvard College Observatory in Professor Pickering's group."

"A computer," I said. "What kind of job is that?"

"I and other women examine photographs of the stars and classify them according to their spectra. But I don't expect you to understand all that."

"Does thee believe a woman's voice should not be heard?"

"What I believe is not pertinent. What we are discussing is your ceasing to care for my cousin's wife."

"Thee may inform Irvin, if thee wishes, that I am a practicing midwife, not a detective." I kept my voice soft but firm. "I do not meddle with the police. Sissy has engaged me to provide her with midwifery services, and I intend to honor our agreement." I planned to consult directly with Sissy about her care. If she wanted me to continue, continue I would.

THIRTY-FOUR

After delivering her warning, Nalia had left without a goodbye or a fare-thee-well. I watched her make her way to the road and turn right toward town. I hadn't really expected any kind of polite parting salutation based on the tone of her voice when she spoke to me. And now my brain was even more scrambled than before. Had Irvin commissioned her to deliver his doubts and she'd lied about him? Was she even his cousin? And why had Sissy given her my address? Maybe Nalia had lied about how she learned where I lived, too. She was a woman who had surely fought battles to achieve the education and experience necessary to become an astronomer at Harvard College, of all places. I found it hard to believe she would support Irvin in trying to remove me from Sissy's labor and birth.

On the other hand, what if she and Irvin were stepping out, and she wanted to do away with Sissy after she gave birth? Irvin would be a father and Nalia wouldn't have to go to the trouble to bear and deliver children. I shook my head. This was only too reminiscent of what had happened in the winter, when the husband of a pregnant client of mine had an amorous affair with a young woman at his workplace. How could men be so stupid, so heartless, to conduct such affairs when their wife was carrying their unborn child?

I frowned and tapped my mouth, trying to think if I had asked Irvin questions about Mayme's death. I stared at the small narrow leaves of the pennyroyal plant. Why would Irvin suspect I was working with the police or investigating on my own? Nalia had said she lived here in Amesbury. Maybe she'd concocted the entire story because she'd heard independently I had worked with Kevin on past cases. Or because she herself was guilty of one or more past misdeeds, one of them fatal to its target.

When the first raindrops dampened my face, I shook myself out of my reverie and hurried to stow the shovel and gloves. I was almost to the open back door of the house when I heard the bell of the telephone, so I hurried in without washing my hands and lifted the receiver.

"Rose Carroll speaking."

I smiled when I heard David's voice in return.

"Good morning, my sweet," he began. "You sound breathless."

"I was outside gardening. Thy call and the rain arrived at the same moment."

"I have a direct line to the rain god, you know." He was clearly smiling.

"Is that so? Except she's a goddess, thee knows," I joked. "When she saw I'd finished planting my seedlings and weeding my herbs, she decided to deliver the watering they needed."

"Have I told you I loved you recently?"

"I believe thee did as we were saying our goodbyes only twelve hours ago." I blushed to remember our caresses in David's buggy after he'd brought me home. I counted. Only two and a half months to go before we could deepen our intimacy to our hearts' content.

"I might very well have."

"How is thee this fine morning?" I asked.

"I am in good health, but two patients under my care are not a bit well. I was making the rounds at the hospital this morning. I'd finished checking on the lady who took a fall yesterday when I was called to the bedside of a foreigner, name of Scanpatski or some such unpronounceable name."

I sucked in a breath. The man from Poland? The possible brother of Merton?

David went on. "He was hit in the back with full force by a carriage traveling far too fast in the Point Shore area of Amesbury near the Chain Bridge this morning. You know, after the Lowell Boat Shop but before the road turns toward the river."

"The poor fellow. Is he going to live?"

"I can't say at present. He has damage to his internal organs, most definitely. He also had broken bones, which an orthopedic colleague is currently setting, as well as a terribly lacerated face. We're going to watch him closely. If he stabilizes, if he regains consciousness, we'll consider exploring inside to see if there's anything we can fix."

"If he isn't conscious, how does thee know his name?"

"He carried a passport and some kind of court papers in his coat. Some were in English. A sheaf were in another language I guessed was Polish, based on the travel documents, which are in French, of course."

"Of course." I had never been to another country except the French part of Canada to our north, but I knew passports and other international papers always included a translation into French, as it was the universal language of diplomacy. I also knew David spoke the tongue quite well. "David, does the man's name begin with a string of consonants, some of which are the letter Z?"

"By George, yes. How did you know, Rose?"

"It's a bit of a long story, but the man might be associated with the husband of the woman who, uh, died this week." I was cognizant of the fact that the switchboard operator often listened in on calls. She wasn't supposed to, but it behooved any user of a telephone to be prudent in his speech.

"You don't say."

"I do. I'll have to let my, ah, friend Kevin know."

"Of course," he said. "But this news isn't why I called. Mother wants to start preparing the invitations to her garden party."

"It's two months away. Why now?"

He chuckled. "Please don't ask me to explain the ways of what she calls proper society. Mine is not to ask why but to comply, at least in this case. So she'd like a guest list from you and Dorothy."

I groaned. "All right, I'll write to my mother this morning. But it'll take a few days to receive her reply." We said our goodbyes and hung up. I waited only a moment before connecting again. I had something more important to do than arrange a guest list.

"I need to speak with Kevin Donovan at the police station, please," I said to the operator.

After a few clicks and background murmuring, Kevin came on the line. "Detective Donovan." His tone was clipped, official.

"Kevin, it's Rose. David Dodge tells me a man with a Polish passport was seriously hurt this morning. A carriage hit him straight on in the Point Shore neighborhood. I thought thee would want to know. I think it's likely to be the person for whom thee was searching. David said the name on the passport could be the one I mentioned."

"Thank you, Miss Rose. I expect it is. Did the man survive?"

"Yes, but he's unconscious at the Anna Jaques Hospital."

"Very well. I'll have them notify me when he wakes up. Anything else?"

I opened my mouth to tell him about Irvin and Nalia, then closed it. "Possibly, but I'll write it in a note and bring it by the station. It's not something to discuss on the telephone."

"I'd appreciate it. And Miss Rose?"

"Yes?"

"Please keep yourself safe. Don't go about risking anything."

I smiled at his solicitude. "I won't. I am not interested in coming to harm."

THIRTY-FIVE

BY TEN O'CLOCK I'd written and posted a note to my mother. I also began a draft of my own guest list. All the Baileys, of course, including my niece Faith, plus Zeb and his family. Bertie and Sophie. Kevin and Emmaline. Jeanette and her husband. Annie. John Whittier. I smiled at the unconventional nature of my circle of friends.

I added my maiden aunts in the Cape Cod village of West Falmouth, although I imagined they wouldn't come. My father's elderly sisters, who lived together, were nearly as old as John and hadn't traveled north at all lately. If my aunts couldn't make the trip, David and I would pay the two a visit after we were wed. I'd heard of the custom of newly married couples taking a honeymoon voyage abroad, but those were well-financed members of what Clarinda called proper society. Still, it would be a delight to travel alone with David and take some time away from our work to simply be together. And I'd heard that Cape Cod, in the southeastern area of Massachusetts, was a beautiful corner of the earth. I could trust Annie with any clients who went into labor, calling on additional support from a midwife friend in Newburyport if she needed it.

As a passing wagon bumped along outside, I paused to gaze at my hand holding the pen, then stretched out my other hand next to it. I had long fingers, but I wore my fingernails short and neatly trimmed. These were hands that touched women's bodies, and I cleaned, gardened, and bicycled with my hands, too. Fingernails like Nalia's would be impractical for me. She could manage because her work examining photographs of the stars was entirely cerebral, and she probably had household help, as well.

I thought of the white substance found under Mayme's fingernails and wondered again what it had been. Surely Kevin's team would have analyzed it by now. Perhaps it was as simple as talc, but nothing about this case seemed simple.

Enough with idle musing. Right now I needed to get a note to Kevin and I could pay a visit to Emmaline and the baby while I was out. I would clean my office later. I checked out the window to see that the rain shower had already passed by. Happy to see the sun peeking through, I jotted down what I'd seen last night as well as a summary of Nalia's rather threatening garden visit this morning, and slid the missive into an envelope. I changed into my split skirt attire, washed up, and told Lina I was going out.

Fifteen minutes later I delivered the envelope to the man at the front desk. "My name is Rose Carroll," I told the fellow. "It's urgent for Kevin Donovan to see this as soon as possible."

"Yes, Miss Carroll." He nearly saluted me.

"I thank thee." I turned away, stifling a smile. I'd been in the station enough times, and enough young officers had seen Kevin respecting my opinion, that I knew the detective would get the note.

I remounted my bike and soon enough was rapping the knocker on Emmaline's front door.

"Rose, what a delight to see you." Emmaline answered with a sleeping baby on her shoulder. "Please come in."

"I thank thee. I delivered some information to thy husband a few minutes ago and thought I'd see how Rosalie is faring." I followed her into a house now tidy and bearing the aroma of fresh-baked bread.

"See for yourself." She handed me her daughter. "Do sit down, Rose." She perched on a chair.

I took the baby and sat opposite Emmaline, cradling the infant in one arm so I could feel her face with my other hand. She was warm but not hot and had a healthy color in her cheeks. I leaned down and sniffed her head. "There's nothing like the smell of a baby, is there?" I smiled at Emmaline. "She's still nursing well?"

She nodded. "Thanks be to the blessed Virgin, and to you, Rose." She crossed herself.

"Good." I looked around. "Where is the young doctor?"

"He's at work at the boat shop." She shook her head in wonder as the tall case clock in the corner gonged once for the half hour. "He'll be there the whole day, I expect. Mr. Sherwood watches out for him." She gazed at Rosalie. "What will I do if she turns out to have exceptional intelligence, too?"

I laughed. "Thee will love her and guide her on her way, as thee so ably does with Sean."

"I suppose. It's a marvel how two perfectly ordinary parents can produce a brain like my son's."

"Has thee heard of Charles Darwin, and of Gregor Mendel?"

"The Austrian monk?" Emmaline asked.

"Yes. It's very interesting the kinds of investigations they are doing, looking into the inheritance of traits. I don't understand much of it."

"God certainly has a hand in it."

"Indeed He does." I handed Rosalie back to her mother and stood. "I'll be off. I have an errand in the Point Shore area. Perhaps I'll stop in and say hello to Sean while I'm there."

"He would love to see you. Thank you for helping our family, Rose." Her eyes filled with tears of gratitude.

"Thee is very welcome. Thee is my friend, as is Kevin. Friends help each other." Emmaline's swings of emotion were typical of a new mother's. "Wipe those tears, now."

"You're a good friend, and I want you to know how much I appreciate you."

I smiled as I smoothed down my dress. "I'll let myself out." She didn't know how much helping others fed something at my core. It seemed nearly selfish to serve other people as I did.

THIRTY-SIX

I CYCLED ALL THE WAY down Main Street to where the Powow River emptied into the Merrimack. The street was full of vehicles with purposes both industrious and leisurely. A plodding workhorse pulling a dray carrying coal was overtaken by a sleek buggy driven by a well-dressed young man. A society girl wearing the latest style drove a tidy whalebone. At the edge of the road two maids bustled along with baskets full of market produce, while a peddler pushed his cart of sundries.

I passed the Captain's Well and neared the stately Huntington home near Haverhill Road, the abode of an influential Quaker family. I frowned. A horse seemed to be clopping along at exactly the speed of my bicycle. Normally drivers and equine riders passed me. I slowed and the hooves slowed, too. With a murderer on the loose in town—and me conducting my own version of an investigation—I didn't have a good feeling about this. My insides chilling, I wanted to glance over my shoulder and see if this was friend or foe. But this was a particularly bumpy section of the macadamized road, far overdue for the town to replace the top layer of small broken stones and stone dust and then roll it smooth. I dared not take my gaze off my route. I'd been run off the road before and didn't care to repeat the experience, so I slowed to a stop, putting my foot down for balance.

A black Biddle and Smart rockaway picked up speed, pulled by a roan trotting by me. I stared at the back. Irvin Barclay had a roan and a black rockaway. It flashed on me that I'd glimpsed this carriage near me several times this week. Was Irvin spying on me? Following me? Or had Nalia borrowed his horse and carriage?

I shook off my worries. It was a sunny morning and I was out in public with all kinds of people going about their business. Families heading for the pond. Women hanging laundry in their yards. Children throwing balls in the sun and reading books in the shade. Men doing repairs on their homes. I had to be safe.

I rode on, bumping over the Powow River Bridge, and headed east along the river into Amesbury's oldest settlement. Some of the homes built by the town's first inhabitants dated back more than two hundred years. I hadn't originally planned this visit when I'd left home, but it had occurred to me as I sat with Emmaline that perhaps I could investigate the area of Merton's brother's accident.

The problem was, I didn't know exactly where he'd been run down. David had said the victim of the accident was found at the far end before the road turned toward the Chain Bridge, perhaps a mile distant. I rode past Lowell's Boat Shop, from which emanated sounds of hammering. The smell of freshly sawn wood mixed with the fresh scent of the river, which was still partially tidal here seven miles inland. Several of the shop's signature dories floated where they were anchored near the river's bank behind the shop. They were sturdy but graceful boats, which handled well and were built to last. Lowell's also made whalers and I wasn't sure what else. I would stop in to see Sean on my way back.

The boat shop sat about a quarter mile before the bridge, one of two spans in sequence which crossed the Merrimack River to Newburyport. When I had passed two houses beyond the shop, the trolley came toward me. Its sturdy team of horses plodded steadily along, and the car behind was full with people heading into Amesbury. A little girl hanging her head out of the window on my side pointed at me and clapped. After I slowed and raised a hand to wave at her, she waved back with a delighted grin. Maybe she'd never seen a woman on a bicycle before, or maybe she was simply excited to be riding the trolley.

I wondered what it would be like to ride in an electrified Ellis trolley. They would have to build an entire network of overhead wires to power the vehicles, I assumed. I shook my head. That was the future, and right now I had an accident scene to search for.

I'd barely pedaled on when I saw a large dark splotch on the paving stones. I braked, lowered the bike to the ground, and squatted at the side of the road. The substance was already dried but didn't look dirty from hooves and wheels running over it. I rubbed at the spot with a handkerchief, and what came off onto the white cloth was a reddish stain. I stared at it, then stood. Should I knock on doors to see if anyone had seen the accident? Two barefoot boys about Luke's age walked toward me, fishing poles resting on their shoulders, caps on their heads.

"Excuse me, lads," I said. "Did either of thee happen to see a collision between a carriage and a man on foot here earlier this morning?"

The taller one shook his head. The shorter of the two spoke up. "No, but we heard it. It was a big thud we heard."

"Oh, yes." Taller's eyes grew wide. "We was fishing, but there was quite a noise went up. Then the ambulance bells came over the bridge."

"We ran up here to look. They was loading the poor gent into the wagon." Shorter shook his head. "I think he was dead. He wasn't moving even a little." The corners of his mouth pulled down.

"Had the person who hit him stopped?" I asked.

"Nobody was around," Taller said. "The fellow musta left. Didn't help the gent at all."

The shorter boy shook his head. "Mrs. Bailey, though, she heard it. She made a telephone call to the hospital for the man, most likely."

"Which house does she live in?" I inquired.

"The big one there." The taller one pointed to a well-appointed home on the water side. "But she went out not long ago. She's got herself the prettiest drop-front phaeton you ever seen."

"A Bailey, 'course," the other boy added.

"I appreciate the information," I said.

"Sure, miss." They touched their caps in unison and continued wherever they were going.

I stood there for a moment thinking. I watched as a mottled young eagle flew near the shore with a wriggling fish in its talons. I couldn't ask whichever Bailey matron lived in the house—likely it was Lydia Crowell Bailey—but Lowell's was nearby. Maybe someone there saw the accident.

Two minutes later I greeted Jonathan Sherwood, the kindly supervisor I'd met in the winter and the one overseeing young Sean, according to the Donovans. We stood in his office with the door open to the shop, which smelled of fresh sawdust. My ears filled with the bangs and taps of hammers, the back-and-forth wheezing of saws, the rasping of sandpaper, the *sheeooh* of planes.

"It's a pleasure to see you, Miss Carroll." Jonathan smiled. "What can I help you with? Are you planning to take up boating?" He was a lean man in his forties and wore spectacles much like my own.

"No boating at this time, but I'd like to say hello to Sean Donovan, if I might. I am a friend of the family, and his mother told me her son was spending time here."

"Certainly." He started to turn away.

I touched his arm. "But first, may I ask if anyone here witnessed an accident several houses away this morning?"

He faced me again, his eyes dark. "Yes. And it was the Donovan boy who saw what happened."

"Truly?" My voice rose.

"Yes. He was quite shaken by it, but he's calmed down by now. Come along, I'll take you to where he's working."

We passed boats in all stages of construction, from skeletal to half ensheathed to finished and in the process of being varnished. I had visited the shop when it was snowy outside and the river was frozen, but now windows stood open and sawdust flew in the breeze. I followed Jonathan down a narrow staircase to the lower level where Sean, with a work apron tied around his waist, stood planing a board secured by clamps. The apron came down nearly to the floor and the ties were secured in the front. A man in his twenties planed opposite him. While I watched, the man stopped and corrected Sean's technique before resuming his work.

"Master Donovan, you have a visitor," Jonathan said.

Sean looked up and his face split into a surprised smile. "Hello, Miss Rose. What are you doing here?" A smear of light-colored sawdust clung to his flushed cheek.

"I was in the area and wanted to see thee at work."

"I'm learning all kinds of useful things about cutting and measuring and making the boards nice and smooth." Sean pointed to the tool in his hand. "This thing is called a plane, Miss Rose, and it leaves those curls of wood on the floor." He pointed down to a floor covered with curly shavings. "It's hard to keep it going flat. You have to keep the pressure steady."

"He's a quick study, I'll say that." The man helping him smiled. "Needs to work on those muscles yet, though."

I should think so. Sean wasn't a hefty child. He did have a sturdy build like his father's, but he couldn't be more than four feet tall.

"Miss Carroll was asking if anyone saw an accident this morning," Jonathan began. "I told her you had."

The smile slid off Sean's face. "I did. The poor fellow."

"How did thee come to witness it?" He wouldn't have been able to see the road from down here. The shop was built on the banks of the river. In front of us more windows looked out onto the water, but behind us the wall had no apertures, being set into the slope.

Sean looked up at Jonathan, who nodded for him to go on. "I was working upstairs," Sean said. "A man knocked at the door to the road. It was standing open for the air. I'm the most junior apprentice, so I went over to see what he wanted. He was a thin fellow and all he said was the word 'bridge,' gesturing an arch with his hand and pointing at the river, over and over. Even then I could barely understand him. He wasn't from around here, Miss Rose." He took a deep breath, but his voice quavered. "I don't think he could speak much English. So I walked out with him and pointed toward the Chain Bridge."

"Was he carrying anything?" I asked. "A bag or a valise?"

"Nothing. He gave me a pat on the shoulder and walked off. But then this carriage came racing up behind him. I saw it run him down. The driver swerved the horse away from the man at the last minute but the vehicle hit him and knocked him to the ground. It was terrible." When his upper lip wobbled, Sean pressed his hand against his mouth and blinked away a tear.

I laid my hand on my young friend's shoulder. "It must have been very hard for thee to witness that assault."

Sean only nodded.

"I heard the collision and ran out," Jonathan said. "The carriage didn't even stop, but kept on in the direction of the bridge. Sean was in shock from the sight, so I sent him inside and hurried to call for the ambulance wagon. I went back out and saw Mrs. Bailey covering the gent with a blanket. She didn't cover his face, so I knew he was still alive."

"Sean, did thee note the type and make of carriage? What kind of horse was pulling it?"

He let out a breath through his lips, then brought his eyebrows together, as if thinking. "The carriage was a Stanhope runabout. Black with narrow red striping."

I stared at him. The Settles had a Stanhope runabout. I'd seen it at the house. I wasn't sure about the red striping, but such a detail could be checked.

"You're very observant, Donovan," Jonathan said.

Sean smiled. "I like to train my eye. My da says it's important for his work, and I want to be able to help him one day. The horse, now let's see." He squinted into the distance. "That's right, it was gray with a dark mane, but it went too fast for me to get a good look at it. Mr. Sherwood, we should tell my da about the accident."

"I have already sent along a message to that effect," Jonathan said. "Did you see the driver's face, lad?"

"Not clearly. He wasn't a thick man, but I didn't see anything else to distinguish him."

Not a thick man. Neither was Merton. Had he attempted to kill his brother? Of course, Adoniram didn't have a thick build, either. Perhaps Merton had dispatched him to do the deed.

"I thank thee, Sean. This information is very helpful. I'll let thy father know, since it appears to have been a purposeful attack and not an accident at all. I won't keep thee from thy work any longer." I patted the side of his face.

"I'm glad I could help, Miss Rose. I hope they catch the scoundrel who hit the man."

"Thy father will, I am certain." I turned to Jonathan. "And I thank thee for thy time. Thee can rest assured that, should I decide to become a mariner, I shall purchase my vessel here." I smiled and we shook hands before I headed out. I needed to let Kevin know about the carriage and horse right away so he could check into Merton's transport as well as the whereabouts of both Merton and his gardener. If the Polish man died of his injuries, this would be another case of homicide.

THIRTY-SEVEN

I WAS HUFFING AND PUFFING on Main Street ascending the seemingly endless hill leading up to the downtown area from Patten Hollow. The sun beat down, making it a most uncomfortable ride. I finally dismounted to walk the rest of the way and glanced to my right. Jeanette sat in the shade of a tree to the side of her home, her hands moving on an open book with enormous pages and no discernible printing.

"Good day, Jeanette," I called.

"Rose!" She turned her face in my direction. "Come and sit with me." She patted the chair next to her.

"I believe I will." I did want to get my information to Kevin, but it could wait a few minutes. I wheeled my bicycle up the walk and pushed down the kickstand, a clever recent invention mounted below the handlebars. I sank into the seat and inhaled the scent of a late-blooming lilac. "I've been down on Point Shore and this hill about kills me every time I ride back."

She threw back her head and laughed. "You can't escape hills in Amesbury, it's true. Have you come from bringing a new life into the world?"

"No, not today. Sadly, a man was run down by a carriage this morning, and a boy I know happened to witness the facts. I'm on my way to relay the details to the police."

"Why, was the gent killed?"

"No, but he is not faring well so far. He's unconscious in the hospital." I tried to shake off the image of a person being hit by a speeding vehicle. I had nearly been run off the road myself this winter. "In fact, it appears he is the Polish man for whom thee interpreted in court a few days ago."

"Oh, my. The poor man. Was it an accident?"

"My young friend said it looked purposeful. I am now wondering whether it had to do with Mayme's murder."

Jeanette rocked in her chair. "Interesting. Say, I was in the bank with Mr. Papka this morning. He was conducting some business and I had to wait for him. Mr. Barclay had a visitor with the most unpleasant voice I think I've ever heard. She seemed to speak entirely through her nose."

Nalia? I blinked. "Did thee learn her name?"

"He addressed her as Nalia. They were speaking quite intimately. I'm sure they thought I couldn't hear them or they wouldn't have been."

"I met her at dinner at the Grand Hotel. Irvin Barclay introduced her as his cousin Nalia Bowerman, but between the two of us, they were certainly not acting like cousins."

Jeanette nodded. "Bowerman. I once met a Mr. Bowerman, an older gentleman. I believe he was an avid student of the firmament in his spare time."

"An astronomer?"

"An amateur, but yes. I heard he died only last year. The matter came up in court because he'd died owing money to more than one person."

"Interesting. Looking at the stars is the same kind of work Nalia does down in Cambridge."

"You don't say. She must have acquired a love of the stars from her father. At any rate," Jeanette went on, "what I overheard at the bank wasn't the talk of cousins, either. It was rather more intimate, if you understand what I mean."

"I do. In addition, early this morning when I was gardening, this Nalia came to my house and essentially threatened me."

"She didn't!" She turned her head toward me. "About what?"

"She accused me of meddling in the business of the police, and said Irvin planned to prevent his wife from receiving my midwifery care. Sissy is nearly at term with twins, Jeanette, and she's never expressed the slightest dissatisfaction with me."

"Well, well, well. The plot thickens. Isn't that what they say in the Pinkerton novels?"

"I suppose. I feel bad for Sissy. She's home alone with the cook, who told me her employer had dismissed all their other servants." I shook my head. "Let's not talk about this mess any further. Tell me, where is thy daughter this morning?"

"She's off on an adventure with her papa. I think they planned to play at the lake and then find something sweet to eat." She smiled fondly.

"Thee didn't want to go along?"

"No. He's very good about relieving me of the burden of being the only parent at home during the week. Anyway, I'm in the middle of reading an excellent novel."

I focused on the book in her lap. The white pages were full of raised dots in all kinds of configurations but without a trace of ink. "Thee can read those dots?"

"Yes. It's a writing system called braille. Each letter of the alphabet has a unique six-dot representation." She set the pads of her fingers lightly on the page. She kept one hand at the left and moved the other across the book horizontally. "I can read quite quickly."

"What a marvel. What book is thee reading?"

"It's *Sense and Sensibility*. I'm reading it in French, though. A music teacher at the Perkins School, where I studied, has developed an American braille system. But there aren't many books yet available to be read. Luckily, my French is as good as my English."

It truly was a marvel. A blind woman could sit in her yard in America reading a British novel translated into French and printed in dots.

"Enjoy thy solitary time and thy book, my friend. I'll be off to see my detective friend and leave thee to it." I stood.

"Keep yourself safe, Rose. Seems like we have more than our share of wrongdoing going on in our fair town this week. I wouldn't want you to come to harm."

THIRTY-EIGHT

AT THE POLICE STATION, I finished telling Kevin what Sean had told me about the man being run down.

"I wish my boy hadn't had to see that assault. Not a fit sight for young eyes." He let out a noisy exhale. "But we'll get on it, Miss Rose."

"Kevin, if the Polish brother was here to claim his family's money, Merton would have great cause to wish him harm, wouldn't he?"

"I daresay he might. And speaking of inheritance, I have a piece of information for you. That business of Mrs. Settle and Mr. Barclay sharing some inheritance? It turns out to be a highly restrictive bestowal. The funds were to go only to the blood relatives named. Not their spouses, not their children or anyone else."

"So, in fact, Irvin would get Mayme's portion upon her death, after her estate is settled, not her husband."

"Yes, he would."

"One more piece of the puzzle, but it's not clear where it belongs. Now, what about Bertie? Have you dropped her from your investigation?" I kept my tone firm and my expression serious.

He cleared his throat. "There's been a new allegation against her, I'm afraid."

"An allegation of what? From whom?"

"Chief wouldn't say. But he's breathing fire down my neck to sew up this case, and fast."

I stood. "An allegation without proof is nothing." I straightened my bonnet. "Good day, Kevin. And good luck."

"I'll need every ounce of it. But thank you."

A minute after I left the police station, Bertie clopped up alongside me on Grover.

"What about another picnic by the lake, Rose Carroll?" She gazed down at me.

"Thee has the best ideas, Bertie Winslow."

The two of us sat on a cloth by the banks of Lake Gardner ten minutes later. The breeze off the water refreshed me and her

151

irreverent company was always a delight. I swallowed a bite of boiled egg. "I was hungry from my morning of riding all over town."

"I brought us each a piece of chocolate cake, too." Her straw boater hung from its ribbons down her back like a schoolgirl's. "Good thing the post office closes at noon on Saturdays."

"True words." I looked her in the face. "Kevin said something about a new allegation against thee. He wouldn't say what it was or who leveled it. Is thee worried?"

She shook her head twice, hard. "I am not. He'll have to come up with evidence against me, which is impossible because it doesn't exist. I intend to go on enjoying life and the police be damned." She glanced at me. "And don't you go worrying, either, dear Rose. It's all going to be fine."

"Very well." I fervently hoped so. "Say, I saw the most remarkable thing a little while ago. I stopped by a client's home, my friend Jeanette Papka's."

"The blind lady? I see her everywhere around town."

"Yes. Did you know blind people can read books printed in raised dots? It's a system called braille. What a marvelous invention. Not only that, but she was reading Jane Austen, in French, on white pages with nothing printed on them for the sighted."

"I'll say that is most marvelous, indeed." Bertie took a swig from a bottle of ale she'd brought for herself.

I shuddered at the memory of my foray into drunkenness.

A man and a woman, each holding a child by the hand, strolled the lake from the direction of High Street. They slowed when they caught sight of us. As the man gazed at Bertie, his face pulled into an angry mask. He muttered something to his wife, who hustled the children toward the far end of the shore, glancing once over her shoulder as if she was afraid she was being followed. He stalked in our direction.

He halted and stared down at Bertie. "Your ilk shouldn't be allowed in public." He folded his arms. "It's despicable."

"Good afternoon, sir." She smiled mildly at him. "It's a free world, in case you hadn't noticed."

"It shouldn't be, not in your case." He spat on the ground near her feet and stomped away.

"My stars and nightgown, Bertie," I murmured. "What a rude, awful man."

She picked up a pebble and tossed it after him, but he was long gone. "I'm used to it, Rose. He's biased, and I can't change his ilk, as he so stupidly put it. Don't concern yourself about it."

"Hmm. That will be easier said than done."

"Tell me, any new developments on the murder case?" she asked, lowering her voice. "I mean, real ones?"

"I'm not sure." I told her about the attack on the Polish man. "But I don't know if it's related or not."

"Poor fellow. Hope he survives."

"I do, as well." I watched the lake, which sparkled in the sun like a sea full of diamonds. Several children splashed at water's edge and a father and son tossed a ball back and forth. Three ladies picnicked near us, while a couple strolled arm in arm toward the woods beyond. "Have you ever encountered a woman named Nalia Bowerman?"

"I heard her give a lecture sometime in the last year. About the stars."

"So the star part is true."

Bertie raised an eyebrow. "Part of what?"

"She might be intimate with Irvin Barclay."

My friend swore in a most unladylike way. "The man who ratted on me, who said I was lurking around the Settle house? I don't like liars, Rose."

"Kevin told me Irvin saw thee riding by because he was passing the house himself."

"You think he might have killed Mrs. Settle? I can see the title on the newspaper story now." She lowered her tone to a dramatic one. "Money Man Murders Matron."

"Thee is full of such titles this week. In fact, Irvin did deliver candy via his wife on the night of Mayme's death, candy that might have been poisoned. Maybe he went over and sneaked in to make sure the sweets had done the trick."

"Then I hope he's caught and hanged. Nobody deserves to be murdered. Not even a woman who cast aspersions on me right and left."

"Murder aside, I'm concerned if he's stepping out with a lady — an astronomer notwithstanding — who isn't his wife." I frowned. "I wish I knew how I could learn more about Nalia."

"I believe she lives up near the top of Powow Hill in the house she inherited from her late father."

So close to my own abode. "Is that so?"

Bertie bobbed her head. "I had to deliver a parcel out there once and I noticed her house has an actual observatory in the back."

"One of those domes that opens." I'd seen a picture of one in an article about Maria Mitchell in the newspaper after her soul was released to God, or she crossed the Dark River, as Orpha would put it.

"Exactly."

"I've never seen it. I heard her father was an amateur astronomer. Perhaps he built the stargazing structure. Regardless"—I shook my head—"Irvin should not be having a dalliance with anyone except Sissy. He's the father-to-be of twin babies, I think I told thee. The ones I'll be helping his very pregnant wife to deliver sometime soon."

"Ouch." Bertie wrapped her arms around her knees and stared at the lake.

"Ouch, indeed." I tore off a piece of bread and nibbled on it.

Bertie gazed at the lake as if she hadn't heard me. I knew my friend well enough to sense her thoughts were elsewhere. I waited a moment more before speaking.

"Berto, what are you thinking so hard on?" I nudged her shoulder softly. Maybe this time she'd tell me.

She turned to look at me. A cloud had passed over her mood as dark as the one that scudded over the sun. "I'm a twin, Rose."

I stared at her. "*Thee* is a twin? I never knew that." She was finally ready to relate her twin story, for which I was grateful, although it seemed it would not be a happy one. "Does thee have a sister or a brother?"

"Had. Alberta, an identical twin sister. But she was a tiny thing, always weak and struggling despite having a cheery spirit like my usual one. Albie died when we were four."

Oh, my. "I'm so, so sorry. Her death must have been terribly wrenching for thee, and for thy parents."

She nodded as if it pained her to do so. "It was. Seeing her laid out is one of my first real memories. It was like a part of me had died, too. I still feel the pain, even though it's been nearly forty years."

"Twins have a very tight bond."

"Mmm." Bertie blew out a breath. "You know how I never see my mother?"

"Yes, and thee has never told me why. She's right across the Merrimack in West Newbury, isn't she?"

"She is, in the house where I grew up."

"Is thee estranged because she disapproves of thy feelings for Sophie?"

"No." Bertie paused for a moment, then went on. "She treated me very badly after my sister died. As if it was my fault we'd lost Albie. I needed more love than ever. I received far less. I tried to make her understand and finally gave up the fight when I became of age." Bertie blew out a noisy, half-sobbing breath. "Now she herself is ill and writes to me every month. But I can't reconcile the hole in my heart. She made it so much bigger than it needed or deserved to be."

Such hurt on both sides. Surely Bertie's mother was devastated to lose a daughter. Taking out her pain on the remaining one was no way to heal, though. Early on in our friendship I'd playfully called my friend Roberta and had been surprised when she forbade me to address her by her legal name, saying her mother called her Roberta. Now I understood why the name—so similar to her twin's—was like ripping apart a barely healed cut for Bertie, despite the decades that had passed.

"I thank thee for opening thy heart, Bertie. Thee was deeply wounded, as was thy mother."

"Daddy tried to help, but he died too, when I was fifteen." She sniffed. "Sophie thinks I should make amends before Mother dies. She says I am only hurting myself. What do you think?"

I took a moment before speaking, and then I trod carefully. "I think thee is a clear-headed grown woman happy in thy life at home and in thy chosen profession. Thee will make the decision that is right for thee." I touched her shoulder. "I also think thy mother might be able to speak about thy twin's death to thee as an adult in a way she was unable to when thee was younger and the pain was so much more acute. Reconciling with her could help to heal thy wound. But it's not my decision to make. It is thine alone."

She let out a deep sigh and nodded.

Over her shoulder I spied an open buggy pulling to a stop some ten yards away. John Whittier sat next to the driver and raised a hand to me in recognition. The driver climbed down and stood at the horse's head holding its harness.

I gave Bertie a quick hug and rose. "I'll be right back. John Whittier is there and I want to say hello. May I?"

"Go." She gave me a wan smile. "I'm fine. I'll sit here and ponder my life."

"Good afternoon, John," I said when I reached him. "It's a lovely day, isn't it?"

"Hello, Rose. Yes, indeed it is. I needed a spot of fresh air and an even bigger spot of inspiration. I am attempting to write a poem in lieu of appearing at a gathering to which I have been invited, but I'm afraid my heart is not strong and it seems to be affecting my ability to compose. Gazing at water has always had a salubrious effect, so here I am at the lake."

"I'm pleased to see thee, as always. I hope the inspiration will flow like the water over the dam there."

"I am also glad to have encountered thee. I came across a piece of information in which thee might be interested." He glanced at his driver, leaned toward me, and lowered his voice. "Regarding the death of Mayme Settle."

"I am all ears."

"It has come to my attention that the gardener with the unusual name—"

I broke in. "Adoniram?"

"Yes. The man took classes in the botanical sciences from Harvard College. A friend came to call yesterday who had also studied botany and now makes a great study of poisonous plants."

Poisonous plants? My eyes went wide.

"He mentioned an odd classmate who was interested in the same subject matter but never finished his degree. When I heard the name, I knew it had to be the one you mentioned."

That was quite a fall for Adoniram. He'd studied at Harvard College but now worked as a gardener? I wondered what had happened to cause his descent in position.

THIRTY-NINE

I BRAKED MY BICYCLE to a stop one house before the Settle abode. Bertie pulled Grover to a halt beside me. At the lake I'd told her what John had said about Adoniram, and she'd agreed to accompany me to speak with him. I knew going alone a second time to visit a possible murderer would be a stupid thing to do. We'd hatched a plan to say she needed some seedlings, too, since he'd invited me to come back for more the last time I was here. I also wanted to get a look at the side of Merton's Stanhope runabout. If the Polish man had been hurt as badly as David said, the paint might be marred by blood. Perhaps Kevin had already sent someone to look, but if the vehicle was in plain sight, it couldn't hurt to verify it with my own eyes.

We'd stopped by the police station on our way. Alas, Kevin had not been in. I'd left him a note with the gist of what John had said about Adoniram at Harvard, and we'd decided to undertake the investigation ourselves.

"Is this the place?" she asked, shielding her eyes from the bright western sun to squint at the modest lake cottage where I'd stopped.

"No, it's the big gray and white one beyond, the one with the mansard roof. Adoniram is probably around the back in the garden."

"So we're going to ask for seedlings and engage in some casual conversation, is that the plan, Rosetta?" She slid off her horse.

"I suppose. I also want to examine the right side of the Stanhope runabout, if it's here, and take a look at the horse if we can."

"I'll have to put Grover somewhere. A good way for me to look around the carriage house, no?" She grinned at me.

"Of course. I hadn't even thought of this benefit of thee coming along."

"Mostly we have to decline if the gardener offers us anything to eat." She raised an eyebrow. "A specialist in plant poisons, indeed."

"Let's go, shall we?" Even though murder is a very serious matter, it rather seemed like we were on an adventure together, or a secret Pinkerton mission. And there wasn't a soul in the world I'd rather be on a dangerous adventure with than Bertie. "The carriage house is around the side to the right."

I walked my bike and Bertie led Grover as we made our way in front of the house and down the empty drive. The doors to the carriage house were shut, so either Merton's runabout was inside or he was out with it. I half expected Adoniram to be around weeding or planting but I didn't see him anywhere. He was probably out back at his greenhouse.

"Should we open the door?" Bertie whispered.

I pursed my lips. "I don't know," I whispered back. I set my bike on its stand. "Yes. If we're discovered, say you wanted to get Grover out of the sun."

"Good idea." She slid open the right side of the door.

I cringed when the mechanism squealed from lack of oil, but then it was open and all was quiet again. I peered into the darker interior until my eyes adjusted. The scent of hay, manure, and well-oiled tackle floated out as a horse whuffed. I saw the runabout a couple of yards in, illuminated only by mote-filled northern sunlight from a small window.

"What are you waiting for?" Bertie whispered behind me.

I swallowed, my heart pounding hard and fast. "I'm having an attack of nerves."

"We can leave, you know."

We should. I'd told Kevin everything I knew. I should let him examine the runabout, let him question the gardener. This was work for a police detective, not two foolish women.

I heard the crack of a branch behind us. I whirled and gazed past Bertie and Grover, but no one was there. Grover snickered, and the horse in the carriage house whinnied in return.

"Shush, now, big fellow," Bertie murmured and stroked Grover's neck. "He wants to say hello to whoever's in there," she said to me, also in a low tone. "I'm going to take him and find him a drink of water."

"All right. I'll stand watch." I let them pass and stood gazing at the back of the big house. I didn't see any curtains part or a face at a window, but I had the sense I was being observed. I'd heard the expression "My skin crawled," which was exactly the sensation I was experiencing. It was as if tiny creatures were swarming through my pores. The hairs on my arms and the back of my neck stood at alert. My throat was so thick I could barely breathe.

I heard voices from behind the carriage house. Men's voices. And they were growing nearer. *Crikey.* We were in trouble now.

"Bertie," I called into the carriage house in a hoarse whisper. "Come."

But she didn't emerge. Adoniram and Merton rounded the corner, the latter wearing a white bandage wrapped around his head.

"It's simply not clear to me why you thought you needed to do that." Merton shook his head, his eyes on the ground.

Adoniram saw me first and touched his employer's arm to alert him.

Merton looked up. "Who are you?" He looked past me. "I didn't leave the carriage house door open, either." He glared as he pressed his lips together into a tense line.

"This be Miss Carroll the midwife, Mr. Settle. We appear to be quite the attraction today," Adoniram said, his eyes narrowed at me. "What business have you got here?"

"Good afternoon. I came with a friend, who also wanted a few of thy spare seedlings, Adoniram. She's, uh, watering her horse." I mustered a smile, gesturing over my shoulder to the open door. "And I wanted to see how thee fares after thy fall, Merton."

Merton's hand went up to his bandage. "How the devil do you know about my fall, and why are you so rudely addressing me by my Christian name?" His nostrils flared.

"Miss Carroll and I were in the kitchen when you fell, sir," Adoniram said softly. "She used your telephone and called for them medical folks."

"And she's not rude, she's a Quaker." Bertie materialized at my side holding Grover's reins. "Hello, gentlemen."

"This is postmistress Bertie Winslow," I added in a hurry. "Bertie, Merton Settle and Adoniram Riley." I knew she'd be able to figure out which was which of the two men. Merton was dressed appropriately for his class in a dark suit and neatly knotted tie, while Adoniram had dirt on the knees of his trousers and wore a working man's cap.

"Ah, Miss Winslow. I've seen you in the post office." Merton quit glowering. "You've mailed parcels for me."

Bertie extended her hand to him and shook. "Mr. Settle. I gave my horse a drink inside, hope you don't mind."

"Not at all, not at all."

When she extended her hand to Adoniram, he tucked his own hand behind his back.

"You don't want to be shaking my hand, now. Got dirt on it, miss. And I'm afraid I went ahead and planted all the rest of them seedlings, so I ain't got a one to spare."

"Well, we'll be taking ourselves along, then," I said with cheeriness I didn't feel. "I hope thee isn't suffering ill effects from thy injury." I addressed Merton but left off his name so as not to inflame him all over again. When he didn't respond, I sidled over to my bicycle.

"Have a lovely rest of your day." Bertie smiled at the men. She hopped onto a mounting block and threw her leg over Grover.

Merton's eyes widened and Adoniram shook his head at the shock of a woman riding astride. I glanced back at the two from the end of the driveway. Merton faced Adoniram and appeared to be berating him. Adoniram, on the other hand, watched me leave as he had before. This time his stare sent shivers up and down my spine.

FORTY

When Bertie and I had turned onto Thompson Street, she signaled to me to stop in front of a modest house set far back from the road. A large fenced-in vegetable garden was flourishing. Fruit trees of all kinds were scattered about the property, with immature apples, cherries, and pears evident among the foliage. A round, cheery-looking woman in an apron and a straw hat hoed in the garden, but she was too far away to hear us.

Bertie glanced up and down the road before speaking. "The runabout had a dent and a dried substance on the right side, Rose." She leaned both forearms on the pommel, gazing down at me.

I stared at her. "Thee managed to check it!"

"Yes, that's why I didn't come out right away. And it has red stripes, but they're more like piping."

"What color was the horse within?" I asked.

"A light gray mare with a black mane."

"Exactly as Sean described."

She nodded, eyes wide. "Imagine, running down your own brother nearly to death."

"It was a terrible thing to do." I shook my head. "I wonder if he hoped to kill the man so he didn't have to share family monies."

"Probably. Should we hie back to the police station and inform your pal Donovan?"

I tilted my head as I thought. "I don't know. He already knows what his son told me. And Adoniram said something about him and Merton being quite the attraction today. I daresay he meant somebody already investigated the horse and carriage."

"Then why didn't they arrest Settle?"

I shrugged. "Maybe because it's only hearsay? Maybe he claimed the substance was something else, like splashed muddy water or . . ." My voice trailed off. "Or what? It might not have been blood at all, right? The carriage house wasn't very well lit."

"It could have been the gardener who drove the carriage at his employer's bidding, too."

"True. Adoniram could have done the driving."

"Seems possible. Well, thanks for bringing me along on your lark, my friend," Bertie said, raising one eyebrow. "I'm off to prepare a romantic supper for my darling."

"Thank thee for coming. I was most certainly not going there alone. One time was once too often."

We said our goodbyes and off she rode. I pedaled slowly for home, thinking of our "lark" all the way as I bumped along the paving stones.

But when I arrived at Powow Street, I slowed and gazed up toward the top of the hill. It was a perfect spot on which to construct an observatory. The hill's summit was the highest point around, rising seventy-five feet above even Whittier Hill. It would be as free as possible from the illumination produced by the town's lamps and bulbs, which would mar a clear view of the starry firmament. Nalia—and apparently her father before her—would have an excellent window onto the night skies for her studies.

I parked my bike against the fence of the Osgood factory at the corner of Chester and began my ascent on foot. I wanted to set eyes on the dome for myself, and the hill was too steep to attempt by bicycle. I shuddered as I passed a carriage house most of the way up where I had nearly met my demise late last fall. I trudged now, breathing hard as it became steep, until the road twisted to the right and then back left for the final fifty yards to the summit.

The last house on the right was a lovely gabled structure with fanciful woodwork painted in contrasting colors to the walls. And, indeed, behind and to the side was a carriage house, but with a domed roof atop a cylindrical tower sticking up off the back of the building. The dome had a ridge bisecting it from one side up over to the top to the other, which must be where it opened.

I didn't want to be discovered lingering in front of the home, so I kept hiking to the summit of the hill where it flattened. I could see all the way north to Mount Agamenticus in Maine, east to the Atlantic coast off ten-mile-long Plum Island, and Ipswich to the south, a more extensive view than the one afforded from the Grand Hotel. But I wanted to find out more about the woman who lived at the observatory right here on Powow Hill. Why had I never seen her in the neighborhood? Perhaps she'd inherited her father's house last year and only then moved to Amesbury. Maybe she spent most of her time in Cambridge with other scientists at Harvard, or in Boston at the Massachusetts Institute of Technology. It also occurred to me the abode wasn't very far up the hill from the Barclay home on Prospect Street.

I let out a breath. I wasn't going to learn a thing standing rooted in place staring downhill. I resolved to return home, play with Betsy and the twins, and put murder out of my mind as best I could.

But I hadn't taken more than a half dozen steps when I halted. A gleaming black rockaway, made by Biddle and Smart if my guess was right, was ascending the hill toward Nalia's home, the roan pulling it plodding with every step. And Irvin Barclay occupied the driver's seat. I shrank behind a nearby tree so I wouldn't be seen. After the conveyance pulled to a stop in front of the house, Nalia hurried out the front door and down the walk. I watched as she climbed in. Irvin turned the rockaway around and drove away. It was about three o'clock. Where were they off to now?

I waited until the carriage disappeared around the bend to continue my walk. Right before I reached Nalia's abode I saw something I hadn't spied on my way up. A maid was unpinning dry laundry from a clothesline behind the house. My timing couldn't have been better. I made my way along the side of the house toward her.

"Good afternoon." I smiled at the dark-skinned girl, who couldn't have been any older than Faith, and looked even younger than eighteen.

"How d'you do, miss." She finished unclipping a dish towel and made a little bob like a curtsy. She wore a faded blue cotton dress, but it had been neatly mended and the apron over it was clean and white. Her nappy hair was pulled back and covered by a white mob cap.

"I am well, except I seem to have lost my way. I seek a Belmont Street." I knew very well Belmont Street was down the hill a little to the east, but I wanted an excuse to speak with her about Nalia. I decided to be careful not to reveal my faith in my manner of speech, in case the girl happened to tell her employer an odd-speaking Quaker had been nosing around.

"You won't have far to go, miss." She pointed. "Go that way to

163

Prospect, down the hill to the first cross street, and Belmont will be the next downhill street you come to."

"I appreciate the help." I gazed around. "This is a fine spot for a residence. Fresh air up here, and a lovely view."

"So it is, but it's sorrowful hard to reach in the winter snows and ice." She shook her head.

"I suppose it would be." From back here I could see the observatory structure more clearly. "What's that curious thing?" I pointed to the domed roof.

"It's Miss Bowerman's. She looks at the stars from within."

Miss Bowerman. She was a single lady. "She's an astronomer? What an unusual occupation for a woman."

The maid beamed. "She's a right unusual lady. She treats me real good, too, not like some of the ladies in town. She don't pay much, but someone like me can't expect more than a pittance." She shrugged.

One of life's many injustices. "And she's not married, I gather."

"No, she don't have time for none of that. Told me she don't never want to be controlled by some gent. But she does have her gentlemen friends, like."

"I saw a woman climbing into a buggy a few minutes ago. I suppose it was her and one of her gentlemen?"

"Yes. I don't like that one. Mr. Barclay's his name." She chewed on the inside of her lip. "He's married, he is, and he's got no business stepping out with Miss Bowerman."

Nor she with him, but I didn't say it to her employee.

FORTY-ONE

I TRUDGED DOWN THE HILL thinking about Irvin and Nalia. Before talking with the house girl, I had wondered why he hadn't married Nalia instead of Sissy. He already had a pretty young wife, so why was he also stepping out with an attractive redhead? Now it was clear that Nalia wasn't having anything to do with marriage, and Sissy was more than happy to bear him children. All kinds of nagging questions still plagued me, though.

They flew out of my head as I stared at the fence where I'd left my bike not half an hour ago. *What?* My trusty metal steed was not there. I gazed up and down the length of the fence. No bicycle. I was positive I had left it right here. I slapped my leg in frustration. Someone had taken it. I'd seen people lock their bikes in public with a small padlock and a length of chain, but I'd never thought I needed to acquire a measure of security. I wished I had. My bicycle had cost me good money a year ago, and now I was without my favorite transportation.

A moment of quiet dread stole over me. What if Mayme's killer had been following me and took the bike to make it harder for me to get around town and investigate the murder? I glanced quickly around. I stood on a busy street corner in full daylight, but the thought of being followed chilled me and made me shiver.

A fellow emerged from the lower of the two big Osgood buildings carrying his lunch pail. I wanted to ask if he'd seen anyone make off with a bike, but how could he have if he was working inside? And I didn't see anyone toiling outside on this side of the buildings to ask. I looked behind me at the large house on the corner of Powow and Chester. It had bow windows upstairs and down with a good view of this spot of fence. Perhaps someone inside saw who had made off with my transport.

I checked both ways on Powow. I waited for a wagon laden with hay to rumble by, then hurried across the street. A distracted-looking woman with a nimbus of white hair and the scent of turpentine about her opened the door a few moments after I knocked. She wore a large paint-spattered man's shirt over her dress and had a smudge of blue paint on her forehead, too. She wiped her hands on the shirt.

"Yes?"

"Good afternoon, ma'am. My name is Rose Carroll. I am a neighbor of sorts, and a little while ago I left my bicycle against the fence right there." I pointed. "It has disappeared, and I wondered if thee might have seen who took it."

She gave a hearty laugh. "I didn't see a thing, Miss Carroll. I was upstairs painting. When I'm deep in my art, I don't even hear fire bells."

My smile slid away. "I see. Well, I thank thee."

"You're a Quaker, aren't you? I can tell by your manner of speaking. I'm Margery Jennings, and I'm pleased to make your acquaintance. You Quakers do good work, I've heard." She glanced at her extended hand. "Oh, you don't want to shake that. Paint might not be dry." She withdrew it.

"Yes, I'm a member of the Religious Society of Friends, and I'm also pleased to meet thee, Margery. I'll be going then."

"Wait a minute." She tapped her temple, leaving a smear of white next to the blue. "My husband might have spied your thief. He's out tinkering in the barn." She stepped onto the stoop and called toward the open door of a large barn at the back. A bench sat in the sun in front of the building. "Teddy?"

A tall man, equally white-haired, ambled out, wiping greased-stained hands on a rag. "Yes, my dear?"

"Teddy, Miss Carroll says someone stole her bicycle from in front of the fence over there in the last little while." She pointed to the spot. "Did you happen to see the culprit?"

His gaze traveled to the fence. "Why, yes. Indeed I did. I was taking a break from my invention and was sitting on the bench out here watching the world go by. I thought it passing strange at the time. A gent drove up with another man in tow. The second jumped down and rode off on the bicycle."

My hand went to my mouth. It appeared I'd been right about being followed. Unless there was a gang of bicycle thieves operating in Amesbury, driving around looking for unsuspecting souls who left bicycles unlocked and unattended, which I supposed was possible.

"Why was it strange, darling?" Margery asked her husband.

"For one thing it was a ladies' cycle. And for the other? The man wobbled and nearly crashed like he'd never ridden a two-wheeler. It was downright comical." He talked through a smile.

"Would the carriage have been a Stanhope runabout?" I asked. "And the horse a gray mare with black mane?"

Teddy tilted his head. "How'd you know about that carriage and horse, Miss Carroll?"

"It's a long story. I also expect the driver was a man in a suit and the thief a workman in a cap."

"Precisely." Teddy nodded. "A workman with grass stains on his trousers."

"So you've had a run-in with these bandits before." Margery gazed at me with curiosity.

"I have." I smiled without much cheer behind it. "I think I'd better go inform the police of the theft. Thank thee, Teddy, for sharing thy observation, and thee, Margery, for thy help."

He glanced with raised eyebrows at his wife.

She smiled at him. "She's a Quaker."

"Ah, the faith of our esteemed poet."

"Yes, indeed." I thanked them again and trudged toward home. I mused that Merton and Adoniram could be bicycle thieves without being murderers, but why?

FORTY-TWO

THE BAILEY HOUSEHOLD was in chaos when I walked in. Mark was elbow-deep in flour and yellow cornmeal, which was also scattered on the floor and in his hair. Matthew and Betsy were playing Parcheesi at the table and arguing about who was winning. Betsy's hair had become unbraided and was a curly snarled mess. Luke was bouncing a ball, which apparently had already knocked a ceramic jar onto the floor, judging from the shards remaining. Their father was nowhere to be seen, and the room was overheated.

"Auntie Rose, Mattie's cheating," Betsy protested.

"Am not," Matthew countered.

"Thee is, too."

"Auntie Rose, I'm making cornmeal muffins," Mark announced with pride. "How hot does the oven need to be?"

"A medium heat, although it feels warmer than that in here right now. Luke, thee knows the rule is no balls in the house." I gave him a firm look. "And where is thy father?"

He returned my look with a hooded-eye glance of his own, but at least he stopped his bouncing. He was fourteen now and growing increasingly sullen, so I was lucky he'd complied.

"Papa's out with Winnie," Betsy offered.

"I'm in charge," Luke said.

"Is he coming back for supper?"

"We don't know," Mark said, but kept his back to me, and his voice had turned less confident.

I sighed. "Luke, please clean up the broken jar before someone cuts himself."

"Or herself." Betsy folded her arms. "Aren't boys and girls equal in God's eyes?"

I had to smile at the little Quaker. "Or herself." I slumped into a chair, exhausted from everything that had happened today.

"Oh, and a lady called for thee," Matthew said. "She said her mistress is having her twins. She sounded rather worried."

I sat up straight. "Sissy Barclay is in labor?"

"Yes, the lady said Mrs. Barclay."

I had to go to her immediately. I didn't want to leave these young people alone to get up to more mischief, though, not to mention Mark handling a hot oven. Who could I call? They all adored David, but he'd said he had a meeting most of the day today. Bertie? No. She knew the children but she wasn't adept at managing little ones. Faith. I'd call Faith and pray she wasn't occupied elsewhere. And I had to summon Annie to assist me. And tell Kevin about my bicycle being absconded with.

I stood. "Listen, darlings. I must go to this birth. I'm going to see if Faith and Zeb can come and watch over you until Frederick returns." I watched Luke, hoping he wouldn't protest.

"Goody!" Betsy clapped her hands.

"Zeb has been helping me with a carpentry project," Luke said. "I will be glad to see him."

Whew. "I have to make several telephone calls. Please behave yourselves." I glanced at each in turn over the top of my spectacles. "I know thee can."

I headed into the sitting room. First I called Faith, and instantly calmed down when she said she and Zeb would be right over. She would tidy up Betsy's hair and manage her younger siblings far better than Luke was able to, plus he would have Zeb to connect with. Next I got through to Annie's landlord and left an urgent message with him for my apprentice to join me at the Barclay residence without delay.

Now for the police. "I'd prefer to speak to Kevin Donovan," I said after the man answering the call said he would take down the particulars. "I believe the theft is connected to the recent homicide."

He whistled into the device, and the piercing sound went straight into my ear. I winced.

"Problem is, miss, he's gone home for the day. Said his baby daughter is poorly."

"Thank thee. I'll reach him at home." I hung up. Poor Kevin and Emmaline, to have their baby sick again. I couldn't go to them, though. I had to get to Sissy. These calls had already taken too much time, and who knows how long ago Aoife had called about the labor starting. Still, I put through a call to Kevin's home.

After Sean answered, I greeted him and said, "Sean, may I speak to thy father, please?"

"He's helping Mummy with the baby. Miss Rose, she's awful hot again."

"I am sorry to hear it." Very sorry. News about the bicycle theft could wait. "Listen, please write down a name." I waited while he fetched paper and pencil. "Tell thy parents I am urgently called to a birth, so I can't come and help. They must telephone David Dodge of Newburyport. He will pay a visit and assess Rosalie's condition. All right?" I doubted his meeting was over by now, but maybe it was.

"David Dodge of Newburyport," he confirmed. "Is he a doctor?"

"Yes. And if they can't get through to him, they should summon an ambulance wagon and take her with all due speed to Anna Jaques Hospital."

"I will tell them." His voice was solemn. "They are both beside themselves, Miss Rose."

"Thee sounds calm, Sean. Please bring them a basin of cold water and remind them to bathe the baby over and over until she cools. Can thee help in that way?"

"Of course. She's my little sister. I don't want her to be sick."

We said our farewells and ended the call. What a gift to have such a responsible and intelligent child in the household. I closed my eyes and held Rosalie in the Light of God, that she might recover and be well very soon. Then I held myself, too. I was facing a challenge in the next hours and would need divine assistance now more than ever.

FORTY-THREE

TEN MINUTES LATER Aoife had shown me into Sissy Barclay's bedchamber. Sissy sat in a loose tea dress with her legs over the side of the bed, her face pale and her hair in disarray. She had been perspiring with her efforts and her neck was wet. At least air wafted in through the open east-facing window and the room wasn't overly warm.

"I am here, Sissy," I said softly, moving to her side and setting down my birthing satchel. I'd learned how important it was to remain calm and be a strong, quiet presence when helping a laboring woman. "When did thy pains begin?"

She glanced helplessly at Aoife, who hovered in the doorway.

The cook checked the watch pinned to her bosom. "It's now half past five. I'd say around three o'clock. I called yeh right away but yeh was out."

Indeed. Out watching Sissy's husband pick up another woman in his buggy at exactly that time. Did he leave because the labor had started?

"I got here as soon as I could. How frequently are the pains coming?" I perched on the bed next to her.

"Every three minutes or so?" Aoife offered. "Pretty regular like."

Sissy nodded with wide eyes. "It's too early, isn't it, Rose? Will my babies survive?"

I stroked her hand. "We will do our best to make sure they do, Sissy. Thy only job now is to let go and allow thy body to do the work it needs to. There's no going back once the womb has begun the process."

"I already feel better now you're here," Sissy said.

"After the next contraction, let's get thee into a nightdress and then I'll assess where we are, all right?"

She nodded solemnly. Half a minute passed before she let out a groan. "Here it comes." She set her hands on her knees and hung her head. Her forehead was tense with pain and she moaned in a low tone.

I stroked the wrinkles from her brow and murmured, "Thee is doing very well." When she opened her eyes after the pain ended, I said, "Aoife, can thee find a light nightgown for Sissy?" I turned to see her waiting with it in her hands. "Thee is an excellent assistant."

"I bore five babies meself and helped me daughters with their births, too."

"I am glad of thy assistance." We helped Sissy change, and I braided her hair in a long plait down her back. Aoife offered a damp cloth to wipe her face and neck. The day was cooling but labor is hard work. And I liked to get my mothers-to-be settled and tidy at the beginning, because they often don't want to be touched as time goes along and the contractions grow more intense.

"Aoife, I'd like you to please bring a pitcher of water and a glass for Sissy."

The cook bustled off as the next pain began. When it subsided, I asked Sissy to sit back against the pillows on the bed.

"I'm going to check where the babies are, and see how much thy womb has already opened." I palpated her swollen belly. One baby was still head down and the other remained head up. If the head-down fetus came out first, the other would not have such a hard time. The head was the largest part of an infant's body and left the birth canal open for the rest to descend. If the breech were the first, I would have a harder time ensuring both babies' safety.

I readied to slide my hand in and check her dilation. "This might be uncomfortable, so breathe down to my hand." She groaned as I assessed a three-knuckle opening and a nice thinning of the mouth of the uterus, what we called effacement. I withdrew my hand and wiped it on a cloth. "Thee is making good progress."

After the next pain, I pressed the Pinard horn all over her belly and listened for heartbeats, but again detected only one.

Aoife returned with the drinking water as well as a stack of folded cloths. Sissy lay back and closed her eyes, and Aoife beckoned to me.

She turned her back to the bed and whispered. "The mister went out with the buggy earlier this afternoon."

"Had the labor started by then? Does he know about it?"

"He wouldn't be knowing. He spent the morning in the garden but got all cleaned up and dressed proper before he left. Wouldn't say where he was off to. Think I should go a-lookin' for him?"

I knew exactly who he'd cleaned up for. "Would thee have any way of knowing where he went?"

"No, in truth I don't."

"Then we'll let him come home as he may and learn the news at that time, shall we?"

"Rose, help me," Sissy called. "It hurts to lie down." She twisted herself up to sitting on the edge of the bed before I got there. "Sitting hurts, too."

I grabbed a pillow and laid it on the floor next to the bed. "Try this position. Kneel on this pillow with thy knees wide and lean thy arms on the bed. Sometimes it helps. Hands and knees on the bed can be good, too."

"Oh, yes, thank you," she said once I'd maneuvered her into kneeling. "This position takes the weight off my back."

"Good."

"Tell Aoife to go away for a few minutes, please," she murmured.

Why? "Aoife." I twisted to look at her. "Sissy would like a word with me in private, if thee doesn't mind."

"Of course." Aoife headed for the hall.

"I found something," Sissy began after the door closed. "It's . . . wait, here's another." It was an intense pain and she wailed.

"Try to keep thy tone low, Sissy. A low tone opens the throat and helps the womb open. A high voice creates tightness, and thee doesn't want tightness or tension in thy body."

She switched to an eerie low singing until the pain had passed. She spoke with her head on her folded forearms. "I was helping Aoife by putting away Mr. Barclay's clean clothes in his chest of drawers yesterday. I found a small box with a powder in it. It was labeled *Lily of the Valley*. Why would he have such a powder?"

"Mmm." I smoothed damp hair back off her brow. "Was it a talc scented like the flower?"

"No. I left it there. I didn't want him angry at me for going through his things." Now she wept in earnest. "Rose, I feel my life is at an end. I'm sure my husband of only a year is stepping out on me. I know I'm going to die birthing these babies and I'm sure they won't survive, either."

"Now, now, Sissy. None of this talk. Thee is a healthy young woman and thy babies will likely be, too. Remember, women have been giving birth for millennia. Thy body is made to do it." I left her well-founded concern about Irvin unanswered. Only he could address that one. "Come along, dry thy tears."

She lifted her face and sniffed, then moaned again and lowered her head to make her way through the next step on the way to birth.

A stair creaked and Annie entered the room as quietly as I had. I nodded and smiled, but held my fingers against my lips so as not to interrupt Sissy. My heart eased to see my apprentice. I would need her help as time went by.

As soon as I could I would ask Aoife to fetch the powder and hide it in a safe place in the kitchen. I knew many plants had toxic qualities and lily of the valley could be one. Kevin Donovan might very well be interested in a powdered form of it found in Irvin Barclay's chest of drawers.

FORTY-FOUR

Sissy's labor increased in intensity an hour later after darkness fell. Her legs trembled as she gripped the windowsill with both hands. Her pains came ninety seconds apart from start to start and lasted a minute, so she barely got a break. She'd said she had to remain standing, and when possible I liked to follow my clients' lead for what position they wanted to labor in.

I left Annie with her and ran down the stairs to the kitchen. "Aoife, it's time to boil water, but first I have a favor to ask of thee."

"The babies are coming? I'm not sure I can stand the excitement." She patted her chest. "What is it yer needing me to do?"

"Is Irvin back?"

"Not yet, more's the pity." She made a tsking sound.

Still, I kept my voice low. "Sissy told me she found a small tin of powder in his bureau drawer. The tin is labeled *Lily of the Valley*. I need thee to find it and hide it here in the kitchen."

"Why in the name of Saint Bridget would yeh want me to be doing such a thing?" She stared at me.

"I have a suspicion about the tin and I need to convey it to the police after I leave here." When she opened her mouth to ask more questions, I held up my hand. "I can't say more at this time. Will thee go fetch it, please? I need to get back to thy mistress."

"Of course I will, Miss Carroll."

"I thank thee."

She followed me up the stairs but turned the opposite way at the top landing. Before I reentered Sissy's bedchamber, I took a moment to hold Kevin and Emmaline's Rosalie in the Light of God, and Sissy and her babies, too, that they all would survive today's ordeals. When I went in, Sissy sat naked and panting on the edge of the bed, which had had the covers removed. Annie was mopping up the floor in front of the window with a cloth.

"Well, well. It looks like thy water broke." I quickly washed my hands in the basin and hurried to the bed.

"Just now." Annie sat back on her knees.

"Very good, Sissy." I stroked her shoulder.

Her nostrils flared. "It doesn't feel good. It hurts like the very devil." She slid down and squatted on the floor, gripping the bed behind her with both hands.

"Thee has lost the cushion of the waters, but this also means the first baby will come that much sooner." I waited until the next pain and her accompanying guttural groans passed. I knelt in front of her.

"I'm going to assess thy progress again." A moment later I slid my hand out. She was fully dilated, making the womb and the canal a continuous passageway. "Thee can push any time thee feels the need. Squatting is a good open position for bringing out the baby, too, if thee can tolerate it."

Annie washed her hands, too. Without being asked, she brought me a large towel. She laid out the scissors and cord string on the dressing table, and squeezed a bit of oil into a small bowl. A stack of baby blankets was also at hand.

I tucked the towel between Sissy's legs. Childbirth could be a messy affair.

Half an hour of pushing and growling passed before I spied light hair at her opening. "I can see a head, Sissy. Thy first baby is almost here. Give me a good hard push now."

But even as she bore down, the door burst open. Irvin stood in the opening.

"Cook said you . . ." His voice trailed off and he stared, mouth agape.

My heart chilled. Was he here in anger? Had he discovered the missing tin?

"Go away!" Sissy cried.

Aoife appeared in the doorway behind him. "I told him not to come up here but he wouldn't listen."

Annie hurried to his side. "Mr. Barclay, this is no place for a man. Your babies are about to be born, and we'll come and get you after they are." She ushered him out and Aoife followed. Annie shut the door with a firm click.

Whew. He hadn't said anything about the tin. He must have thought the babies were already born and wanted to meet them. "He's gone," I said to Sissy, rolling my eyes at Annie. "One more good push for me now."

Sissy put her whole body into the effort, and we were rewarded with a tiny baby girl sliding into my waiting hands.

A baby who lay pale and limp. I hurried to suction the mucous from her mouth and nose with the rubber bulb syringe, then turned her onto her belly on my left hand and rubbed her back vigorously with my right. "Come on, baby," I whispered. "Breathe for me." I held her up by her heels and gave her back a gentle whack.

She filled her lungs and wailed, waving her hands and kicking her feet when I laid her down.

"Thee has a daughter, Sissy." My voice was full of emotion, as it invariably became at the moment of every birth.

Annie wiped a tear from the edge of her eye.

"I do?" Sissy asked. "Praise God. Help me up, please."

Annie stepped in without my asking and helped Sissy onto the bed and then sitting up supported by pillows. A minute later I'd cut the cord and laid the baby in Sissy's waiting arms, skin to skin, with a blanket covering the baby. The new mother's smile as she gazed at her daughter was as tender as I'd ever seen.

"I didn't die, and neither did she," she murmured.

"You both did very well," Annie said in a soft voice.

"Yes," I said. "Remember, thy second baby will be along by and by."

"How long until that happens?" Annie asked. She hadn't assisted me at a twin birth before.

"It can be a matter of minutes or up to an hour."

But nothing happened for quite some time. With our help, Sissy put the baby to her breast but the newborn was so tiny she had trouble latching on. I estimated her weight at about five and a half pounds. At least her breathing seemed healthy. The lungs were always at risk in a premature infant.

When I palpated the second twin's position, my heart sank. It still seemed to be rump down. I listened for a heartbeat now the first twin was out and at first I couldn't hear anything. Finally I thought I detected a beat but it was so faint I might have been mistaken. I prayed the baby was alive. If it had died in utero, its little body would already be in a state of decrepitude. The labor would be harder, too. Live babies seemed to stimulate the uterus to keep contracting. And of course Sissy's sorrow would have a great impact on her healing and on her ability to mother the living twin.

A full fifty minutes after the little girl was born, Sissy's contractions finally started up again.

"I can't do it again, Rose," she whimpered.

"Of course thee can." I removed the baby and handed her to Annie. "Wrap her up good for warmth, please." The best place for a newborn, especially such a small one, was against her mother's skin, but in lieu of that, a tightly wrapped blanket would keep her warm and feeling secure.

Sissy stayed where she was as her womb began to contract in earnest. She raised her knees and gripped them, once again resorting to the deep, guttural, animal-like vocalizations so many women involuntarily produced.

Sure enough, the birth was not an easy one, despite her passage already being open from the first twin's emergence. The baby's derriere came out with both legs tucked up inside. With another push, one popped out, then the other and most of the torso. One shoulder seemed to be hung up. Annie stood near Sissy's head, encouraging her, rubbing her shoulders, but when she glanced at me my apprentice look distinctly worried.

My thoughts went to Orpha and to a shoulder dystocia birth from over a year ago. I knew what to do. After a great deal of maneuvering to turn the shoulders, I had to make sure the head was born promptly. It's exceedingly dangerous for the chest to be out and not the head, because the brain can be starved of oxygen. The tiny boy's size helped, and at last he lay in my hands.

"Thee has a son," I murmured to Sissy. But he was as flaccid and pale as his sister had been at first. I once again massaged a twin, clicked the soles of his feet, held him upside down, and willed him to take a breath. I could see his heart beating in his chest but he was even smaller than his sister. When he gave a sickly wail I heaved a breath of relief.

His twin gave a cry in response. I glanced at Annie's worried face before I handed Sissy her boy, again covering them both with a flannel blanket.

"A son." She beamed down at him.

"Hold him close and rub his back, Sissy. I fear he is quite weak."

She looked up in alarm. "Why is he weak?"

"Both twins are at least six weeks early. Thee knows that. Speak to him as thee holds him close. He has spent months hearing thy voice from within and it can be a comfort. He may well thrive, with thy warmth and care."

Or he might not live through the hour.

FORTY-FIVE

THE LITTLE FELLOW did live through the hour. He was smaller than the girl and had even more trouble suckling, and his breathing was strained. I was not hopeful about his future.

Aoife popped her head in the door. "May I?"

I looked to Sissy for the answer. She sat propped up in bed with a wrapped baby in each arm, a shawl draped over her shoulders.

"Come in, Mrs. O'Malley, please, and meet my children." Sissy's voice was strong. She was recovering remarkably well. But she was young and her labor, while arduous, had not been overly long.

Aoife hurried to the bedside. "Ah, take a gander of the wee ones." A smile split her broad face. "What have yeh got there, Mrs. Barclay?"

"A son," Sissy lifted the boy a little, "and a daughter."

"Bless our sainted Mary, so yeh do. They're tiny bits of things, then, aren't they?"

"Yes, they are," Sissy said. "But they'll grow, won't they, Rose?"

All I could do was nod. Their growth was in God's hands, not mine. "Is Irvin still about?" I asked Aoife.

"He's downstairs. Shall I fetch him? He's about to pace a hole in the carpet, he's that eager to meet his babies."

"I'll go and get him in a few minutes," I said.

"I'll nip down and let the man know." She slapped her head. "I'm after losing my mind, I am. I came up to see if I can bring yeh some nourishment, Mrs. Barclay. A nice bowl of soup, a piece of pie?"

Sissy blinked. "Why, yes, I find myself quite hungry all of a sudden."

"And for the midwives?" Aoife smiled at Annie and me.

I shook my head. "We'll have something before we leave, but I thank thee."

After we helped Sissy clean up and don a fresh garment, I washed up, too, and left her and the babies with Annie. I hadn't been anywhere in the house except the kitchen and Sissy's bedchamber, and when I reached the downstairs hall I wasn't sure behind which closed door to find Irvin. I picked one on the right because I heard voices. Perhaps Aoife was discussing something with him.

When I pushed open the door, Irvin stood with his back to me in front of a large desk. He was speaking not to the cook but into a telephone.

"And good riddance, too, that's what I say. That woman was no good for anyone."

That woman. Mayme Settle or his first wife? Either way, I should not be standing here listening. I turned to go, but the doorknob was slightly loose. It clicked when I grasped it.

Irvin whirled. He dropped the telephone receiver on the desk and took several strides to loom over me. His eyes narrowed and his mouth turned down in rage.

"You're spying on me. I knew it. This midwife business is only a nasty guise to get into my house and snoop around." Spittle flew out of his mouth.

I stepped back into the hall and held up both hands. "Thee is wrong, Irvin. I just spent an evening helping thy wife deliver premature twins. I came down to say thee may go up and meet them now."

His eyes widened and he shook off his anger. "Do I have a son?"

I sighed inwardly. The only care of so many men was a male heir. "Yes, a son and a daughter, too." At least his mood had switched, but he wouldn't have reacted as he did if he were not worried about what I'd overheard.

"He will be Irvin William Barclay, Junior." He began to push past me but I laid my hand on his arm.

"Wait. Thee must know the babies came very early. They are both quite small, and the boy in particular is weak. It is possible he will not survive. Please treat Sissy with care. She's been through an ordeal." And it isn't over yet.

"Balderdash." He batted away the idea. "Any son of mine will be strong and hearty." He hurried up the stairs with great clomping steps.

I followed him up at a slower pace. When I entered Sissy's room, Irvin was sitting on a chair holding one of the babies. I couldn't see the face, but assumed it was the boy.

"Aren't they wonderful, husband?" Sissy asked, beaming at him.

"Yes." He frowned and gazed at me. "Why is his breathing so noisy, Miss Carroll?"

I glanced at Annie, who gave me a small nod. "His lungs are not fully formed yet." I went to Irvin's side. The newborn fought to breathe even more than before I'd gone downstairs, and he made a rasping sound with each inhalation. "He's having trouble getting the air he needs."

"Can't you do something for him?" He gently stroked the baby's cheek with his forefinger, which looked monstrously large against the tiny face.

"Sadly I cannot. We have no medicines to improve his condition." Sometimes steam could ease breathing, but with someone so small, steam that was too hot could burn him, and it was very hard to manage holding a newborn over a steaming bowl. The little fellow would make it or he wouldn't.

Sissy had been listening. Now she looked at me, horrified. "Do you mean he might die?"

I nodded slowly. "It's possible."

"Then we need to summon a priest immediately! He needs his last rites."

Annie, who also attended the Catholic Church, laid a calming hand on Sissy's shoulder. "I'll go telephone for Father Nilan." She hurried out.

Irvin curled his lip at his wife. "Papist poppycock."

"Irvin, I told you I wasn't going to give up my faith when I married you," Sissy said, her tone harsh. "I didn't then and I will not now. My children will be raised in the Roman Catholic Church and that's that." She held her daughter close.

This was not the time for marital strife. I cleared my throat. "Let us focus on the twins' health, shall we?" Irvin grasped the baby boy rather too tightly. "Irvin, please calm thyself and don't restrict thy son's body quite so closely. Instead thee might walk him about and rock him gently." I kept my voice soft.

Irvin did as I suggested. He took the baby near the open window and rocked him, humming softly. The rasping quieted. Sissy sat with her daughter but her gaze was on her husband. Annie slipped back into the room.

"He's coming," she murmured to Sissy.

But before the priest could arrive, Irvin's shoulders slumped and he stopped moving. I went to his side.

"He's gone." His voice shook. "My boy is gone."

FORTY-SIX

THE NEXT HOUR was a difficult one, with distraught Irvin and Sissy unable to comfort each other. The food Aoife had brought Sissy sat untouched. I held both parents, as well as the baby's released soul, in God's Light for a moment. After five minutes of Irvin continuing to rock his dead son to the tune of Sissy's sobs, I held out my hands.

"Thy wife needs to say goodbye, too," I murmured.

He glared at me, but handed over the now-silent bundle.

Sissy's face running with tears, she extended the girl twin to him. "Your daughter needs you, husband."

Irvin turned away instead, his brow in his hand. Each person had his own way of expressing sorrow, and I had seen couples driven apart permanently by a child's death. Annie took the daughter while I handed the boy's body to Sissy. The black-garbed priest blew into the room in a flurry but was perfunctory in his ministering. He offered his condolences, said a short prayer in Latin over the baby, and touched his forehead with oil. The smell of alcohol on the priest's breath was a jarring touch to the grief in the room. When he left abruptly after he was finished, I didn't mind.

Annie looked exhausted and sad. She'd never seen a baby die shortly after its birth. As for me, I knew by now I would feel the impact on my own emotions later. As a midwife, I couldn't allow my own grief to interfere with caring for my clients, who had a much greater need. Such sad deaths were not frequent but did happen in our practice. Still, I had to remind myself my competent apprentice was only eighteen. Annie hadn't had my years of experience. I expected she was famished, as well. My own stomach was distinctly empty.

Aoife had come back upstairs when she heard Sissy's wails and hovered like the mother hen she was. Irvin finally left the room. I held my breath a moment, hoping he wasn't going to his own room to discover his possession missing, but the thud of his heavy steps diminished as he made his way down the stairs.

"I'd like thee to try nursing thy daughter again before we leave,"

I said to Sissy. I took the boy and laid him gently on the bureau, lifting the blanket up over his face. I didn't know what arrangements they would make for burial, but suspected Sissy would want to bring his body home to her mother and sisters if she could.

Annie handed Sissy the little girl, who now squirmed and started to cry. I gave Sissy several pointers on how to position herself and the infant, and how to make sure the little mouth opened wide enough and latched on adequately to be able to take nourishment without hurting her mother.

Sissy looked up in wonder. "She's got a strong suck for such a tiny thing." She sniffed away a last—for now—tear.

"Excellent," I said. "She just needed a little time."

Aoife beamed from the corner where she sat, the rocker creaking with each back and forth. "Good. My babes did, too."

"The first milk is a thin substance full of many nutrients. It's called colostrum." I nodded encouragingly. "Thy true milk will descend in a day or two." I watched as the baby nursed and then closed her eyes. "Blow gently on her face to wake her. She'll need to eat frequently to gain weight, and thee should be sure to feed her on both sides every time."

We stayed until the baby was sated from suckling both breasts. "We'll be going, now," I said. "Aoife, please make sure Sissy always has fresh water to hand, and eats plentifully of fresh vegetables, meats, and milk."

"You're eating for you and your baby in a different way now." Annie smiled at Sissy. "Shall we say a Hail Mary together?"

Sissy nodded, and the two young women recited their prayer, with Aoife chiming in from her rocker.

"Rose, I think I'll stay on a little longer," Annie said.

"As thee wishes. Aoife will bring thee something to eat, if I'm not mistaken."

The cook stood. "Right away. I'll walk yeh down, Miss Carroll."

I touched the baby girl's cheek. "What will thee name her?" I asked Sissy.

Sissy gazed at me with steel in her eyes. "I will name her Irvina for her father. Perhaps having his name will help him to love her."

I gave a single nod. "I think thee is a wise young woman. Keep

Irvina close beside thee in the bed, and feed her whenever she wakes. I shall return tomorrow to visit thee and the baby." First Day notwithstanding, I often had work that called me on the Lord's day of rest. I moved to the bureau where Irvina's twin lay. He would never play with her, make up a secret language together, quibble over toys, nor be her constant companion and best friend as twins so often were, even boy-girl sets. I touched his cheek and sent up a prayer his death wouldn't irrevocably split this new family.

Once downstairs, I told Aoife I wanted to say goodbye to Irvin, and that I'd meet her in the kitchen. This time I knocked on the study door so I wouldn't further raise his ire. He pulled open the door before Aoife even reached the kitchen.

"What do you want?" His eyes looked haunted, but his sorrow didn't prevent him from glaring at me.

"I wanted to say good night. I'll be back tomorrow to see how Sissy and the baby are doing."

"You'll do no such thing. I've a mind to bring a lawsuit against you for killing my son. I don't ever want to see you again, you, you, midwife." He spat out the word like it was an obscene thing.

I took a deep breath and let it out before speaking. "Thee is grieving and I understand."

"How could you understand? I've wanted a son with all my heart for decades. I told my wife to go to the hospital to deliver the babies, especially after she learned there were two. Use a real doctor, not some fly-by-night charlatan like you. But would she listen to me? No. And now my boy is dead." He gripped my shoulders. "Dead! How are you going to explain his death, Miss Carroll?"

I removed his hands and took a step back. "The baby wouldn't have survived anywhere, believe me. I am deeply sorry for thy loss." I drew myself up tall and strong. "But I must insist on visiting Sissy tomorrow. Many things can still go wrong with her health after childbirth. She is my responsibility."

"You're not exactly a responsible lady, in my opinion," he scoffed. He glanced behind me. "I'll be going out, Mrs. O'Malley. And I don't know when I'll be back." He pushed past both of us. A moment later the door slammed, shaking the house.

FORTY-SEVEN

I AWOKE WITH THE HEAVY DARK FEELING I am invariably seized with in the aftermath of a tragic birthing outcome. I could only imagine Sissy's own awakening, although she at least had a living baby to delight in and grow to know, a tiny thing who very much needed her. My other mothers who had lost newborns had only the one with no one to replace him or her in the days after the demise. Aoife had promised to keep a careful watch on Sissy until I returned to help her with nursing, if need be.

Still, I had business to conduct this morning before Meeting for Worship. Conveying a small parcel to Kevin Donovan was foremost, and I also wanted to see how Rosalie was faring. I would visit Sissy and baby Irvina this afternoon. With any luck, Irvin would have gone out again so I wouldn't have to encounter him.

I gazed at the paper-wrapped package Aoife had slipped me last night after Irvin had stormed out. She'd tied it in string and it looked for all the world from the outside like a purchase of buttons or tobacco. I had slipped it into my satchel, then sat down for soup and pie before trudging home. Now it lay on my desk. Was it poison? Was it the weapon that dispatched Mayme Settle to her final resting place? If so, this case might be finally solved.

Outside the day glowered, too. Rain clouds had blown in as I slept and the ground under the young swamp oak out front was dark with fresh rain. I dragged myself out of bed, washed up, and dressed. Once I opened my door, aromas of meat and coffee drew me to the kitchen as if I were being pulled by a rope of delectable fragrance.

In the kitchen, by some miracle, Frederick had started the fire in the stove and was stirring a pot of porridge. Sausages sizzled in the skillet and a bowl of strawberries had been washed and trimmed. Had some alien being descended from another planet and occupied the body of my brother-in-law? Frederick never prepared food.

"Good morning, brother."

"'Morning, Rose. Coffee's ready."

I thanked him and poured myself a cup. "Where are the children?"

"Upstairs planning a play they want to put on. Except for Luke, who's sleeping, of course."

I smiled. The ability of teenaged Luke to sleep deep and long was legendary in the family. I helped myself to strawberries and porridge. "May I?" I pointed to the sausages.

"Of course."

I added one to my plate, then sat with my breakfast. The morning's newspaper was open and I idly perused it as I ate. My eyes widened when I glanced at the section advertising employment. One read, "Lady computers wanted for Professor Pickering's group at Harvard College Observatory. Applicants must have completed high school and have good eyesight and an aptitude for numbers." This must be where Nalia worked. When I read what the job paid, though, I was astonished. It was a pitifully low number for such a skilled occupation. My breakfast cooled as I thought. Jeanette had said Nalia's father had died leaving debts, and her maid had said she was paid only a pittance. Nalia had a house to maintain. Where was she getting her money? And how often did she work in Cambridge? Going back and forth must be terribly onerous, and was the reason Jeanette's husband stayed near Harvard during the week. Maybe Nalia lied about being in the Pickering observatory, or perhaps she was formerly employed there and had been fired for not arriving on time.

A sausage popped on the stove and Frederick swore softly, rubbing his hand. I didn't think I'd ever heard him utter such a word, but the children were nearly always nearby, which might explain it.

I gazed at his back, putting aside my thoughts. "Frederick, I don't believe I told thee David and I have finally been able to make a plan for our wedding. It will be in early Ninth Month."

He turned. "Thee must be very happy about having a date certain."

"Indeed I am."

"And I might share that Winnie has accepted my proposal to wed." Frederick's cheeks pinkened. "Not quite sure what she sees in me, but I am grateful to have the company of a fine woman like her."

"I'm delighted to hear this news."

He cleared his throat. "Thee knows no one can replace Harriet."

"Of course. I do not judge thee, Frederick, and I know the children love Winnie. I will return the use of thy parlor to thee as soon as I become David's wife. I was most grateful for thy offer to me after Harriet died, and I have greatly enjoyed being part of thy family in this home."

He turned back to the stove and pushed around the sausages before looking at me again. "I owe thee an apology. I have acted badly in the past. My dear betrothed has helped me see the error of my ways. I'm afraid thee has borne the brunt of many of my ill tempers."

Another wonder atop the first. "I accept thy apology. Thy life has not been easy these few years, I know."

"Thee is correct."

"If I might," I continued, "I think it would be good to also apologize to thy children, as Way opens. I am an adult. I have ways of dealing with thy actions. They are innocents who have been hurt and bewildered at times by thy behavior."

He whirled. "I've already done it," he snapped.

Ah. So perhaps this new Frederick wouldn't last. How quickly he'd reverted to his normal way of being.

He turned back to the stove, taking in a deep breath and letting it out before speaking. "I have taken each child aside and had a quiet conversation about my bad moods, and have spoken with Faith, as well. The apologies have been made. I have also been eldered by my younger daughter about the term 'moron,' for which I apparently have thee to thank."

I concealed my smile as I stood and carried my dishes to the sink. I rinsed them before going to stand next to Frederick. We had never made a practice of embracing, unlike my cuddling habits with the children, so I extended my hand. "Peace between us, Frederick."

He took my hand and covered it with his other hand, as well. "Peace between us." He made eye contact for a brief moment, then looked away.

At a rapping on the side door, Frederick dropped my hand and called, "Come in."

Winnie pushed open the door. "Good morning, dear. Hello,

Rose." Her bright blue eyes shone in her barely lined face, and her black hair was a bit mussed under a summer boater. She was also a Friend, but had told me she didn't care for bonnets, and that was that.

Maybe Winnie was the impetus for the nice breakfast. I approved. "Good morning to thee." I smiled at her. "I want to say how pleased I am that thee and Frederick will join in marriage." I held out both hands. "I'll be out of thy parlor in early Ninth Month, too. David and I have a date firm, at last."

She took my hands and squeezed. "I'm so happy for thee, Rose. I have some good news of another sort, too." She dropped my hands and removed her hat. "Several friends and I have decided to continue Mayme's knitting project for the little babies at the Alms Farm, and to sponsor other of her good works, as well. We're calling it the Mayme Settle Benevolent Society."

"That's splendid. I'm sure her daughter Helen will be happy to hear about it."

"I have already written to let her know," Winnie said.

"Well, I'm off on an errand. I'll see thee both and the children at Meeting for Worship. Thank thee for the breakfast, Frederick."

"Don't mention it." His voice grew gruff, as if all this honest talk of feelings and making amends had unsettled him.

FORTY-EIGHT

I WANTED TO DELIVER the tin to the police, but I also needed to see how Rosalie was faring, and the Donovan home was in the opposite direction from the police station. I slid the wrapped tin into my pocket, not needing to bring my satchel, and donned bonnet and the oiled rain cloak David had purchased for me.

After I stood at Kevin and Emmaline's front door on Boardman Street for five minutes knocking and calling out, I gave up. They were clearly not at home. I prayed Rosalie was not so ill she'd had to be taken to the hospital. Maybe Kevin had been called into the station to pursue a murderer and Emmaline had taken the children to her mother's. But no, Emmaline had said her mother was away. Frowning, I reversed my steps and walked back to Market Square and along Friend Street to the police station.

As I started up the steps, a tall angular woman in her thirties pushed out through the door. Her eyes were red in a narrow face. She wore a black dress cut in a simple style and a black bowler atop her dark hair.

There was a trace of the familiar in her visage. I greeted her. "My name is Rose Carroll." I took a guess. "Would thee be Mayme and Merton's daughter?"

She halted, peering at me. "Yes, I'm Helen Settle. How in tarnation did you know that, Miss Carroll?"

"Thy face resembles thy father's." I hoped that wasn't a rude thing to say to a woman, and if I'd known Mayme when she was younger and perhaps less full of figure I might have seen more similarity with her and her daughter. "May I offer my sympathies on the passing of thy mother?"

"Thank you." She sniffed. "You knew them, I take it?"

"Not well, but I was at their home the night Mayme died, in fact, at a knitting circle thy mother led."

"Not many seem to be grieving for her."

"That's a pity." I clasped my hands in front of me. Merton hadn't seemed to grieve at all for his wife, alas.

191

"My mother was a difficult woman, as you might know. But she was still my mother, and didn't deserve to be—" She brought her hand to her mouth as her shoulders shook. After she regained control, she said, "Forgive me. It's all so hard to fathom."

"There is nothing to forgive." I reached out and touched her arm. "Thee is devastated and rightly so."

"I came as soon as I could, but I had to administer final exams. I teach at Smith College and it's end of term." She blew out a long, sad breath. "My father appears to be helpless in the face of this tragedy, so it's up to me to make all the arrangements."

"Such as the funeral?"

"Yes," Helen said. "And talking with the police, I'm afraid." She jutted her head forward. "Do you work with them? Why are you here on a Sunday morning?"

I laughed lightly. "I have a small bit of business with the detective, but no, I do not work for the police."

"I see."

"Thee is staying at the family home, I assume."

"No. I'm with a friend while I'm here." She cleared her throat. "It's, uh, more comfortable there." She didn't meet my gaze.

More comfortable than the big well-appointed home she'd grown up in? Perhaps she was estranged from her father, too.

"Well, I'd best be off," she said. "A pleasure to meet you, Miss Carroll. You're a Quaker, I gather."

"Yes. I'm pleased to have met thee, as well." I extended my hand. "I wish it had been under happier circumstances."

Helen shook hands with a firm grip. "You aren't alone in that wish." She trudged down the steps and away toward town.

I entered the station and, to my surprise, Sean sat on a high stool at the front desk. He wore a too-large patrolman's hat. His face split in a big grin when he saw me.

"Miss Rose!"

"Hello, Sean. Is thee now employed by the Amesbury Police Department?"

An officer of a more appropriate age sat at the desk behind Sean. He waved at me. "I'm here if need be."

I nodded at the officer and said to Sean, "I was at thy house but no one seemed to be at home. How is thy sister faring?"

His expression sobered. "She's not very well. She and Mummy had to go to the Anna Jaques Hospital."

My heart sank. "Oh, my. I am indeed sorry to hear this. They went yesterday?"

"Yes. They called your doctor friend, Mr. Dodge, and after he examined her he took them himself in his carriage. So I'm here working with Papa."

"I'm sure they will help her at the hospital, Sean. Thee shouldn't worry, all right?"

"Very well." The boy spoke so softly I could barely hear him.

"Now, I must speak with thy father. May I go to his office?" This question I directed to the man behind Sean, who had now put his feet up on his desk.

"Go ahead on back." The officer gestured toward the door to the back. "The chief ain't here and it's Sunday morning."

"I thank thee. I'll see thee before I leave, Sean."

He saluted in the most adorable fashion. He beckoned me closer. "Papa's quite concerned about Rosalie."

I nodded. "I'll see if I can help in any way." I shed my rain cloak and hung it on a hook, then made my way through the door until I stood in the open doorway of Kevin's office. He stood backlit at the window, gazing out with his hands clasped behind his back. I knocked on the jamb.

"Kevin?"

He turned. "Ah, Miss Rose. Top o' the morning to you." His words were jovial. His tone was anything but, and the skin below his eyes looked bruised from worry and lack of sleep.

"Sean told me Rosalie had to go to the hospital. What a pity. Thee and Emmaline weren't able to reduce her fever?"

"No. But your Mr. Dodge is a fine fellow, he is. Took the wife and the babe in his own carriage and wouldn't accept a red cent in payment."

My throat thickened in sudden emotion. "He is indeed a fine man. Did he say if they might offer a treatment for the fever?"

"He seemed to think they would. Something to do with willow bark, perhaps."

"Yes. It contains a substance that can help lower fevers." David must have decided on an appropriate dose for an infant and perhaps used a buffering agent, as well. "Has thee had word this morning yet?"

"Emmaline left a message here that the nurses are offering a measure of hope for our baby."

"I'm glad to hear it. May I sit?'

"Of course. Forgive my lack of manners."

I perched on the chair facing his desk while he sat on the other side. "Have there been any developments in Mayme's murder?"

"Not much at all, more's the pity."

"Kevin, my bicycle was stolen from Powow Street yesterday in the early afternoon. A neighbor, a Ted Jennings, said he saw two men drive up in a runabout. One jumped down and rode off on the bike."

"Blatant criminals!"

"Exactly," I agreed. "And their descriptions matched Merton and Adoniram."

He cocked his head. "I don't quite fathom why they would make off with your metal steed."

I thought it was quite easy to fathom but kept my thought silent. "How about the Polish man who was hit in the Point Shore area? Has he survived?"

"So far he is clinging to life but isn't awake to talk to anyone about the assault." He drummed his fingers on the desk, his brow furrowed. He rubbed at his carrot-colored hair with his other hand.

"The birth I attended was at the Barclay home," I said.

"Oh?"

"Yes. And Sissy Barclay revealed something quite interesting during the throes of her labor." I pulled out the package and set it on the desk. "She said she discovered the tin in this package in her husband's dresser drawer. It's a powder labeled *Lily of the Valley*."

He peered at it. "Most likely belonging to Miss Nalia Bowerman." Kevin checked a piece of paper on his desk. "I found what you related in your note yesterday most interesting. I investigated her a bit. She is an astronomer, as you said someone told you. She and Mr. Barclay are, in fact, cousins of a sort, but it's a distant relationship, second or third cousins, something along those lines."

"Interesting. Irvin and Mayme were cousins, too. Does that make Nalia related to Mayme?"

"No. Her connection is through Barclay's father's side, and Mrs. Settle was his aunt's daughter."

"Does Nalia have any criminal background?" I asked.

"Now you mention it, she does. She was caught trying to lift a stylish topper from Forbes Haberdashery in Boston."

"Stealing seems odd, doesn't it? She's very well dressed, so she must have money from her family. It's not from her job. Only this morning I glimpsed an advertisement for the Harvard group I believe she works in."

"She's one of Pickering's women, I believe," Kevin said.

"Exactly. The pay is ridiculously low, though. And I also heard her late father left debts when he died. Is thee sure she is still employed there? It's quite the trip from Amesbury to Cambridge and back."

He nodded slowly. "Good point. I'll investigate that further. Either way, perhaps Miss Bowerman thought she had to steal the hat to maintain her style. You ladies operate in strange and unknowable ways. Including you, Miss Rose, purloining this package from a private home."

I winced. "I thought it could be important evidence. Does that justify my thievery?"

"We shall see." He chuckled as he cut the string on the package with a penknife and tore off the paper. "Lily of the Valley, you say? Some kind of ladies' dusting powder, I assume." He peered at the powder within, then wet his index finger and touched it.

His hand was halfway to his mouth when I gestured for him to stop. "Don't taste it!"

"Why in blazes not?"

"Mayme Settle was poisoned, correct? What if this is the poison?"

"Lily of the valley is a plant growing everywhere. You think it's poisonous?" He took out a handkerchief and wiped off his finger.

"I don't know. But Irvin Barclay is a serious gardener, as is Adoniram Riley. And Adoniram studied plant poisons at Harvard, as I relayed to thee. It might very well be the toxin we are looking for."

Kevin's eyes widened. "Very interesting. I'll send it along to our chemist. Do you think Barclay could have gotten the poison from Riley? That they're in cahoots?"

"That would seem to be an odd pairing, don't you think?"

"Odder things have happened." He wagged his head. "This case confounds me, Miss Rose. I don't mind admitting it to you. Everyone is lying, but who is lying because he's a killer, and who because he has other secrets?"

FORTY-NINE

TWENTY MINUTES INTO MEETING FOR WORSHIP and my head was exploding. I had sought the peaceful respite of our unprogrammed Meeting, praying for a soothing of my week's concerns. Some First Days the worship ended up completely silent, allowing, as John had written, the outside world to fall away and leave us God alone. Today? Not so much.

A merchant with a self-satisfied air had been droning on for five minutes about justice and injustice. I stopped listening to his words but I couldn't escape hearing his abrasive voice. He finally ceased and sat, causing the pew to give off a mighty creak. I enjoyed only two minutes of blessed silence before another Friend stood. She clasped her hands in front of her and closed her eyes, then proceeded to quote a long Bible verse about recognizing the immigrant as citizen. When she was done, the next message arose not three minutes later. And the morning proceeded thusly. A few of the spoken ministries were brief and uplifting, but many more were long-winded and dire. Not all First Days were like this. Some weeks worship remained completely free of messages. Alas, not this day.

It was all I could manage to stay seated and not leave. At last one of the elders signaled the end of the Meeting by initiating the handshake of friendship. I filed out amid the two hundred other members and made my way to where John Whittier stood on the front lawn.

"We had quite a busy worship, did we not, Rose?" John now asked me, his dark eyes twinkling, both hands resting on the silver-tipped cane in front of him.

"I daresay I might have more gainfully communed with God by sitting alone by the shores of Lake Gardner."

"God also shows Himself through the shared messages, thee knows this." He kept his chiding gentle.

"Yes, I know, of course." I kept my sigh to myself.

"I expect thee wished for silence so thee could array thy thoughts about Mayme Settle's passing in some more harmonious pattern."

I blinked. He knew me too well. "It's true. The current investigation is plaguing me."

"Not in any physical way, I hope. Thee isn't venturing into dangerous situations?"

"Not if I can help it. It does appear Merton Settle is originally Polish, although what his native country has to do with the case I am not certain." I turned my back on other Friends straggling out of the simple white building or talking in small groups on the grass before dispersing for home. I kept my voice low. "I told Kevin Donovan what you shared about Adoniram's history with poisonous plants, and he's following up the lead."

"I have faith that, with God's guidance, thee and the good detective will discern the truth, as Way opens."

My faith didn't feel so firm on the matter right now.

"I did learn from the esteemed Judge Cate that Mayme Settle's funeral is to be held tomorrow morning," John said. "I thought thee might be interested to know about it."

"I am, very much. I met the daughter this morning. She said she was handling the arrangements. Where will the service take place?"

"At Saint Paul's, the Episcopal church on Main Street."

"The one with the red door. I thank thee for this news." I frowned. "John, has thee heard of a Nalia Bowerman? A lady astronomer?"

"Why, yes, I have had occasion to meet her. She studied with Friend Maria Mitchell, who introduced me to Nalia. Does thee know her?"

"Not exactly, although I have met her. She might have a connection to the case, though."

"By way of committing a criminal deed?"

"Maybe."

He stroked his beard thoughtfully. "It's possible someone mentioned her as having come under suspicion for some unlawful act, but I can't recall which or how I know this. I'll think upon it, Rose."

"Was it the theft of a hat in Boston?"

"I can't recall at the moment."

"Please send word if thee remembers. Or better yet, let Kevin know."

"Thee has my word. Now I must make my way homeward for First Day dinner. Mrs. Cate doesn't approve when I arrive tardy to the table."

We said our goodbyes. I was unsettled and stood for a moment. The Baileys would be having their own First Day dinner at one o'clock, at which I was expected. Winnie and Mark were preparing the meal together. What a blessing Frederick was now cooking, too, to provide a positive example for his sons. At least it would be a blessing if he continued. His reversal in mood seemed rather too dramatic to trust.

I'd invited David to dine with us, but he was occupied elsewhere. We'd spoken briefly this morning by telephone and I'd mentioned that the twin births had taken place. I hadn't gone into the details of the labor or the outcomes on the telephone, of course. He'd promised to fetch me for a drive later this afternoon, so I could tell him then. I needed to visit Sissy and the baby sometime soon, but I didn't want to go without my satchel in case there were supplies I needed. It wasn't yet midday. I made a quick decision. I had time to dart home to grab my bag and then proceed on to the Barclay home. An invisible string tugged me toward the Settle home, but I mentally cut it. I wasn't about to go there alone, and didn't have a reason in the world to pay either Merton or Adoniram a visit.

FIFTY

FIFTEEN MINUTES LATER I knocked on the kitchen door of the Barclay home, satchel in hand. Trepidation filled me at the prospect of encountering Irvin. I hadn't let fear stop me from caring for any of my mothers before, however, and I wouldn't let it stop me now. Aoife welcomed me in but held a finger to her lips.

"Mr. Barclay's in a bad way. I'd advise yeh to keep yer voice down, then."

I grimaced. "Bad sad or bad angry?" I asked in a soft voice. My stomach growled at the scents of roasted meat with fried onions and potatoes, but I ignored it.

"The second, but coming from the first, no doubt. He's been right raging about, he has."

"I'm sorry to hear it. I hope he has not directed his rage at Sissy or the baby."

"I don't think so."

"How are the two doing?" I asked.

"Mrs. Barclay has the weepies, she does, but she's feeding the little girl and keeping her close by. She ate breakfast earlier, and just finished her dinner in her room with that good of an appetite. I think they'll both be fine."

"I'm glad to hear it. I'll go up and take a look for myself in a moment. Tell me, what have they done with the body of the twin who didn't survive?"

She rolled her eyes. "Mr. Barclay laid him out in the parlor for all the world like he's a dead prince."

I brought my hand to my mouth. "Oh, my. He can't leave the body there long. It's Sixth Month and will only be growing warmer. They need to get him buried."

"I told the mister as much but he was having none of it." She set her fists on her hips. "What can the man be thinking?"

"I'm sure he doesn't want to let his son go. And somehow I doubt Sissy has much sway over his decisions, although she certainly put her foot down about having the priest come."

"She did, and I was proud of her for doing it."

"Is Irvin in his study?" I glanced at the door to the hall.

The cook nodded. "Either there or watching over the sainted corpse. But there's a back stair, if yer after wanting to go up unseen." She pointed to a door in the corner of the kitchen.

"Back stairs will suit my needs perfectly. I'll be back down in a little while." I trod the steps as lightly as I could and eased into the hallway, then made my way quietly to Sissy's room.

She lay on her side with tiny Irvina sleeping beside her. The room was tidy and the window was open a few inches, allowing in a portion of fresh air. I suspected Aoife's motherly hand.

"Hello, Rose," Sissy murmured, half asleep herself.

"Good afternoon, Sissy." I moved to her side and touched the baby's forehead. She was warm but not hot and was breathing regularly and comfortably. I perched on the edge of the bed. "How is thee feeling?"

"I'm sore down there, and I can't seem to stop tears from coming out of my eyes." Her eyes were red and moist.

I nodded but let her continue.

"This little girl, though? She's a hundred percent sweet. I can't even believe how much love fills me when I look at her. And she's a good nursling."

"I am happy and satisfied to hear this. Of course thee is sad about her twin. Thee is barely a mother and thee has already lost a child. Thee will never forget him."

She swiped at her eyes and sniffed. "No, I won't. My husband is worrying me, though. He insisted on taking our son's tiny body downstairs and has barely been back." She pushed her lips out in pity, gazing at her daughter. "And he hasn't held his namesake once. Will his actions change, Rose?"

"I can't say. I hope so. He is clearly grieving quite deeply and needs to be left to do so. May I examine the baby?"

"Of course." She pushed herself up to sitting and watched as I took the baby into my lap and pulled up her little gown.

Irvina awoke but didn't cry, instead regarding me with the deep calm eyes of a newborn.

"My older sister sewed the nightie for my baby, and several other little garments." Sissy smiled sadly. "I wish she were here."

"Has thee sent for her?"

"No. I wanted to but Mr. Barclay didn't allow it."

I liked Irvin Barclay less with each new thing I learned about his overly controlling behavior. "When thy daughter grows a bit stronger, thee can pay thy family a nice long visit." I laid my hand lightly on the baby's chest and felt her heart, which had a strong beat. Her cord stump was clean and looked normal. Her reflexes were good, too. I covered her again and laid her to the side.

After I'd examined Sissy, satisfied her womb was firming up and returning to normal, I returned the baby to her arms. "Thee is a first-time mother. Does thee have questions for me?"

She frowned. "How soon can I go out? We have to hold a funeral mass for my son."

I thought for a moment. "He is going to need to be buried soon. Normally I would not recommend venturing out in public for several weeks until thee has thy strength back. A carriage ride could be uncomfortable and jolting until then. But I understand thee must be in church for this rite. As long as thee promises to go straight there and come directly home after the burial, I can't see a problem."

A shadow slid off her face. "Oh, good. I'll make the arrangements with Father Nilan." She lifted her chin. "And Mr. Barclay can come or not come, but he's not stopping me. I'll have Mrs. O'Malley drive me if he's not willing."

I loved what motherhood had done for this young woman's backbone. "Thee is lucky to have Aoife."

She nodded several times in agreement. "I know. She's been taking good care of me. She's a real motherly sort."

I wanted to ask her about Nalia but I didn't want to upset her. On the other hand, Nalia seemed to have gotten my address from Sissy, so maybe talking about my address was the way to ease into it. "Sissy, I didn't mention this last night, but a woman named Nalia Bowerman paid me a visit yesterday morning. She said she is thy husband's cousin, and that thee gave her my home address."

"Oh, her. She is my husband's distant cousin, but she's a bit of a pest, isn't she? She's always calling, bothering Irvin for something or other. She wouldn't tell me why she wanted to see you, but I thought it wouldn't hurt."

Interesting. Sissy didn't seem to have a clue Nalia and Irvin might be up to more than what cousins normally did.

"She actually said Irvin didn't want me to care for thy pregnancy," I said. "It was rather in the nature of a warning or a threat."

"Too late for that now, isn't it?" She laughed softly. "Don't worry, she's harmless."

I certainly hoped so. I stood. "I'm glad to hear it. I'll be going now. Summon me if there are any changes, if thee starts bleeding copiously, if thee has questions Aoife can't answer."

"I will. And thank you, Rose. I couldn't have done any of this without you." Her eyes widened. "Oh! I need to pay you. There, in the drawer to my dressing table, you'll find an embroidered bag. It has my secret cache of coins." She smiled and hunched her shoulders as if delighted at sharing her secret.

I extracted my few dollars. "I thank thee." I made my way out and back down the maid's stairs. I pushed open the door to the kitchen and instantly regretted the move. Irvin was pacing back and forth in the empty kitchen. He whirled when he heard the door. I froze.

"You!" He advanced on me. "You . . . you thief, you." He shook an index finger in my face.

I took a step back and clutched my satchel in front of me for protection. "I don't know what thee means." Where was Aoife?

"Going through my belongings. Stealing from my personal possessions."

The tin. "I did not go through thy things, I can assure thee." I lifted my chin.

"If that wasn't bad enough, you let my son die, and now you're trespassing in my home. I forbade you from returning."

"Regarding thy son, I told thee last night. He was simply too small and weak to live. No one short of God could have made it happen. I also informed thee I would not shirk my responsibility toward thy wife and daughter."

His mouth turned down in a terrible glare. "I'm about to telephone the police but first I think I'll wring your Quaker neck." He stretched his meaty hands toward me.

FIFTY-ONE

"AOIFE," I yelled even as I raised my satchel.

The cook pushed through the swinging door from the hall. "Mr. Barclay! What would yeh be after, now?" She rushed forward, grabbing an iron skillet from the counter as she came. She laid a hand on his shoulder. "Don't yeh dare be hurting the midwife. She's only doing her job, and taking better care of yer wife and wee babe than yeh are."

He twisted toward her as if to wring her neck, instead.

She raised the heavy pan in air. "Don't yeh even dare."

He turned his glare on her. But he stopped. After a moment he dropped his hands. "Women," he snarled. "And you," he added, looking back at me. "I mean it. You are never to set foot in this house again." He stomped past Aoife and pushed into the hall, leaving the door whapping behind him.

I brought my hand to my neck and blew out a breath. "I thank thee for rescuing me."

"I'm that glad yeh called for me. I was just dusting in the hall." She set the skillet down and shook her head. "What was he going on about, then?"

"I think he's noticed the tin was missing," I whispered.

"Ah." She nodded once, also whispering. "The sign of a guilty man, all upset and after blaming others about losing something he shouldn't ought to be owning in the first place."

"I expect so. At least Sissy and the baby are well. Thee is doing a good job of caring for them."

The invariably cheery woman lifted the corner of her apron to wipe a tear from her eye. "She needs a mama right about now, and since my darlings are all grown and gone, I like to help when I can."

"She wants to have a mass for the boy. I gave her leave to go out, but she isn't sure her husband will take her. Thee can transport her, if necessary?"

She made a *pshing* sound. "Of course." She lowered her voice to a murmur. "That woman came a-callin' this morning, she did. Right here to the house, if yeh can believe it. I don't know how she dares."

"Nalia Bowerman?" My eyes went wide.

"The very one, all tarted up she was, too, in her fancy green dress. Said she wanted to 'pay her respects to her cousin in the matter of the deceased child.'" Aoife pronounced the words in a mocking tone.

"Interesting. I don't suppose thee overheard any of their conversation."

"Nay, not that I didn't try." She winked. "They were speaking in the parlor with the boy's body, but they closed the door and talked soft like."

A clock somewhere in the house donged once. "Oh, my," I said. "I have to get home for dinner. Sissy knows how to reach me should she need me. I've enjoyed getting to know thee a bit, Aoife. I hope to see thee again." I smiled and held out my hand.

She shook it heartily. "And I you, Miss Carroll."

"Since I am banned from the premises, Sissy should pay me a visit with the baby in two weeks' time. Will thee let her know?"

"Of course. I'll bring her meself. And we'll send yeh a message about when the mass is to be, in case yeh want to come sit silently amidst our fancy church trappings and music. I know yeh Quakers aren't much for the gab in yer own church."

I laughed. "Indeed we aren't." Not usually, anyway. Yet as I walked the few blocks home, I wished I knew what kind of gab the brazen Nalia had exchanged with Irvin during her visit.

FIFTY-TWO

I SAT OPPOSITE ORPHA in her rocking chair at three that afternoon. I'd excused myself after the family's dinner dishes were done, feeling the need to talk through Sissy's births with my mentor. And perhaps discuss Mayme Settle's murder, too. My trek over here had seemed overly long. I needed to regain my bicycle and soon.

Orpha regarded me, wizened hands folded in her lap. "I see you're still troubled, dear Rose, or perhaps troubled anew." She rocked gently.

"Thee knows me too well. I am once again confronted by the caprices of our lives. The first matter is that Sissy Barclay's babies were born last night."

"So soon?"

"At least six weeks premature, possibly up to eight. The first baby, a girl, was vertex. She came out without an overly long ordeal and, while small, seems to be thriving. The second was a frank breech and didn't make his appearance for nearly an hour after his sister. He was very poorly in the first minutes, but I rubbed life into him. To no avail, as it turned out." I pressed my eyes shut against sudden hot tears.

Orpha rocked, waiting. She had been in my shoes many times, suffering a delayed reaction to a trauma.

I sniffed and wiped away the tears. "His breathing was not strong even from the beginning, and he was smaller than his sister. He died less than two hours later in his father's arms."

"May God rest his innocent soul."

"Sissy called for the priest, Father Nilan, but I tell thee, the man was intoxicated. The only solace he provided was what Sissy took from her child receiving the ritual blessing." I rocked in time with Orpha even though I sat in a stationary chair. The movement was oddly comforting.

"How fares the mother?" Orpha asked.

"She seems to have grown a spine with motherhood. She stood up to her bullying husband about the priest, and is determined to hold a mass for the little boy. Irvin forbade her from having her mother or sisters with her for the birth, but I am sure she will take her daughter for a good long visit with her family when she's up for the journey north to Portland."

She gave a soft laugh. "I meant to ask how Mrs. Barclay is doing physically."

I smiled at my mistake. "She's doing well. She's twenty and in good health. Old enough to endure the labor and birth, young enough to recover easily." I frowned. "The father, on the other hand, seems obsessed with his son's body. He has laid him out downstairs and is mourning deeply."

"As any first-time parent would, of course."

"Yes. Also, he is older and Sissy told me he has wanted children for many years. Or, rather, a son. He's paid no attention to his living child, though. His daughter, whom Sissy named Irvina in his honor."

"More's the pity." Orpha made a tsking sound. "These men and their obsession with male heirs. The couple probably hasn't made burial plans yet, but they'll need to."

"I know. On top of everything, Irvin told me never to come back to the house. He said I am responsible for the baby's death. In fact, he told me not to return last night, but I paid my postpartum visit this morning regardless. Unfortunately I encountered him in the kitchen after I left Sissy and he nearly attacked me. The cook saved me by threatening him with a heavy skillet."

"Oh, my, Rose. Such violence."

"I know. It was quite the shock."

"This cook seems a brave woman, indeed."

"Very much. And a caring one, too. She's stepped into the role of mother for Sissy, benefiting both of them."

"Mr. Barclay shouldn't be coming after you, though. Man ought to be ashamed of himself." Orpha rocked in silence for a long minute as she regarded me. "Something still plagues your soul, and this old lady imagines it's the business of the murder."

"It is. Kevin has not made an arrest. The investigation of suspects and events seems to be a tapestry woven from many kinds of thread in the most confounding of patterns."

"You spoke before of Mrs. Settle's gardener, the one whose

daughter we could not save postpartum. I assume Mr. Riley is one of those threads?"

"He is."

"I now remember an unusual conversation I witnessed when I returned to assess the baby boy's health the day after his birth four years ago." She laughed in her throaty way. "Perhaps not unusual so much as unsettling. Mrs. Settle was leaving the Riley home, that is, the son's, where the birth took place."

"The son who is now raising the little boy as his own."

"The very same, over on Carpenter Street. I was still a ways up the hill and across the road from the house when I saw Mr. Barclay approach the matron. By his stance and expression, he appeared quite self-satisfied. I kept approaching, minding my own business but taking care to listen as closely as I could. When I grew near, he held out an open palm and said to her, 'Pay up or I'll tell the world.'"

"He did?"

She gave an emphatic nod. "As sure as I sit here today."

"He must have learned her son was the father of Alice's baby."

Orpha whistled. "I think they call that blackmail."

"How did Mayme react?"

"I was trying to recall. I believe she scoffed and turned her back. I wonder what became of his threat."

I wondered, too.

FIFTY-THREE

DAVID TURNED ONTO SPARHAWK STREET at a little past four o'clock and walked his mare along the new road that curved from the downtown area to join Highland. He'd fetched me for a ride with the top down on the doctor's buggy, saying only that he wanted to show me something special. The morning's glowering clouds had blown through to allow a sunny, breezy afternoon. Light glinted off Daisy's sleek roan coat.

After we passed the imposing brick church where Father Nilan presided, Daisy clopped on the paving stones down to a small hollow. A stream ran under the road here, a stream I'd nearly crashed into last winter after I was attacked while driving a buggy alone at night.

"It's pretty here, isn't it?" David asked, pulling the horse to a halt.

I nodded. It was, with all the trees in full new leaf and lady slippers blooming in the understory. Except I barely saw it.

"You're preoccupied, Rosie," he went on. "It's the murder case, isn't it?"

"Thee is correct."

"Here's a new thing to think on. The man who was hit? He regained consciousness and it looks like he'll live. I put in a call to Detective Donovan and he's going to pay a visit when he's able."

"I'm so glad the man survived. I had told Kevin he would need to contact Jeanette Papka about translating."

"Yes, he mentioned her."

"I had quite the midday myself." I told him about the tin, and Irvin's rage this morning.

"How dare he attack you!"

"I have to admit he had told me yesterday not to come back."

"But you had midwifing to do and you weren't going to stay away." David covered my right hand with his left.

"Exactly. I didn't tell you that the second twin died shortly after its birth last night. The pair came so early it's a marvel the girl lives and is strong enough to nurse well. And now Irvin blames his only son's death on me."

"It's not your fault. Such is life in our time. It's a sad but true fact. A scientist needs to devise a substance which mimics the lung fluid premature babies are missing."

"And one day someone shall, I have no doubt. It's a good thing Aoife is a big strong woman." I giggled, remembering. "Thee should have seen her hoist her iron skillet in the air against Irvin."

"I wish I had. I'd like to thank her myself for saving you, my sweet."

Matching black geldings pulling a surrey trotted by, filled with a group of young women in summer finery. One of them waved a white-gloved hand.

"Hello, David!" she called out. "Hi, Rose."

He waved back. "Am I ever glad Mother has ceased pressuring me to marry that silly girl. She's sweet, but she thinks of nothing but clothes and parties." He squeezed my hand. "And you're the only woman I have ever wanted to marry."

"And thee the only man for whom I have had those feelings." I smiled. "I want to thank thee for helping Kevin and Emmaline. Has Rosalie's fever come down?"

"I believe she's on the mend." He clucked to Daisy.

We rode up a gentle incline, then turned left at the corner of Whittier Street. He pulled the horse to a halt again. Across the street a new house was nearly complete. It had fish-scale slate shingles on the conical top of the tower, whose cylindrical shape extended all the way to the ground. Several harmonious rooflines and inset panels gave the house an attractive look, and a big sugar maple in the back would shade the structure from the midday sun in summer. It looked like the carpenters had only to finish the wraparound porch and paint the outside. Large windows stood open, and I could see the inside was nearly complete, as well. A gentle wind cooled the air up here.

"Do you like that house?" he asked.

"I do. It's very pretty and well situated. Bertie lives just blocks farther down this street. And the house isn't ostentatiously large. I wonder who is building it." Much building of new homes was going on in this neighborhood, mostly by mill and factory owners and managers, but also by bankers and lawyers.

He didn't speak for a moment, then cleared his throat. "I am," he murmured.

"What?" I whipped my head to my right and stared at him with my mouth open. "Thee is?"

He nodded. His cheeks were pink and his smile tentative. "I hope you don't mind. I wanted to have a fresh new abode to bring you home to."

I laughed out loud. "Mind? Of course I don't mind. I'm simply surprised. I was wondering where we would reside, and hoped very much thee wouldn't expect me to live in thy parents' home." "Under Clarinda's roof" was what I'd been about to say but softened my words in the nick of time. I gazed at the house with a different set of eyes altogether and brought my hand to my mouth at the thought of finally, at last, being able to sleep every night with my love. I sniffed, tears springing up unbidden.

David drew his arm around my shoulders and squeezed. "I hope those are tears of joy. I wasn't able to keep my secret any longer."

I could only nod.

"It has four bedrooms upstairs, so we'll have plenty of space for little ones when they come along, and it has an indoor toilet and bathroom. There's a small maid's room off the kitchen in case you want household help to live in. But we don't have to if you don't care for having someone," he hurried to add.

"We can discern the need as Way opens." The side of the tower under the roof featured four inset panels. Three were decorated with cut-out stars, and one with a crescent moon. "What a delightful touch those are." I pointed. "Were they thy idea?"

"Yes, because you are my moon and my stars." He smiled, no longer looking nervous. "Also, I made sure to specify an office for you on the first floor with a separate entrance on the side. We can order carpets and furniture together this week so the decor is exactly what you prefer."

"David Dodge, I cannot believe my good fortune." I turned and kissed him full on the mouth, not caring that a passing carriage full of matrons stared at us with pursed lips and frowns of disapproval.

FIFTY-FOUR

DAVID HANDED ME DOWN off his buggy in front of the Bailey house and we said our farewells. He'd just climbed back in when Luke trotted up on Star, Frederick's gelding. The horse nickered to Daisy, who whuffed in return and stomped a hoof.

"Hello, David," Luke said. "Aunt Rose, I think I spied thy missing bicycle."

"My purloined bike?" I asked. "Where is it?"

"I was playing ball with some friends in that field on the far side of Lake Gardner, out near E. P. True, the ice dealer. I saw the bicycle half hidden in a copse near the dam on my way back. The western light lit up the metal or I would have missed it."

The copse that was not a stone's throw from the Settle house. "What a blessing. I thank thee, Luke. I must go fetch it immediately. I am quite fatigued from having had to traipse all over town on foot for most of the day."

David frowned. "I wish I could transport you there, my dear, but I am due back at the hospital to conduct evening rounds. We physicians rotate the Sunday evening duty. Tonight it's my responsibility."

"I'll take thee on Star and thee can ride the bike back," Luke offered.

I smiled at my nephew. "Yes, of course I can. It's still an hour until sunset." Thank heavens for the long days of Sixth Month. And for Luke's true sweet nature reemerging instead of his recent sullen moods.

"Very well. Thank you, Luke." David knit his brow again. "But accompany her home, will you?"

I waved my hand in the air. "I'm standing right here. And I don't need an escort. Now off with thee, David." I blew my betrothed a kiss and watched his expression lighten.

He smiled at me, then clucked to Daisy and drove away.

I gazed up at Luke. "Let me run in and don my split skirt. I'll be right out."

"Of course. Star needs a drink of water, anyway."

Not three minutes later I sat behind Luke as we trotted down High Street toward the lake. I rested my hands on his slim waist. How had he gotten so big so fast? He was already taller than me and wasn't anywhere near finished growing. As we clopped over the bridge crossing the Powow River, I marveled at how high the spring rains had made the rushing water. We slanted onto Hayes and passed two houses, one on either side of the road. Then there were no more, only a row of trees and undergrowth, and the shadows slanted long. At the end we rounded onto wide Whitehall Road and I glanced left over my shoulder at the Settle home, shuddering as I did.

We passed two large houses on the right before Luke pulled Star to a halt. We were at the end of a second row of trees planted atop the embankment covering the granite dam now nineteen years old. Luke pointed to the cluster of growth nearest us.

"See? It's right there."

I slid off the horse. Sure enough, my bicycle had been shoved behind a bay laurel shrub under a maple tree.

"Can thee extricate it?" Luke dismounted, too, and waited, holding Star's reins.

"I think so." I elbowed aside the bush, grabbed the leather seat, and tugged. The handlebars hung up on a branch and I had to wrestle out the bike. "There." I brushed dirt off the seat.

"Is it damaged?" Luke asked, peering at the bicycle.

"I don't think so, thank goodness." I swung it around so it faced the road and straightened my bonnet.

"Shall I follow thee? David wanted me to." He gazed at me with a worried look even as his stomach gave off an angry growl.

I laughed. "Thee must be starving by now. Following me is completely unnecessary, dear Luke. Go on ahead. I'll be along as fast as my legs can pump." I smiled at him. "And I thank thee for the ride."

"All right. I'll see thee at home." His appetite was as legendary as his ability to sleep. One wouldn't know it by looking at his beanpole shape, but Luke could consume alarming quantities of food. He rode off.

I was about to mount my own steed when I noticed the

handlebars had become twisted. I managed to straighten them so they were again at right angles to the front wheel. I rode along until I reached Hayes and turned left. I coasted with the slope of the road down toward the river and picked up quite a bit of speed. I'd passed the two houses and was nearly to the narrow bridge when a fox darted out in front of me. I slammed the pedals backward to brake so I didn't hit it. But nothing happened. The pedals spun in reverse. I cried out, trying to swerve, trying to stop.

The fox dashed away. My front wheel hit a rock. My hands lost their grip. The bike crashed into the metalwork of the bridge. I flew off, sliding down the bank. I grabbed at a sapling, praying it would hold. If I fell into the river I would be swept away by its roiling spring current.

The young tree held fast. I worked my hands farther down the sapling's trunk to where it didn't bend. I dug my toes into the dirt and hauled myself up until I sat on flat ground. My breath came fast and noisy. My heart beat like the hooves of a galloping horse.

"Miss, you all right there?" A man with his dinner napkin still tucked into the neck of his shirt towered above me. He extended a meaty hand. "Let me help you up."

I blinked, then took his hand. "I thank thee." I stood but my legs shook. I reached out and took hold of the edge of the bridge.

"I heard your shout and ran out to see what happened." His gaze traveled to the bridge where my bike lay on its side. "That your bicycle?"

I nodded. "The braking mechanism failed and I couldn't stop. Then my wheel hit a stone and I went flying."

He whistled. "Give me a trusty horse any day. These new-fangled contraptions aren't to be trusted and there's no two ways about it."

"It's been quite reliable up to now." But I thought I knew exactly who was responsible for it failing. I dusted off my hands, my fear at drowning turning to anger at Merton and Adoniram, scoundrels both. "Return to thy dinner, kind sir. I'll be walking this machine home."

"You take care of yourself, now. You look like a nice young lady." He returned to the back door of the nearest house.

I glanced down at my skirt and groaned. Nice, maybe, but my

new garment had a tear at the shin and a smear of mud up and down the side where I'd slid. There was nothing to be done about it now. I peered at the bicycle but couldn't see an obvious reason for its failure. I brushed off my hands but did so gently, as the skin was tender from the brush scraping it. I picked up my metal steed and began my trudge home, with a hip that felt bruised and a sore knee, to boot. A member of Friends Meeting was well-known for his tinkering abilities. I'd take the bike to him tomorrow and see if he could put it to rights. Or maybe I'd show it to Kevin first.

I supposed it was possible that the mechanism had come with a flaw that caused the braking not to function. But it had functioned fine up until it was purloined, and I thought it much more likely that two murder suspects had deliberately tampered with the brakes before they'd abandoned the bicycle in the copse. They'd want to ensure that if I found it, I would still be slowed in my investigation. That, or removed from the investigation permanently. And they'd very nearly been successful.

FIFTY-FIVE

THE AIR IN SAINT PAUL'S was scented with incense by the end of Mayme's funeral service the next morning. The church bell outside had finished ringing eleven times and the sanctuary was full of the rustling of silks, the quiet clearing of throats, and murmurs but not weeping. An organist played somber music while the pallbearers, including Merton and Adoniram, took their positions around the white-covered coffin at the front. Adoniram had cleaned up for the occasion, wearing a threadbare but respectable black suit and a sparkling white collar. I'd never seen him without dirt on his knees.

My anger at their tampering with my bicycle had risen up again. I'd tried to wash it away by immersing myself in the service. It had, however, been tedious and noisy. The priest had led the mourners in various responsive readings interspersed with an overly long sermon. For someone like me accustomed to silent worship, it seemed the church wanted to keep people so busy they didn't have a chance to connect directly with God. The singing of hymns had been nice, though, with some excellent voices in the congregation joining in.

Nursing my sore hip, I sat at the back between Bertie and Jeanette. We'd arrived at rather the last minute and I hadn't had a chance to ask Jeanette if she'd translated for Kevin yet, nor to share the exciting news about the new house with both of them. I spied Irvin Barclay a few rows up, which surprised me. He hadn't liked Mayme. Maybe he wanted the satisfaction of seeing she was good and gone. I couldn't see if Nalia was with him due to a lady's large hat blocking my view.

As I observed the ornate decor of the church, I finally listened to the small voice inside that had been nagging at me since David had showed me our new house yesterday. This sanctuary presented a stark contrast to the light-filled simple Friends Meetinghouse where I was so completely at peace during worship. Was our home-to-be also overly ornate? The design was not a simple one, with all those gables and rooflines. With four bedrooms it was also much larger than we would need, at least at first. And even when children came along, one bedroom for the girls and one for the boys would be sufficient. Wouldn't it? I supposed my husband might want to use one room as a study, and as the Bailey boys and Betsy grew into adulthood, there might come a time when one of them would want to reside with us.

I resolved to speak with David. At the very least we could keep the design of the interior simple. I did not want to slide into luxury simply because we could afford it. I certainly wouldn't spend extravagant amounts on furnishings like Sissy had done. So many among us in modern society were in far greater need of such monies.

I wrenched myself back to the present, in which the priest was leading the pallbearers toward the back of the church. As he swung a small globe from a chain, the smell of incense increased. Behind the coffin followed Helen, the only person in the church with wet eyes.

I confess to sliding behind Jeanette when I saw Irvin approaching down the aisle. I didn't need any more of his ire, especially in public like this. We three were among the last to file out, with Jeanette tucking her hand through my elbow. Outside all the black-clad mourners gathered in the street behind the funeral wagon, which now held the coffin.

"Are you going to the burial?" Bertie asked me from where we stood on the second step.

"I can't. I have a prenatal client coming at noon."

"I must return to the workplace, too," Bertie agreed. "The post office calls."

"And I have to get to the court," Jeanette said.

"Jeanette, remind me to tell thee about a little friend of my niece's. She's blind and has a thirst to learn but isn't attending any school. Betsy reads to her when she can and they play together."

"I'd be happy to pay her and her parents a visit. The Perkins School offers scholarships for needy children, and my dear friend is the head of that department."

"That would be most helpful. I thank thee." I wouldn't mention the word that had sparked the conversation about Betsy's friend. Jeanette didn't need a reminder of society's attitudes about her incapacity.

"Oh, and I met with Charlie's father. He said the baby's mother was indisposed, but I helped him out quite a bit, I believe." Jeanette turned her face toward the crowd in front as if listening to something I couldn't hear. "Rose, your detective transported me to the hospital this morning to translate for the man who was attacked by the carriage," Jeanette said. "The poor fellow's pretty bad off."

"I'm glad thee could help." I was about to ask what he'd said when Kevin approached the funeral wagon. Two officers were with him.

"Ooh, something's up," Bertie said.

The crowd grew quiet, with only the sounds of one of the harnessed horses stomping and whuffing. "Kevin and two policemen have walked up to Merton," I whispered to Jeanette.

She nodded as if she'd been expecting it.

We had a great vantage point to watch what transpired from the steps here. Was Merton about to be arrested for murder?

Kevin reached out his hand. Instead of touching Merton, though, he touched Adoniram's arm. "Mr. Adoniram Riley. I arrest you for assault with intent to commit murder on Vladislaw Szczepanski."

"Mr. Settle told me to do it, but I swerved!" Adoniram yelled. "I didn't murder nobody."

"I also arrest you for the murder of Mayme Settle." Kevin's voice rang out strong and satisfied.

A great gasp went up among the gathered mourners. Kevin had forgotten to mention bicycle thievery. I didn't care. These charges were much more important.

"I didn't do it!" Adoniram protested. "I didn't do none of it."

"Quiet, now," Kevin said.

"Mr. Riley!" Merton stared at the gardener in horror. "How could you?"

The white-robed priest, who stood nearby, hung his head. In sorrow at the shocking disturbance to his ceremony? Or at one of his congregants being involved in a murder, perhaps.

All focus was on the arrest, but I noticed another uniform moving to Irvin's side. Nalia stood with the banker. Kevin left Adoniram with his officer and pushed through the crowd. This time he rested his hand on Irvin's arm.

Irvin's eyes went wide. "Take your hand off me, man," he snarled, trying to twist away.

"Mr. Irvin Barclay, I arrest you for the murder of Mayme Settle."

Both of them? I couldn't wait to ask Kevin what he'd uncovered. Maybe the chocolates had been poisoned, after all.

"I never did," Irvin proclaimed, chin in the air. "You can't prove it."

"We'll see about that." Kevin nodded to his man. "Cuff him."

The big banker struggled, but the policeman managed to secure his hands behind his back.

"You'll pay for this, Detective." Irvin glared at Kevin.

"Not another word out of you."

"I tell you, I didn't do it," Adoniram shouted above the buzz of shocked words passing through the onlookers. He gestured with his chin to Merton. "He did. I saw him!"

FIFTY-SIX

"I WAS WATCHING. I'd just brought Mrs. Settle her tea," the gardener shouted. "The lady was sick that night but she was quite alive. Her husband pressed a pillow to her face until she stopped moving."

White stuff. Kevin had mentioned a white substance under Mayme's fingernails. She must have struggled, trying to rip off the pillow. *And tea.* Kevin wouldn't have arrested Adoniram if he didn't have evidence. They had to have found traces of poison in her teacup. Why hadn't he washed it out?

"This is getting interesting," Bertie said with a delighted look on her face.

Merton's face drained of color. He shook his head, hard. "He's lying. I would never kill my dear wife."

Helen stared at her father, her face equally pale on an expression of disbelief. Her head wagged back and forth.

Kevin hurried back to the wagon. "Why didn't you say anything earlier, Riley?"

He held up a hand. "I got my loyalties to my employer."

"Until your own life is threatened," Jeanette remarked to us. "Then loyalty has a funny way of disappearing in a trice."

"You can't believe him," Merton protested. "He's only a gardener, a simpleton."

Merton certainly wasn't returning the loyalty. Adoniram narrowed his eyes and tried to lunge for Merton, but the policeman held him back. Another one took Merton firmly by the arm.

I saw a movement of green at the edge of the crowd, which had doubled from passersby wanting to witness the excitement. Nalia strode up the sidewalk away from everyone. She was heading for the intersection where the new statue of Josiah Bartlett presided.

"Stop that woman," I called out. I pointed. Some cousin, she was. She wouldn't be trying to escape if she weren't also guilty.

Kevin glanced at me, nodded, and blew his police whistle. "Police! Stop!"

Nalia ignored them. She wasn't running, but she was moving

fast, as if she was late to an appointment. Perhaps she was, or maybe she was trying to make her escape.

I unhooked myself from Jeanette "I'll be right back." I lifted my skirts and sprinted after Nalia. My legs were strong from bicycling and I ignored my bruised hip for the moment. I reached her side before she turned left toward Patten's Hollow.

"Nalia," I said, stepping in front of her. I suddenly didn't have a plan other than stalling her until Kevin could catch up. I launched into a greeting, trying to keep my voice casual. "How good to see thee again." I tried to slow my breathing. She didn't need to know I'd had to run to catch up with her.

She blinked. "Good morning, Miss Carroll."

"Quite the excitement back there, wasn't it?" I glanced over her shoulder. Kevin was hurrying toward us. "It's unfortunate about your cousin being arrested."

"It's a mistake, of course." She gave a little shake of her head. "Damn fool policemen. Filthy Irish, no doubt. They don't know a thing. Make false arrests all the time."

Judge thee not, lest thee be judged, I thought.

"He'll be out before the sun sets, I'm quite certain," she went on, but she didn't meet my gaze when she said it.

"Was thee off to arrange a lawyer for him?" I asked sweetly.

She paused. "Ah, yes. Yes, that's exactly where I was off to. Now, if you'll excuse me."

Kevin appeared behind her and I moved back to allow him room. "Not so fast." He stepped between us and touched her arm. "Miss Nalia Bowerman, you are under arrest as an accessory to the murder of Mayme Settle."

FIFTY-SEVEN

"I NEVER DID! That's a ludicrous suggestion." Nalia's eyes narrowed at me and the corners of her mouth pulled down in a look of loathing. "You and your meddling. You'll pay for this, Rose Carroll." She lunged toward me, her long fingernails extended like talons.

I ducked back as Kevin grabbed her arms.

"That's enough out of you," he said.

Nalia fought against the detective, hurling a string of shocking invectives at him, but he managed to cuff her wrists.

"Nice work, Miss Rose. She was next on my list." He gave me a wink before hustling her off to the police wagon.

I stared. Four people involved in murdering one matron. If it was true, this was unprecedented, at least in my experience. I was dying to learn what evidence Kevin had against the astronomer, but I was going to have to wait for that. I made my way back to the church, where Bertie and Jeanette still stood on the second step. The police wagon's rear compartment was now crowded with three accused killers and an officer.

Merton was ushered into the front seat.

"Father," Helen cried.

The priest took her elbow, restraining her from approaching the police wagon. Merton stared straight ahead, not acknowledging her. An officer shut the front door and went around to the driver's seat.

I watched as the wagon clattered away toward the station. Only poor Helen and a few stalwart mourners were left to accompany the priest, following the funeral wagon as it made its way down Main Street on the way toward Mount Prospect Cemetery.

"Rose to the rescue," Bertie exclaimed, clapping her hands.

"You caught her, I assume," Jeanette said.

"I did, and I engaged her in polite conversation until Kevin caught up."

"Why did you pursue her?" Jeanette asked.

"It seemed like the act of a guilty person to flee the scene the minute her cousin, with whom she is intimately involved, is arrested. Kevin gave me the nod, so off I went."

"She could have attacked you, though," Bertie said.

"I suppose, although it's a very public corner up there, and she didn't. He arrested Nalia as an accessory to the murder. I can barely believe it. It appears four people were involved in killing one unpleasant woman." I kept my voice low.

"I assume Miss Bowerman worked with Mr. Barclay to achieve the evil end," Bertie said, also in a soft tone. "But it sounds like Mr. Settle and his gardener had independent plans."

I told them my theory about the pillow. "So Merton's might have been a crime of opportunity, as they say. He saw a chance to get rid of her and acted in the moment. Poison, though? That's a planned killing."

"You know, I caught a snippet of conversation between Mr. Barclay and a lady inside the church," Jeanette offered. "I listen rather more acutely than most people, and I knew his voice from the bank. He was telling her something had disappeared and she seemed furious with him."

"That must have been Nalia. The something was a tin of poison his wife discovered in his drawer," I said. "I secreted it away from the house, with the cook's help, and gave it to Kevin."

"That would explain Miss Bowerman's anger." Jeanette nodded.

"What did the Polish man say in the hospital?" I asked.

"He insisted he is Merton Settle's brother. He said Mr. Settle's carriage purposely ran him off the road, with Mr. Riley driving. He also thought it passing strange the cook was mysteriously gone from the house and no maid was about, either. Which left only the gardener doing for Mr. Settle."

"As Adoniram told me." I thought. "Did Kevin ask him about pushing Merton in the front hall?"

"Yes. Mr. Szczepanski claims his brother tripped in his rage to get rid of him, and Mr. Settle fell and hit his head."

"One man's word against another's," Bertie observed.

"Yes," I said. "We might never know the truth about what really happened, but at least Merton was not seriously hurt in the fall."

"So he'll be able to stand trial for murder," Jeanette said.

"Precisely," I agreed.

The curious crowd was dispersing in front of us as the church bell tolled once, signaling eleven thirty.

Bertie clapped me on the arm. "Well done, lady detective. I'll be seeing you, Mrs. Papka." She grinned and hurried toward the post office.

"Walk me to the courthouse, Rose?" Jeanette asked.

"Certainly." I extended my elbow for her to tuck her arm through, and off we went through a town safe again after a week of uncertainty and danger.

FIFTY-EIGHT

I SAT WITH EMMALINE and baby Rosalie late that afternoon in the garden behind the Donovan home. Kevin had called. He'd said they were home and asked me to stop by for a visit. At the edge of the yard Sean pushed a toy tin wagon hitched to a wooden horse along an elaborate structure made of pieces of discarded wood, which Emmaline said was a city he'd built himself.

"What a blessing Rosalie is well again," I said, watching a cool baby sleep on her mother's lap, shaded by a tall elm tree.

"Thanks to God, you, and your wonderful husband-to-be."

"David is wonderful, isn't he?" My cheeks warmed.

"He told us the fever might have returned because her little body hadn't yet rid itself of the germ causing the illness." Emmaline gazed down at Rosalie. "I hope she's not to have a life of being frail and poorly, Rose."

I batted away the suggestion. "She's going to be fine. Little babies are learning to live in our world of germs, and every time she falls sick and recovers it strengthens her for the next time."

She smiled. "May it be so. Now, my husband tells me the murder is solved—with four people under arrest!"

"Yes. I've never seen such a thing."

"I hadn't either," Kevin said, appearing behind his wife. He carried a tray filled with glasses of lemonade and a plate of ginger cookies. He set it on a small table and plopped into the chair next to Emmaline's. "It's thanks to you, Miss Rose, I was aware of Nalia Bowerman and the tin of poison in Barclay's drawer. It was you who told me Barclay sent candies to the victim and about Riley's past with the victim. You also alerted me to the Polish brother. I am greatly in your debt."

"We all are." Emmaline nodded.

I ignored the praise.

"Please, Miss Rose, have a refreshing drink, and you, too, my Em. Here, give me the baby. You have to drink a lot while you're feeding our daughter. Your midwife told me so." He grinned at me as he lifted Rosalie off Emmaline's lap. An experienced father, he was careful to support her head. He gazed down with pure love as he cradled her in his arms.

"Have any of the four confessed?" I asked him.

"Riley did," Kevin said. "Said it was an eye for an eye. He claimed Mrs. Settle had killed his daughter and, with the cook away, he finally had a chance to return the favor. He'd put some kind of poison in her tea but it hadn't killed her."

Emmaline frowned. "Wasn't Mr. Settle as responsible for the girl's death as his wife?"

"I asked Riley," Kevin replied. "He said Settle was so browbeaten by his wife, he just went along with whatever she said."

"And it's true that household matters like a maid taking leave would have been in Mrs. Settle's purview." Emmaline sipped her lemonade.

"It was stupid to leave the teacup with dregs in it," I said. "Perhaps he didn't have a chance to retrieve it before Merton came in to finish off the deed."

"Mr. Settle, however, says we can't prove he used a pillow on her." Kevin shook his head.

"Mr. Riley's word won't be enough?" Emmaline asked.

"Perhaps. We're checking Settle's wardrobe for feathers, rips, any signs there might have been a struggle. Say, Miss Rose. You saw Settle earlier the night his wife was killed, when you said he hurled a hateful look at his wife after she spoke down to him. Do you recall what he was wearing?"

I thought back. "A silk smoking jacket. Blue, I think."

He nodded. "Thank you. I'll get one of my men on it."

"The candies Irvin sent over must have been poisoned, too." I sipped my drink.

"They were." Kevin nibbled a ginger snap. "The chemist suspects the lily of the valley powder, thanks to you."

"Poor Mrs. Settle must have been quite sick that night if she drank poison in her tea and ate poisoned candy, too," Emmaline remarked.

"Adoniram was watching," I said. "I wonder if it was not to catch Merton at anything but to observe Mayme die." The thought sent a shudder through me.

"It's possible. Barclay, the rat, claims it was Miss Bowerman who put him up to the deed, though. He insisted she was the one who injected the toxin into the chocolates. Being accused of homicide really brings out the worst in people."

"How does thee know she did? Thee arrested her, too."

"She happens to have a much larger tin of the same poison in her home, which her maid kindly relinquished to us." Kevin's smile was a satisfied one. "And I heard back from Harvard today. You were right—she's no longer employed there and must have been feeling quite the financial pinch." He wagged his head.

"I can understand Adoniram and Merton's motivations, not that I think they were justified," I said. "Thee can add bicycle thievery and vandalism to their charges if thee wishes. I reclaimed the bike yesterday. Luke saw it abandoned near the Lake Gardner dam."

"You don't say." Kevin's eyebrows went up.

"We went to fetch it, but as I rode home, I found the brakes not functioning and I nearly was washed away down the Powow." I rubbed my sore hip.

"Oh, Rose," Emmaline exclaimed.

"I managed to rescue myself, but I believe those brakes had been deliberately tampered with. They had functioned perfectly prior to the theft."

"Duly noted," Kevin said. "I'll stop by and take a look later."

I shook my head, remembering my close call with death. "Kevin, I have one remaining question. Why would Irvin want to kill Mayme?" It struck me that poor Sissy would be alone with her infant daughter now. I hoped she would move back to Portland and live with her mother and her sisters. Perhaps she could take Aoife with her if she decamped. "And why did Nalia help him?"

"We did some digging into that very matter. It turns out Barclay had borrowed a considerable sum from Mrs. Settle to make an investment in a property. The land turned out to be swampy and malaria-ridden and couldn't be built on. All the debt landed on his head. That's why Mrs. Settle refused to rightly share the inheritance with her cousin. I think Miss Bowerman put him up to the deed of murder in order to claim the full inheritance. Not much future with a man who doesn't have any money."

"A married man, no less." Emmaline pressed her lips together.

I gazed at Kevin. "And after Nalia lost her position at Harvard, she thought Irvin's potential to secure Mayme's share of their inheritance would benefit her, too."

"Yes."

"Orpha told me yesterday she witnessed Irvin telling Mayme four years ago that she needed to pay up or he would tell everyone. We thought it must have been about the fact that the Settle son had impregnated Adoniram's daughter and then abandoned her. The girl died after giving birth. I would imagine Mayme would go to some lengths to protect what she regarded as her reputation."

"Blackmail, eh?" Kevin raised an eyebrow. "We'll see. For now, we've done our job. It'll be up to the lawyers and the courts from here on out. But the streets of Amesbury are safe once again, and for this I thank you, Rose."

"And I thee, Kevin."

Sean ran up and took a swig from his father's glass. "Papa, I've thought of a new way to locomote. Instead of trains and horse-drawn carriages, why don't they put electricity into carriage bodies? Just think, one could motor around free of having to take care of big animals!" His eyes were bright. "I'm going inside to draw up some plans."

"That's my boy." Kevin watched his son disappear into the house, shaking his head, fond vying for proud on his face. "Maybe next he'll invent a way to prevent crime."

ACKNOWLEDGMENTS

MANY HEARTFELT THANKS are due to the following:

My fellow Amesbury Quaker (and Scorpio sister) Jeanne Papka Smith for inspiring me to create Jeanette Papka, who is equally as comfortable in the sighted world as Jeanne. She gave the manuscript a close read and set me straight on a couple of points about living as a blind person.

Barbara Ross for her great-great-grandfather's name of Adoniram. As far as I know her Adoniram was never suspected of murder.

The West Falmouth Quaker Retreat House, where I wrote a draft of the first half of this book in a week.

Dear friend, author, and crack editor Ramona DeFelice Long for another expert developmental edit.

Midwife Risa Rispoli for once again reviewing my birth scenes.

Jessie Crockett for advising me to let the boy twin die—sadly, such deaths were not only a fact of the time, but this one helped the story, too, in ways I didn't expect.

Many friends who shared details of their own unmedicated twin birthing experiences.

Artist and neighbor Margery Jennings for updating my bookmarks every year in a barter deal—and for letting me use her, her house, and her husband in a scene.

My fellow Wicked Authors—blogmates, dear friends, and lifeboat. Readers, please join us over at WickedAuthors.com. Meet these fabulous writers—Jessie Crockett, Sherry Harris, Julie Hennrikus, Liz Mugavero, and Barbara Ross—including all their alter egos, and read their books.

My family, my Hugh, my friends and fellow Friends, my Sisters (and Brothers) in Crime—I couldn't do it without you.

Finally, Bill Harris and the expert team at Beyond the Page Publishing, for picking up this series midstream and offering it a new home. I'm grateful for the warm welcome Rose Carroll and I have received and the professional product Beyond the Page produces. Long live the midwife!

About the Author

AGATHA- AND MACAVITY-NOMINATED AUTHOR Edith Maxwell writes the Amesbury-based Quaker Midwife historical mysteries, the Local Foods Mysteries, and award-winning short crime fiction. As Maddie Day she writes the Country Store Mysteries and the Cozy Capers Book Group Mysteries. A longtime Quaker and former doula, Maxwell lives north of Boston with her beau, two elderly cats, and an impressive array of garden statuary. She blogs at WickedAuthors.com and KillerCharacters.com. Read about all her personalities and her work at edithmaxwell.com.